THE SURFACE

A Novel

Rebecca J. Kelly

For my parents.

Prologue

Excerpt from a Medical Case Journal

Dr. Tess Avrakotos – Medical Director – NASA

I have seen many interesting cases since I became a doctor over two decades ago. The case of Eta Shepard remains the most intriguing case I have ever come across. Even her name is interesting. It's pronounced with a long e: "Eeta." As in the seventh letter of the Greek alphabet. She's so compelling, in fact, that studying her and publishing my findings will be the most notable accomplishment of my long and tenured career—of this, I am certain.

Background <small>(see footnotes for broad historical references)</small>

Eta's fascinating story begins with her mother, Millicent Shepard. Millicent, who preferred to go by her nickname, Nu, also a letter in the Greek alphabet, was an astronaut with NASA approximately two decades before this writing. She was one of the most decorated members of the astronaut fleet and had earned the coveted position of commander of the Delta Space Station.[*] She was on board the station, serving as commander, at the outbreak of the Great Nuclear War.[†]

It was understood by NASA and the other participating space agencies that the crew of the Delta, which included Nu and two other crew members, Andrei Fedorov of Roscosmos and Vincent Cho of NASA, departed in the Russian Soyuz Capsule MV-54 approximately two days after the initial nuclear strikes, shortly after the loss of satellite communications. Debris from this spacecraft was found scattered across Siberia three days later.

Unknown to all but the crew, Nu Shepard did not depart on MV-54 with her two colleagues. She stayed on the Delta in hopes that communications would soon be restored. We know this now because Nu kept detailed notes in her flight log on the Delta. These notes were recovered many years later. A full-scale search of the debris site for MV-54 was never completed due to the pressures of the war. Also, at the time, all parties assumed that the Delta Space Station deorbited somewhere between twelve and eighteen months after the war. No debris was ever located for the space station, but this was during the period of heaviest fighting after the initial nuclear strikes, and the satellite blackout severely hindered communications with other countries.

Nu Shepard realized four weeks into her prolonged stay on the Delta that she was pregnant with Andrei Fedorov's child—a child conceived while the two were flying their mission. She kept detailed medical logs during her pregnancy and NASA recovered these logs shortly before the Delta's ultimate demise. Her daughter, Eta, was born approximately eight months after Nu lost communication with the surface.

Eta is the only human conceived, born, and raised in space—an incredible scientific specimen. There's no doubt that Nu understood the danger her daughter was in, and despite this, she believed it was safer to stay on the Delta than take the remaining escape capsule, Soyuz MV-49, down to the surface. During those years, Nu spent an astonishing amount of time scanning the Earth's surface in hopes of reconnecting communication with the ground and obtaining a rescue.

Nu would eventually lose her life in a battle with an aggressive form of inflammatory breast cancer when Eta was fifteen years old. Eta continued monitoring the surface for an additional three years after losing her mother and finally made a radio connection with NASA after the launch of a new set of communication satellites.

Her point of contact was Alexandros (Alé) Bakas, a NASA engineer in the satellite communications department, who happened across her distress signal during a routine control check of the new satellites. Alé and Eta became very close over the few months that followed as they worked to create a plan to bring her home. A group of twelve engineers assisted on the rescue mission, including myself, serving as flight surgeon. Eta had contact with all participating engineers at some point during the mission and with the managing director of the mission, Jade Stanton. However, Alé was her primary contact since she felt most comfortable speaking to him during the five months and sixteen days she remained in space after her discovery. We monitored Alé's communications with her since the start of the mission and the bond seemed to be strong and shared by both parties.

The Delta, still in orbit after twenty years, was well past its prime operating age of eight to ten years, and with no supply missions to deliver new parts or maintenance supplies, it was destined to fail sooner rather than later. Despite the lack of supplies, Eta did an exceptional job keeping the station in orbit all those years. An issue with the ion engine ultimately led to the decay of the Delta's orbit, to a point at which it could not be repositioned to a safer orbit without the use of a liquid-fueled engine. At the time of this writing, NASA, after suffering a complete dismantle during the war, has yet to put a human in space. Because of this, there was no spacecraft available that could safely reach the Delta and save it from reentry.

The choice to bring Eta down in Soyuz MV-49 was made and approved by NASA upper management. The crew of engineers prepared three spacewalks for Eta to repair damage to the Soyuz spacecraft. It had, after all, been sitting in a vacuum connected to the U5 docking port on the Delta for over eighteen years at the time of the rescue. It was exposed to numerous collisions with space debris, as well as solar radiation. This, combined with the loosening of the protective blankets on the outer hull of the Soyuz, exposing it to extreme heat and cold, meant it was unflyable without serious modifications. Eta was able to perform said modifications with a few minor complications and undocked from the Delta two days after completion of the spacewalks.

Eta had limited help from the NIX‡ unit #2437. Nu, who was a gifted computer programmer, made some interesting upgrades to unit #2437. She facilitated these upgrades by taking additional computing hardware from the Delta computers and uploading custom programming to the unit. Because of the added computer power, #2437 offered companionship and served a greater role in performing duties on the Delta than simpler units of the past. In fact, #2437 was integral in raising Eta from a young age. Nu depended on the robot to provide entertainment for the child and included it as another member of their small family. Eta affectionately referred to the unit as "Nix" and it responded to the name.

Eta's battle to keep the Delta in orbit ended five months and sixteen days after her initial contact with the surface when we were able to successfully bring her through reentry using the modified version of the Soyuz MV-49. The original plan included bringing #2437 down to the surface in the Soyuz along with Eta, but an unfortunate encounter with space debris caused the need for the robot to stay back on the Delta and manually release the Soyuz from its docking port. Without its sacrifice, Eta would not have been able to undock the ship.

Shortly after Eta entered Earth's atmosphere and landed in New Mexico, the Delta disintegrated upon reentry over the Atlantic Ocean. That was two days prior to the time of this writing. Eta escaped the reentry with her life, although she suffered multiple injuries during the descent and the subsequent roll of the Soyuz capsule along the surface, which lasted approximately twenty-two minutes. Injuries included fractures of the fifth and sixth ribs on the left side as well as the fifth rib on the right side. The broken ribs caused punctures in both lungs, requiring surgical repair by a thoracic surgeon. The pelvis was fractured in three places and there was a fracture of the femoral neck.

She was in surgery for approximately twelve hours while two of the most accomplished bone surgeons in the country worked to put the bones back in place. Artificial bone pins, made to simulate human bone growth plates, were added to the ribs, pelvis, and femur. Dissolving stem cell capsules were inserted at various points around the bone structures to ensure quicker healing. Because of these advanced medical procedures—indeed, these procedures are not even available to the public as they have yet to gain full governmental approval—I expect Eta will heal much faster than someone receiving typical medical care for this type of injury.

Conclusions

What can we learn from Eta? Her knowledge and expertise in the field of spacecraft maintenance and general problem-solving are surely second to none. Her unique physiology is one of the most significant scientific discoveries of our modern time. To be able to study her adjustment to surface gravity and explore how her body works when compared to humans born on the surface will give us invaluable information for future long-term space missions. Indeed, we see now that it *is* possible for humans to live, work, and even procreate successfully in a microgravity environment—perhaps without any long-term physical effects.

Eta can teach us a great many things about her mental capacity as well. Despite being cut off from the Earth's surface for eighteen years, she did have access to a vast archive of entertainment and learning material on board the Delta's computers. Being a long-term space habitat, the Delta was equipped with thousands of books, encyclopedias, magazines, newspapers, movies, songs, and social media archives—all prewar information, of course. Because of the archive, she grew up with a reasonable working knowledge of how people interact with each other and how people on the surface live day-to-day lives (prewar), and she even knows many pop culture references. In addition, she's fluent in Russian, Spanish, and English. Her education, under Nu's tutelage, was extraordinary considering the strange circumstances surrounding her upbringing.

There is the ongoing question of how we (NASA) should respond to the budding relationship established between Eta and Alé. Watching their interaction and how deeply they seem to care for each other despite having never met in person is fascinating. It's a clear indication of how someone such as Eta, completely cut off from the rest of the world and humankind, can develop connections just like you or me. Still, it could present a danger— not to Eta per se—but to our research and plans regarding Eta's role in future space missions.

Recommendations

We have only begun to scratch the surface when it comes to learning from this extraordinary young woman. I, personally, consider it an honor that John Patrick, NASA administrator, has entrusted me to head this project—the search to explore, study, and understand the most unique human to have ever lived.

Continued monitoring and documentation of Eta's physical and mental state is essential for us to glean as much knowledge as possible from this remarkable girl. Alé should be kept at a distance for the time being, at least until Eta has recovered from her injuries. When the time comes to bring the two of them together for a meeting, the relationship should be monitored closely to ensure he poses no risk to our subject or to our work.

Footnotes

*The Delta Space Station was a fourth-generation spacecraft built by an international consortium of space agencies. It was modular, similar to stations of the past; however, it included a large centrifugal force module which provided limited gravity for the station inhabitants, allowing astronauts to spend more time in space with less bone and muscle atrophy. Because the station was meant to support life farther out in the solar system, it was also equipped with a large garden, allowing the crew to grow food and supplement oxygen.

†The Great Nuclear War began with a strategic nuclear attack by the Guerrero dictatorship of Brazil in collaboration with the Kim dictatorship in North Korea. The initial bombing was followed by a cyberterrorist attack that took out the world's satellite communications network. Many nuclear strikes followed, and civilians around the world were forced to move underground. The Trusted Allies, a group of countries including the United States, Canada, Britain, France, Germany, Russia, China, and others, finally defeated Guerrero at the Battle for Sao Paulo ten years after the initial nuclear strikes, ending the war.

‡Nautical Intelligence Experiment (NIX) units were the robots included on space stations of the time. They had been in use since the Beta station nearly three decades before the Delta. These units had limited computing ability but were essential for keeping up with station maintenance as they were sturdy enough to operate in the vacuum and could leave the spacecraft through their own secondary airlocks, eliminating the need to activate the larger, primary airlock.

Part I

After Touchdown

Chapter 1

West Texas

Time Since Touchdown: 42 Days, 9:59 a.m. CST

We crossed the border about thirty kilometers ago. I could feel the difference in the air. It was as if there was a sudden pressure drop right where the edge of New Mexico stopped and the edge of Texas began. The West Texas air was lighter, wavy, almost fragrant with heat.

On the border, we encountered miles upon miles of cotton fields. No living plants, just the skeletal remains of what was once the largest cotton-growing area in the US. Nothing new has been planted here in years. Not since the war. Not since the drought.

Beside me, in the driver's seat, he's holding the wheel tight. Almost like he's afraid that if he lets go, we might be back there. Back in the holding facility again. And he can't stand that thought. So, he holds tight to the wheel, holding tight to the dream of escape.

I consider him for a moment. Tufts of dark, curly hair fall over his forehead. The sides of his head are shaved, faded up into a thick mop on top. He's wearing a sweater over faded blue jeans, despite the searing West Texas heat that pushes down on the car windows from all around. The sweater is navy blue with a tiny logo of a crocodile on the left breast. He has the sleeves rolled up, exposing his forearms.

I reach over to him and touch the skin on his right arm. It's dark and firm and hot to the touch. He allows it for one second, and then, without warning, he pulls his arm off the wheel and down to his side. I quickly retract my outstretched fingers and lay my hand in my lap.

"Alé," I say. "Where are you taking me?"

He's been facing forward, eyes knitted tight down the centerline of his forehead. A man on a mission. But now, his face softens slightly and he turns my way. Not completely my way, he won't look me in the eye, but he turns enough so he can speak in my direction.

"East," he says, resuming his position, hands on the wheel, gaze glued out over the hood of the blue car. I don't know what kind of car it is. It's the first car I've ever been in. There is a flashing NASA emblem rotating on the holo-screen built into the dash.

I glance over the steering wheel and see the cruise control is set to 105 mph—I forget that they don't use the metric system here. I'm not sure if there is a speed limit on this highway, but I'm almost certain we're exceeding it. And why not? He has kidnapped me, after all. Any kidnapper in their right mind would drive as fast as they could to get as far away from the scene of the crime as possible. I know this and yet, I'm not afraid. He saved my life, after all. He brought me to the surface. He freed me from the Delta Space Station, a prison I was born into and lived in for eighteen years. And now, he's kidnapping me to free me from another sort of prison. I can't blame him for that.

I can only hope what we're doing is right.

Chapter 2

Five Weeks Earlier

Maryland

Time Since Touchdown: 1 Day

The desk was rich, dark mahogany with a wood grain so unique, Alexandros Bakas was sure he'd never seen anything like it before. He traced the grain with his eyes from one end of the massive desk to the other and found that although it ebbed and flowed in shape, it never ended. It was hundreds of continuous lines of dark chocolate-colored wood seamlessly melded together by nature and time. He imagined the tree it came from and how beautiful it must have been before someone severed it at the stump to make this desk.

He had seen the desk many times before, but this was the first time he really paid attention to it. As he was contemplating the life of that ill-fated tree, Jade Stanton, his boss at NASA, walked into the room. She didn't walk so much as glide through the open doorway in what looked like a single, seamless motion.

Jade was a tall woman with long, graceful legs which allowed her to move like a gazelle. She wore a sharp, tailored suit: blue with a starched white button-down shirt underneath. Her long, slim fingernails were painted a bright coral red to match her lipstick. The color struck the perfect contrast to her clear, dark skin. Her hair was curly and black, cropped short. She wore black Gucci glasses and her earlobes flashed thick diamond studs which Alé was sure cost an entire year of his salary... times two.

She made her way around her enormous desk, her eyes pinned to the small holo-screen she held in her hand. Alé watched the holographic image on the screen flicker as the light from the overhead fixtures passed through it. It was a file icon, rotating slowly clockwise, something Jade had no doubt been searching through as she walked down the long corridor which led to her office. Jade was like that, working at every moment, even while she walked. She flicked the icon with a quick touch of her index finger and the screen went empty as she took a seat in the enormous leather chair behind the desk. She placed the holo-screen on the desk in front of her and waved her finger across it again to shut it down.

Only then did she finally look at Alé, a slight smile curving her lips. "Alé, thanks for meeting me on such short notice."

Alé was the nickname everyone but his mother used when referring to him. Jade crossed her long arms in front of her body and swung one leg over the other. This was her power position and Alé had seen it many times before. She looked down at him over the top of her glasses, cementing the intimidating body language into place. "As you know, things have been a little crazy around here over the last twenty-four hours."

Alé *did* know how crazy things had been. He had been in charge of the mission to bring Eta Shepard home from the Delta Space Station before it burned up in the atmosphere. Eta was special in every way possible. She was the first person ever born in space. She had lived her entire life in space, on the Delta, and nobody had known about her presence there until Alé's team at NASA stumbled across her distress signal mere months before the Delta deorbited. Since that fateful day, when Alé first heard the strange signal with the call sign *Delta*, it had been a roller coaster of a ride at NASA trying to organize a rescue mission to get Eta home alive.

Along the way, Alé had grown attached to the eighteen-year-old girl. He marveled at her ability to adapt and survive.

They had spent hours speaking to each other over radio communications throughout the six months between when he intercepted Eta's distress signal and when she finally boarded the Soyuz capsule that would ultimately bring her home. He had been her primary contact during that time and he had grown to love her in a way he could never describe or replicate. The sound of her voice made his heart feel like it was floating in midair.

It had been the most intense few days of Alé's life, preparing Eta to leave in the banged-up Soyuz space capsule, which had been orbiting alongside her on the Delta for over eighteen years. There was more than one instance where they didn't believe they could save Eta in time.

But the technology had worked and some amount of blind luck had been on their side. After a violent reentry that severely injured Eta in the process, the spacecraft punched through the atmosphere intact. When the Soyuz finally touched down safely in the New Mexico desert, Alé had to excuse himself from the Mission Control room at Goddard Space Flight Center in Greenbelt, MD. He didn't want the crew of engineers in the room to see him break down with relief after such a stressful reentry.

What he hadn't expected as he'd closed the door to Mission Control that day, was to find two NASA guards standing in his way. The mission had been run under the highest security protocol, which meant the select group of people working the mission were allowed only limited contact with the outside world. They were required to sign ironclad confidentiality agreements and agreed to twenty-four-hour surveillance of their homes and holo-phones if NASA deemed it a necessary action.

There were always guards outside the Mission Control room, as per the security protocol, but they had mainly spent their days lounging in chairs against the wall playing card games on their holo-screens. They would give a nod and perhaps a hand wave when he left the command center, but that was it.

On the day of the landing though, Alé encountered a guard as he exited the door to Mission Control. The guard was standing directly behind the door to stop any person from leaving the room. Alé was so distracted, he ran right into the man, a bulky fellow with an enormous head covered in shaggy brown hair that continued down his sideburns into a full beard and enormous hands to match. He was one of the regular guards and his name tag read "Jeff."

"Oh, I'm sorry," Alé said after hitting Jeff dead center in the chest. "I didn't realize you'd be standing right here. I just needed to get some air."

Jeff looked down at him and grunted. "Nobody leaves the room. Orders from Patrick."

Alé's eyes grew wide with disbelief: John Patrick, the administrator of NASA, had ordered this. No one had ever physically barred him from leaving the room before. "I just needed some air," he repeated to the guard.

Jeff looked over Alé's head at the second guard standing across the hall. This man was even taller than Jeff, who Alé guessed was at least six foot three, and Alé had yet to see him hanging around Mission Control. Unlike Jeff, he wore no name tag, only the starched, black combat gear that all the members of the NASA Guard wore. This man had impeccably groomed hair, black as night and combed across his head with a sharp part running down one side. He wore no scruffy beard like Jeff; rather, his skin showed not a sign of errant facial hair. In fact, if Alé were to guess, it wouldn't surprise him one bit if this man didn't even need to shave, his skin was so smooth.

As the guard with the neat black hair considered Alé, he ground his huge jaw under that fair, clean-shaven skin. He tilted his head to one side before giving Jeff the slightest nod. It was obvious who was in charge. Jeff understood the order and stepped to one side.

Alé, shaken by this encounter, watched the strange guard as he walked down the hallway that led to the stairs. It wasn't until he reached the stairs to the ground floor that he realized Jeff was following behind him, no doubt on orders from the taller man.

That night, after Eta was taken to the secure NASA facility in White Sands outside of Las Cruces, New Mexico, Alé asked Jade if he could leave right away to go see her. After all, he had been working with Eta for months preparing for her escape from the Delta. He had gotten very close to her over that time and he knew she was in rough shape after the ballistic reentry. Alé wanted to be as close to her as possible in case something else went wrong. He longed to see her in person, and it surprised him how badly he *needed* to see her.

To his great disappointment, Jade had denied his request that night. She had shooed him away with the promise that they would discuss the issue the next day when they'd all had a good night's sleep. Dejected, he had grudgingly left the Goddard campus.

Alé always took the same route to and from work, but that night, he decided to take a different route to clear his mind. That was when he noticed a car following him. It was a NASA Guard vehicle. He knew it because of the shape: a bulky black box van with no identifying marks or plates. Alé stopped at a light and peered back into the van, where he caught a glimpse of Jeff behind the steering wheel… following him.

The whole experience had left Alé uneasy and he'd had a rough night of sleep. He was here, now, in Jade's office, to ask again if he could go to New Mexico. But he also wanted to address the strange guard presence from the night before.

"No, thank you for meeting with me," Alé said. "I'm here to talk about New Mexico. I need to be there, Jade." He wasn't asking. He was going to get to New Mexico some way or another and he needed her to know that.

Jade's left eyebrow ticked up toward her hairline and her lips pursed in response. It was clear his words held a vague threat and she was not a person who took threats lightly. "Is that so?"

He nodded. "I'd like to leave today, if possible. I understand there's work to be done with the mission, but it's important for me to see her. I checked outgoing flights and..."

A click of the door interrupted Alé. He turned to see the tall guard member from the night before wearing black combat gear, striding through the now-opened door. The man swiveled around on one perfectly shined black boot and snapped the door shut behind him before taking a seat in the chair next to Alé.

"Ahh, just in time," Jade said to the man before turning back to Alé. "Alé, this is Carter Kane, the *head* of the NASA Guard." She managed to put enough emphasis on Kane's title to give Alé an uncomfortable feeling. "I believe you two spoke last night."

"We didn't actually speak," Alé said, raising his eyebrows and looking away from Kane.

"No, we didn't." Kane crossed his arms in front of his chest. "But I am aware of your background, Mr. Bakas. I know you've been in charge of the mission to bring the subject down to the surface. We've been keeping track of you for a few weeks now. Checking your activity on the NASA cloud, internet browsing, cell usage, and so on. And we've been listening to your conversations with the subject."

"Stop calling her the 'subject,'" Alé said, anger welling in his chest, making it difficult to breathe.

Kane ignored this. "We've also noticed you've become somewhat close to the subject. Perhaps a little too close. It's something we hope won't be a problem going forward."

Alé didn't respond. He felt violated. Instead, he pointed his dark eyes at Jade, daring her to explain herself. She held his gaze, her eyes just as dark but much colder.

"It's true, Alé. We needed to keep an eye on things to protect the security of the research," she said. "We've never seen a case like Eta's before. Someone born and raised in low-Earth orbit... well, that's too special to mess around with. I would have called you in myself to discuss the issue, but things were moving so quickly with the rescue mission. It was our top priority to get Eta back here safe so we can study her, and we needed to make sure you were one hundred percent on board to make that happen since you were the first one to make contact with her. She trusts you."

Jade sighed and released her arms, allowing them to fall to the armrests on her chair, her hands dangling off the edges. "Look, I get it," she continued. "You like the girl. Hell, I like her too. From the brief conversations I've had with her, she's great. She's brilliant and interesting and you're drawn to her. I get it. But it's time to distance yourself from her... at least for the time being. Tess is in New Mexico. She went there yesterday morning.

She'll take good care of Eta." Jade was referring to Dr. Tess Avrakotos, the flight surgeon in charge of the medical team associated with Eta's rescue mission. Tess would also be in charge of Eta's medical care on the ground.

"We need you here in Baltimore," Jade said. "We've got bigger plans in the works and you're integral in those plans. All of the mission data we pulled from the Delta before it disintegrated must be compiled. We're talking about billions of bytes of information to sort through. We need you and the rest of the team working on this."

"What about Eta?" Alé asked.

"Well, for now, she needs to heal and rest. Tess is putting together a research team to study her. We're going to learn so much from her—anatomy, psychology, genetics, you name it. This is the biggest scientific discovery of the century, a girl born and raised in space! We're not going to miss out."

"But has Eta agreed to this? I mean, you can't study her without permission."

Kane chimed in, "That's not for you to worry about at this time." He looked as though he was going to continue, but Jade waved him off.

"I understand you're worried about her," she said. "Trust me, she's in good hands. Project Diamond is almost ready for human tests and with the information we learn from Eta, we may even be able to launch sooner than anticipated. It's a very exciting time here at NASA. I assure you, Alé, you'll get to go to New Mexico to see her. For now, I need you fully engaged in analyzing every bit of data we took out of the Delta. Nobody knows the details of the mission like you do. Is that clear?"

Project Diamond was the crewed space program NASA had been working on for the last six years. It seemed they had found themselves the perfect test subject when they discovered Eta's rogue distress signal. Not only could they study the effects of long-term space exposure on the human body, but they could use Eta's advanced knowledge of her space station to better outfit their new space vehicles.

"So, this is why you've been keeping Eta's existence a secret from the world? This is the reason for the heightened security?" Alé asked, pointing his thumb in Kane's direction. "You're planning to keep her under wraps to study her. That's been the plan all along."

A smile spread across Jade's red lips. "You're sharp. That's why I like you. I'll ask again, are we clear?"

Alé glanced over at Kane who cocked his head to the side, daring Alé to dissent. "I guess I have no choice. But promise me one thing—I want to see her. Soon. You make that happen and I'll do whatever data mining you want me to do."

"Done. There's a planning meeting set for Project Diamond in New Mexico in four weeks. You can go along on the jet then. It will be the perfect opportunity for you to start uploading medical data. I'll pencil you in." Jade nodded her approval and Kane shifted his gaze to her. "Anything else?"

"I guess not."

Alé stood and turned toward the door. Before he reached the knob, Jade stopped him. "Eyes up, Alé. Remember, this is top priority. You'll get your day in New Mexico, I promise."

Alé nodded over his shoulder and slipped out of the room.

***

That night, in his apartment, Alé stared out the window, utterly consumed by his thoughts. Across the street was a seemingly endless string of historic row houses. House after house covered in a brick skin, each a different color and pattern, yet each designed exactly like the next. This area of Baltimore was known to the locals as Pigtown. Alé had lived in Pigtown his entire life, except for the few years he and his family went into hiding during the war.

His tiny apartment sat on the third floor of a similar set of row houses. It was under five hundred square feet and included a combination kitchen, living room, and dining room with a large picture window overlooking Carroll Park on one end and another overlooking the row houses on the other. To the left of the larger main room was the door to Alé's bedroom, which had an attached bathroom. The contents of the apartment were sparse, with a few pieces of basic furniture—the cheap and easy-to-get variety.

Eighteen years earlier, when Alé was eight-years-old, a full-scale nuclear war had broken out when the fascist Brazilian dictator, Juan Guerrero, dropped nuclear bombs on major cities around the world on one particularly hot day in June. Washington DC was a target and Alé would surely have died in that attack had the bomb meant for the US capitol not malfunctioned and detonated offshore. The events of that day were capped off with a cyberterrorist attack led by a network of underground hackers working closely with Guerrero. The cyberattack had been almost as costly as the nuclear strikes in that it had taken out the world's satellite network, crippling people's ability to communicate. The event marked the beginning of a decade of fighting that forever changed the way people lived and the way governments controlled their citizens.

Only in the last five years had the world economy bounced back enough from the war that companies started to manufacture home furnishings like sofas and dinette sets. Rough gray upholstery covered the sofa Alé now sat on, reminding him more of the burlap sacks they used to store root vegetables during the leanest years of the war than it did a sofa covering. Still, he wasn't picky. He rarely spent much time in the apartment anyway.

He had been staring out the window overlooking the row houses for the last thirty-two minutes, motionless, thinking. His mind consumed by his conversation with Jade earlier that day, wondering how he could have been so stupid to assume she would simply allow him to leave and go to New Mexico. He hadn't thought much of it at the time, but now that he looked back on how the mission was run—the heightened security, the ever-present watch of the NASA Guard, the threat of surveillance, the lack of transparency with the press and the general public—the warning signs were all there. They'd been planning to keep this a secret all along and he cursed himself for not having known better.

What he didn't understand was why Jade cared so much about keeping him in Baltimore. Why not allow him to go to New Mexico and be with Eta? *They must think I'm a threat.* His mind wandered back to seeing Jeff in the NASA van following him home. Knowing he'd missed these red flags made him shake his head in anger, breaking his gaze out the window. How could he have been so stupid?

He dropped his head in his hands, ran his fingers through his hair, and gripped it forcefully. If he'd had any sense about what he was doing the last three weeks, he would have talked to Jade about this long ago. He would have demanded to know what NASA's plans were for Eta.

The idea that they would have the gall to believe it was acceptable to *keep* her made him even more angry. He released his hair and a loud growl escaped his lips. Shaking his head, he knew his only option now was to play ball with them. If he wanted to see Eta, he would need to follow the rules and do what they asked. But he decided that along the way, he'd find out as much as he could about their plans. There was no harm in arming himself with knowledge.

He stood from the faded gray sofa and walked closer to the window. Jade had been right when she'd said Eta needed time to heal. This gave him a few weeks to figure out what to do next. So perhaps it wasn't a bad thing that Jade had kept him from going right away. He would need the next few weeks to come up with a plan, and he would need Eta to be as strong as possible if it came time to implement the plan.

As he gazed over the city in front of him and watched the sun take its final bow over the horizon, he decided he would play the game. No matter how angry it made him, he'd need to carefully consider every move he made from now on for the sake of Eta's best interests.

NASA would never communicate their plans with her, nor would they ask her permission to use her body and her mind for their own experimentation. They weren't going to look out for her wellbeing.

But he would.

Chapter 3

Maryland

Time Since Touchdown: 1 Day

John Patrick strolled down the east wing hallway of Building Thirty-Six in the heart of the Goddard campus. As the long-standing NASA administrator, Patrick rarely made his way out to Goddard anymore. He was firmly entrenched in his administrative duties at NASA headquarters in downtown Washington, DC, but the last twenty-four hours had been a momentous time at the space agency and it was the people at Goddard who had made it happen.

His twelve-hundred-dollar Prada loafers made an echoing tap on the tile of the empty hallway. It reminded him of the beat of a military cadence during his army days. He had to chuckle thinking back to those times when he first enlisted. So young and naive, he had been first in line to serve his country in fighting the South American army. No draft card necessary.

Now he was at the top of one of the most important government agencies to rise from the ashes of the war. And he had made it so.

When Patrick came to NASA, they had just started to rebuild the war-ravaged infrastructure around the country and he proposed to Congress that the world's greatest aeronautics agency could be instrumental in that rebuild, considering the vast resources and facilities it had at its disposal. The only thing he asked in return was the funding to start a new crewed space program. This time, though, NASA would start from scratch and truly make space travel economical and useful. No more tiny capsules limited to a single use or bulky space "planes" that were more deadly than they were efficient.

Patrick's vision of human spaceflight included commercially feasible missions to bring back valuable minerals, fuel sources, and building materials from the Earth's nearest neighbors like the Moon, the Asteroid Belt, and Mars. He wanted to see luxury space travel as the ultimate vacation getaway for rich and powerful people all over the world, not just in America. These were the types of products that private industry was interested in—not experiments or research, but real, physical commodities that could be bought and sold.

Congress, in a desperate quest to pump up the postwar economy, had jumped on board with Patrick's vision for a commercially viable space program. And so, he began his quest almost six years earlier by setting up a mining operation on the Moon. Project Diamond would be the first feather of many in his cap.

Oddly enough, as the Project Diamond astronauts were ramping up their training schedule in the deserts of New Mexico, some lowly engineer at Goddard had picked up a strange distress beacon. Patrick had to admit when he'd first heard from Jade about the girl who was "lost in space" he'd been skeptical. It seemed a waste of time and resources to take staff away from the Diamond mission to save one girl. Yet, the more Patrick thought about it, the more he realized that bringing this girl, Eta, down to the surface, could be an asset to his space agency.

There were so many questions about the feasibility of long-term space travel for humans. When he'd first gone public about the planned mining mission, the critics came out in droves to tear down the plans because they involved real, long-term mission time frames. The initial plans called for astronauts to spend six years on each mission with the possibility to bump that time out to ten. It was simply too expensive to rotate astronauts out any sooner than that and one thing Patrick was good at was finding ways to squeeze the absolute most out of his resources— including people.

The problem was the safety concern. Before the war, decades of research and experimentation had been done on four generations of space stations to see how the human body could adapt and function in space. Even after all that time and energy wasted on space station research, they still had no real idea of how the body would handle years, if not decades, in space. After the war, with no long-term space vehicles in orbit and no functioning satellites, there was no way to calm those critics.

Patrick's solution was to simply go quiet. He shut down all communication with the press about upcoming missions. Prior NASA administrations had felt the need to inform the public whenever they made a move. They paraded everything from new mission approval to astronaut selection in front of the press. He took the opposite approach and went completely mum: no more press conferences, press releases, or question-and-answer sessions. He never liked the press anyway and eventually, they stopped asking questions. With so many more important infrastructure projects in the works postwar, they had plenty to keep themselves busy.

Then, like Sir Isaac Newton and his fabled apple, the answer to Patrick's problem fell from the sky. On a Soviet-era spacecraft, no less! He couldn't help but chuckle at the irony of it. Here was actual, living proof that long-term space travel was possible and, better yet, safe. According to initial reports he'd received, Eta had a rocky landing, but aside from a few broken bones and punctured lungs, she was stable and in good condition.

The medical research she would provide would be priceless and he had plans for her even beyond that. Eta Shepard was going to more than make up for the millions he'd spent rescuing her from the Delta—she was going to be instrumental in their next step in space.

As Patrick continued down the hallway, he stopped briefly in front of a darkened office window to check his appearance. He brushed the sleeves of his tailored suit and straightened his signature red tie. One of his rules regarding wardrobe was that all men working at NASA wear a button-up white shirt and either a blue or gray tie at all times. Patrick liked to stand out from the crowd and nobody was allowed to wear red except him.

After squaring his shoulders, he ran his fingers through his thinning blond hair. He was in the midst of hair-growth treatments and leaned in closer to the glass to inspect his hairline. He was skeptical about whether the treatments were working, but now as he examined it, he imagined that perhaps his hairline had grown slightly thicker. Good. He smiled at his reflection and continued down the hallway.

As he reached the door to Jade's office, a man opened the door and walked out, allowing it to slam behind him. The man, shorter than Patrick but well-built with thick, dark curls, had a troubled expression on his face. He looked up at Patrick as he passed and Patrick raised an eyebrow at the man who awkwardly raised one hand in acknowledgment and simply kept walking down the hall, head down in thought. Patrick turned to watch him for a moment before he shrugged and opened the door.

Inside, Jade sat at her desk, arms crossed, sharp eyes resting on the face of Carter Kane, who turned to see Patrick and immediately stood from his chair in reverence to the administrator. Patrick nodded his approval and Kane resumed his seat.

Patrick liked Kane. He had appointed Kane himself when he realized that if he was going to keep the details of his missions private, he would need a much better security force than had ever been present at NASA. Kane had been instrumental in building up the NASA Guard from a few hundred members to several thousand, run like any true military-style organization. Patrick and Kane had served together in the army and he trusted Kane entirely.

Jade set her eyes on Patrick as he strolled to the empty chair next to Kane. The air of importance he put on for others didn't fool her. The two had a long history, including a passionate love affair many years earlier. She had known him when his hairline was still intact and he wore secondhand boots. When Patrick was appointed administrator, Jade was one of the first people he hired as a project manager and he had personally brought her up through the ranks to her current position as senior manager in charge of satellites.

"So happy you could join us." She raised a single eyebrow, her words icy with sarcasm.

He made a partial bow of his head and lifted his hands as if in surrender. "My apologies. You know how the Metro can be."

Jade chuckled. "When was the last time you took the Metro?"

Patrick smiled. "You've got me there. Again, my apologies." He settled back in his chair and crossed one leg over the other, gesturing toward the door. "Was that the engineering kid? The one who picked up the signal?"

Jade nodded. "Alé Bakas. He was the first one to talk to her and was instrumental in the rescue operation. He's one of my best project engineers."

Patrick glanced at Kane. "How are things going with him? Is he on board with the next phase?"

"Well, sir"—Kane cleared his throat in preparation for his speech—"we've been keeping an eye on him for a few weeks now. As you know, he became very close to the subject during the planning of the rescue. We've got a shadow on him and we're planning—"

Jade held up her hand to stop Kane midsentence. "He's fine, Kane. I told you he's on board. Just trust me on that one." She shot him a look that could pierce even the thickest hide.

Kane's jaw flexed and a flush of hot blood creeped up his neck and into his face.

Patrick watched the exchange with a raised eyebrow and opted to diffuse the situation. "Jade is an excellent judge of engineering talent and when she says he's on board, I believe her. But you've got a point, Kane. He did get very close to our subject and we wouldn't want to muddy this up with emotion." He turned to Kane and directed his steely blue eyes at his head guard member. "Keep a loose eye on him. I'm sure our engineering friend will come to understand his place."

Kane gave a tight nod and allowed his tense back to relax slightly into his chair.

"So how is our girl doing?" Patrick continued. "What's the latest status report?"

Jade leaned back in her chair and pulled up the report on her holo-screen. She maximized it and swiveled the holographic image toward Patrick and Kane so they could all see. It showed the current status on Eta's medical stats: heart rate, metabolic rate, oxygen levels. At least fifteen lines, each a different color, jumped and pulsed on the screen against a background of normal readings so they could compare. "She came out of surgery six hours ago and so far, all looks great. Her ribs are broken but the lung punctures were small. The surgeon was able to patch them up, no problem. They put pins and stem cell caps in her pelvis and leg to speed up healing in the bones. According to the doctor, the stem cells are top of the line and should have the bones healed within weeks, maybe less. She could be up and walking in as little as two."

Patrick nodded, his brow wrinkled. "That's good. It's critical that she survive the injuries from reentry. We can learn much from her body, but we can learn much more if she's still alive. I want our best staff members taking care of her. Is Tess down there?"

"Yes. She left last night and plans to stay and oversee medical care until Eta's healed."

"What about security?" Patrick asked, looking at Kane.

"We've coded it as a top-priority mission, the highest security clearance only. Holo-watch recognition required for all entrants to her room and all staff has been notified of the delicate nature of the mission."

"Good." Patrick nodded his approval. "Good. I don't want this leaking to the press."

"And do you ever plan on informing the outside world of our miracle girl?" Jade asked.

"Perhaps. When the time is right. For now, everything stays tight, got it?" Patrick waited for the synchronized nods from Jade and Kane before continuing. "I want us to be especially careful with the information kept on the NASA cloud. Anyone with a B-level security clearance can access that database. Our research could easily fall into the wrong hands."

Kane leaned forward and cleared his throat. "Sir, I assure you, any information on the NASA cloud is protected with the highest encryption standards. Those files are the safest files in the world."

"Really, Kane?" Patrick stared down the end of his nose at Kane, who held his gaze, not backing down. "You saw what that hacker network did to our satellites eighteen years ago. You really think they can't get through your firewalls? If you believe that, I may have the wrong man for the job." Kane dropped his eyes and shifted in his seat. A slight smile came to Patrick's lips at the concession. "I mean it. Only those with the proper security clearance should have access to her files. And that's especially important for anything involving Project Diamond. Is that understood?" He leaned back in his seat and habitually straightened his tie.

"Yes, sir," Kane replied, taking care not to look at Patrick.

"Good." Patrick smiled and tented his fingers in front of his face, elbows resting on the armrests. "Now, where should we go for lunch?"

Chapter 4

New Mexico

Time Since Touchdown: 21 Days

The days are starting to form into separate blocks of time, rather than one, continuous span of minutes strung together like links in a chain. It's easier to make out the difference between day and night, and time has become less fluid and more rigid.

On my left wrist, a thin metal band is cold against my skin and a tiny screen on it flashes:

Subject: Eta Shepard
Mission: Delta Space Station Extraction
Estimated Age: 18

There is a window in the corner of this room, but it's covered in thick blinds. Only a sliver of light seeps in around the edges. From the moment I noticed the window a few days after I woke up, I wanted to go to it and look outside, but they haven't let me do that, even though I've asked about a hundred times. Tess says the light is much too bright for my eyes. I have stopped asking now because it seems to make her angry any time I bring it up. Her eyes slim and her mouth tightens when she's put out with me and I've learned it's best to let it be.

I don't think it's a real window anyway. The light from the edges of the blinds bends and fades as each day slips by, but in a strangely consistent way, almost like it's on a timer meant to imitate the sun. They know, of course, that I'm not used to the normal sunrise and sunset that happens on the surface. I've only ever known the sun as it exists in orbit, rising and setting every ninety minutes. Even so, I've seen enough movies and pictures of sunlight to at least have an idea of how it should act, and the light in that window doesn't seem right.

There's a stopwatch app on the holo-screen they've given me so I can read books and listen to music if I like, and I started timing the light to see how it changes day to day. From what I understand of the sun and the weather here on the surface, this light should be changing. Some days there will be cloud cover. Some days it will be raining. Some days there will be full sunlight. But the light from the edges of the window is always the same. It begins to fade each night exactly six minutes later than the night before.

I have a consistent routine. I'm sleeping less and I'm much less groggy when I wake. They've taken most of my pain medication away now, which is fine with me. I hated the way it made me feel during those first few weeks after the Soyuz touched down. But they're still giving me a tray full of about thirty different pills to take every day. There are tiny blue pills and fat yellow ones, chalky white round pills and thin, oblong red ones. I have no idea what they are, and the few times I've asked, I've received a mouthful of medical jargon. They speak of stem cells, blood pressure, nutrient retention, and active healing, whatever that means.

Some of the medicine gives me weird side effects like nausea, stomach cramping, or severe fatigue. There's always an explanation for it and when I complain, they switch them up to something different. But I'm a bit confused about why I need so many different medications. I feel as though I'm getting better with each day, stronger, less hobbled. One would think they would try to wean me off of the medicine. Instead, they seem intent on adding to my daily dosage. They even watch me take them to make sure I don't spit anything out.

I spend most of my days reading and trying to get caught up on the happenings of the world. My holo-screen has some limited internet access, but it seems heavily filtered by NASA. They did supply me with a large library of e-books to help me get accustomed to the world since the war.

There are days when even reading is too much for me. The weight of gravity and the atmosphere and my place here in this sterile room hit me full force. It's those days when I think about the station. The Delta was my home for eighteen years. It was all I knew and the sadness of knowing it no longer exists is enough to send me spiraling in on myself.

I think about my mother. There were times on the Delta when she would allow the sadness to overtake her too. On those days, she would quarantine herself to her sleep compartment and leave me to my schedule: chores, schoolwork, exercise, sleep. Sometimes when she disappeared, that's what I called it as a child—disappearing—I would peek in on her curled up in a ball under her covers, sometimes sleeping, sometimes crying quietly, sometimes just staring into oblivion. She would see me poke my head in to check on her and give me a weak smile before waving me away with a flick of her fingers. Sometimes she couldn't even muster that and she would simply turn around on her cot and face the wall, tightening her body as if to provide an extra shield of protection against the outside. That's what I do on those days when the memory of the Delta is too much. I tighten up into a ball to create my shield against the world.

She died when I was fifteen. The cancer started in her breast and took over the rest of her body in the span of a few weeks, like a virus might infect a naive population. I remember she came to me with her worries about the lumps in her breast and, before I could even process the development, she was gone, taking her last breath while I held her in her bed, sucking the stale air out of the small room as her spirit left the station for good. Nix, the station robot, had taken her body outside and sent her on her way back to her earthly home.

Despite the sadness of it all, her legacy wasn't her tragic end—it was me, surviving and making it down to the surface. I am her legacy. She wanted my life to reach beyond the five modules of the Delta. She wanted me to experience the whole world.

As I spend my days healing in this room, I wonder what she would want me to do now. Would my mother want me to stay trapped in this room, allowing these scientists to study me, test their medications on me, watch me through the lenses of the overhead cameras? I'm not even sure why I ask myself the question. I know the answer.

***

I finish lunch and lie back in bed to read a book. This is the third book I've read in seven days. This one is about how they rebuilt the telecommunications systems after the war ended. There's a knock on the door and Tess pokes her head inside, dropping by for her daily visit.

She's wearing a dark dress with thick black heels that make a deep "thump" sound as she walks across the room. Over her dress, she wears her usual white lab coat with her name and title embroidered across the left breast: Dr. Tess Avrakotos, Medical Director, NASA. She tucks a single auburn curl behind her ear and takes her usual seat on the far side of the white sofa in the corner. Tess doesn't believe in staying too long, so she sits right on the edge of the cushion. That way she can make her exit as swiftly and efficiently as possible.

"Good afternoon, Eta. How did you sleep last night?"

"Fine. Same." I don't look up at her from my holo-screen.

"Really? Are you sure you didn't have nightmares again? You look pretty tired."

Tess is referring to the nightmares I started having after they took me off the pain medication. I would dream about being on the Delta as it broke up in the atmosphere. I woke up screaming and would pull my monitoring electrodes off while thrashing about in bed. They had to come in and sedate me a couple of times. Eventually, they stopped putting the monitoring equipment on me at night.

"No, no nightmares recently," I say, flicking to the next page in my e-book before looking up at her. "I think that medicine you gave me has helped." That's not exactly true. She prescribed a little blue sleeping pill which she said would help alleviate the nightmares, but all it did was put me into a sleep so deep, I felt like I'd been out for days. I was sleeping for twelve hours straight and, when I did eventually wake, I could barely function. I started hiding the blue pills in my cheek and into a rip in my mattress after the night nurse closes the door to give me some privacy. Tess doesn't know about this, so I play along. I'd rather have nightmares than be totally comatose.

"Great," she says. "How have you been feeling? Is the pelvic pain getting better? How about the lungs?"

"Good. Lungs are fine. I've been working on my breathing exercises and I can hold my breath for nearly two minutes now. The pelvic pain is almost gone." She nods, satisfied. About a week after I landed, she told me about what they'd done to me during the sixteen hours I was in surgery, the artificial bone pins they inserted into my pelvis and ribs, the stem cell capsules they injected throughout my body—these procedures are supposed to promote healing. According to Tess, I am healing at a rate five times faster than someone who would have had the same surgeries under regular circumstances.

I *do* feel like I'm healing much faster than I should be. I feel as though I should be out of bed, moving around, walking. Anytime I need to use the toilet or shower, they roll me to the tiny bathroom in a wheelchair. I've been told specifically *not* to walk there on my own. Yet, I feel good. I feel like the longer I sit here in this bed, the quicker my body will wilt and I can't handle that. I've always been able to take care of myself, even when I was alone on the Delta. I want to be free to move and run again. I want to be free from this white room. I bite my lip and decide to bring it up to her again.

"Tess, I'm feeling much stronger. Why haven't they been helping me get up and out of bed? I've asked a couple of the nurses and they keep telling me to ask you. Even the doctor said I needed to talk to you about it."

"Yes, we should probably get you up and moving again." She drops her eyes from mine for a moment. I've seen her do this before. She's lying to me and she needs a moment to gather her excuses. She looks back up, her response now situated in her mind. "Yes, well, we can start work on that in a few days. Remember, the last time we tried, you were so exhausted, it set you back a week. I don't want to push you too much."

She is right about that. They tried to get me to stand on my own about two weeks ago, just to see if I could. There were six nurses and doctors all standing around in my room to watch me. I heard them speaking about bone density tests and the structural integrity of my skeletal system. It made me shaky and nervous, so many people around me. Looking back on it, it makes me angry to think about it. I'm not used to that. I'm used to being alone. Tess should have known that. She should have insisted they give me space to try on my own.

Yet they were there, all of them wearing their white coats, punching notes into holo-screens, watching me, and waiting for me to perform. When I wasn't able to stand, I cried, mostly out of frustration. Nobody moved to help me. They were there to observe, not to interfere, and when I finally gave up and flopped back down in bed, Tess came over to me, smoothed my hair to my forehead, and said, "Now, now. Don't cry. We'll try again soon."

I shift my eyes to the floor, embarrassed at the memory of that day. Tess smiles and holds up her finger to make a point. "Patience is a virtue after all."

"Hmm…" I nod slowly, lifting my eyebrow. "We certainly want to maintain our sense of virtue."

Tess ticks her head to the side to show me she has caught my sarcasm. I decide to change the subject. There's something else that's been weighing heavily on my mind. "Tess, when can I see Alé?"

I've asked her this question every day for the last three weeks. Of all the strange things I've noticed since I've been here at this facility, and there are many, this is the strangest. Alé and I were so close during my last few weeks on the Delta. He was totally dedicated to me. He saved my life. And he hasn't even been here to visit me yet. The more days that pass without a word from him, the more I wonder if it was all a game. Perhaps he was never really there for me and said he was to get me to do the work necessary to save myself. The more time that passes, the more I doubt my own feelings and the more I question what I thought was reality a few short weeks ago.

Tess sighs. I can tell she's tired of answering this question. Again, she lowers her gaze as she formulates an answer. "He's been very busy sifting through the data sent back from the Delta's computers. So, you know, it could be that he hasn't had the time." She brings her hand up to her ear to sweep that same, loose auburn curl back into place. "He's way out in Baltimore, so it will cut into his time to make the trip. As I've said before, perhaps you should forget about seeing him for a while… until the team gets caught up."

Today's answer is the same as yesterday's and it's been the same answer since I started asking. "You know, he's a young guy," she adds, shrugging and raising her palms. "He's probably busy with his own life. He'll come around eventually."

My face drops and I can physically feel a pain in my chest, in my heart, at these words. How can he not want to see me after all that we shared? She must see my expression. Her mouth turns down in an overstated frown, as if she pities me for wanting to meet the man who saved my life—a man who doesn't want to meet me in return.

I turn away from her and look at the bank of monitoring equipment against the wall next to my bed. She didn't need to add that last bit about him being too busy to see me. That was hurtful. She wants me to believe that I'm not important to him.

And maybe I'm not…

I close my eyes to keep the tears from streaming down my cheeks. I take a few deep breaths and compose myself without looking away from the wall. "Hmm… yes, I suppose so."

"Anyway, things seem to be moving along well with your recovery. I'm glad to hear that the nightmares have stopped. I have two new doctors coming out to meet you tomorrow. They are respiratory specialists and they want to do some scans of your lungs to document the healing process." She stands to leave and as she reaches the door, she adds, "They'll also be taking some membrane samples from your lung lining. So, we'll need to put you out for a few hours while they do the procedure."

She isn't asking me and I don't respond. I have no idea what taking membrane samples has to do with my recovery, but I'm not in the mood to question it. I continue to stare at the wall as she slips out the door. After she's gone, I let the tears go.

Chapter 5

Maryland

Time Since Touchdown: 27 Days

Alé sat in his tiny office on the second floor of Building Thirty-Six in Goddard Space Flight Center's sprawling campus in Maryland. He stared at the large holo-screen in front of him and lightly tapped the end of a pen on the edge of the oak desk. His eyes darted back and forth over a document he had pulled up on the front tile of the screen. As he finished reading it, he shook his head with boredom, touched the holo-screen tile, and flicked it off to the side, dumping it into a folder with other similar documents.

He'd spent the last three weeks since his discussion with Jade minding his business and doing what she'd asked him to do—work on compiling the billions of bytes of data they had received from the Delta's computers before it crashed into the atmosphere. He'd made good progress too, sifting through most of the scientific information and separating it into files to be sent to different departments for further analysis.

One thing he quickly noticed, though, was that the medical data pulled from the Delta's computers was not part of the data dump he received. When he casually asked Jade about the absence of the medical data, she dismissed him with a wave of her hand, muttering something about Tess being in charge of all that.

The fact that Tess was so heavily involved didn't make him feel better either. Something about Dr. Tess Avrakotos gave him pause. She had been instrumental as the flight surgeon in the team of engineers that brought Eta home alive from the Delta. She had been the one to officially clear Eta as healthy enough to make the trip. But Tess had also been a little too excited about Eta's discovery. She had been overly concerned with getting as much data about Eta as possible and less concerned with bringing Eta to the surface safely.

Alé finished up the file he was working on and uploaded the details to the cloud with an encrypted key. This particular batch of files would go to the astrophysics department and contained detailed information on the many course corrections made during the Delta's nineteen-year communication lapse. His good friend Xander Kent would have a ball looking through this information. Xander had helped Alé pinpoint the Delta's orbit months earlier when NASA was still unaware that the Delta remained in orbit and that Eta was on board. The Delta's course correction information would be invaluable for the upcoming Project Diamond mission.

Project Diamond was NASA's first foray into crewed space exploration since before the war. They'd abandoned all prewar technology in an attempt to revamp the program into a commercially feasible space force. The brainchild of John Patrick himself, Project Diamond was on track to send humans deeper and house them longer in space than ever before.

The mission had been top secret from the beginning, with only those few elites in NASA's administration knowing the full scope of what they hoped to accomplish. This was more than just spaceflight for the sake of bragging rights; this was intended to bring actual commercially viable products to Earth through a mining expedition to the Moon.

Project Diamond team members would spend the first two years of the mission assembling a space station similar to the Delta. The new station, dubbed the Diamond Station, would then leave its initial low-Earth orbit and set off for the Moon. Once there, the astronauts would take a specially designed exploratory vehicle called the Gem down to the surface. Waiting for them on the surface would be twelve bundles of supplies and construction materials. These supply ships had, in fact, already gone to the Moon by way of secret launches from Cape Canaveral. All NASA needed to coordinate the launches of the supply ships were the tracking and data relay satellites or TDRS. Alé had been working on that same mission when he'd picked up Eta's distress signal months earlier. Once those satellites were in place, they could track signals from space vehicles anywhere in the solar system. The TDRS were essential to moving Project Diamond forward, and once they were launched and operational, the project had moved into high gear. Eta's discovery on the Delta, although extraordinary, hadn't halted Patrick's plans.

NASA chose the exact coordinates for the landing of the twelve supply bundles for a specific reason: they led to a cavernous lava tube a mere thirteen meters below the lunar surface. Lava tubes were essentially caves made from flowing rivers of lava that traveled under the surface rock millions of years earlier. The tube chosen for the Project Diamond site offered the perfect place to build a lunar colony. It was not too far below the dusty surface and it provided protection from space radiation, as well as protection from the thermal swings that day and night brought on the Moon.

Two of the supply bundles delivered the drilling bots, which were at work drilling their way into the lava tube when Eta's Soyuz touched down in the New Mexico desert. When the astronauts did finally arrive within the next year and a half, the tube would be opened up and ready for habitation. They would unpack the remaining supply bundles and begin building the first underground colony on the Moon.

While one crew of astronauts worked on setting up the permanent habitat, another crew would begin mining the surface. Their goal was twofold: first, they planned to excavate large quantities of rock to send back to Earth in special spacecraft called mining pods. These pods were completely automated, with limited power needs. Their primary function was to protect the mined rock from reentry into Earth's atmosphere. Once on the surface, NASA would market the lunar rock to the highest bidder. Patrick had full confidence that people would pay top dollar to get their hands on building materials shipped directly from the Moon.

The mining expedition's second goal was to find elements within the lunar rocks to help with further colonization. These elements might even include an energy source so important, it could make sense to ship it to Earth in bulk quantities in the future. As far as lunar exploration, the missions to the Moon in the 1960s had merely scratched the surface of what would be discovered on the lunar landscape. This was the real jackpot Patrick was after—a long-term source of energy to fuel Earth's systems for centuries to come.

When it came to Project Diamond though, the outside world had no idea NASA was involved in such an ambitious plan.

Patrick kept a tight rein on the PR department and he believed the public was on a need-to-know basis. After the war that wiped out a third of the world's population and decimated many metropolitan areas, governments were taking a more active role in monitoring citizens. Media and news outlets were now governmentally funded. The now-rebuilt cell service communications systems remained under heavy supervision. It wasn't like the old days when half the people on the planet owned a cell phone with the ability to access the internet on 85 percent of the Earth's surface. In the years after the war, cell service was allotted only to those bequeathed with high-ranking government titles. Permits for individual holo-phone usage were limited and hard to come by, although the government was known to provide holo-phone service to those willing to part with enough cash.

As a midlevel engineer and project manager at NASA, Alé was one of the lucky few who had regular holo-phone access. He was also privy to the Project Diamond files because his work on the satellites was a necessary part of the mission. He knew better than most that the NASA he worked for was nothing like the clunky administration that first sent men to the Moon. NASA as he knew it was much larger, had access to ten times the resources, and was not afraid to monitor the movements of its employees. Alé knew that whatever Patrick had in mind for Eta, Diamond was involved. So, that's where he looked first.

He had been poking around in the Project Diamond files for the last three days. Alé knew that Carter Kane was watching him, so he'd taken the precaution of using a backdoor program that allowed him to navigate the NASA cloud without detection. This little bit of computer programming was something he'd built on his own and he was proud of its simplicity and effectiveness.

The program masked his IP address with a false address from inside the organization, effectively offering him a screen to hide behind. Because he already had the security clearance to look at the files, he was able to get in and sniff around by simply hiding behind the screen. The computer programmers in charge of security would see that he had been in there, but his activity would be coded under a different IP address inside the organization so they wouldn't think anything of it. Alé knew that if someone *really* wanted to find out who was looking at the Diamond files, they could, and it wouldn't take much to crack his program. But he also knew that nobody was actually looking for that sort of thing from within the organization because all the files on the cloud were encrypted with triple encryption standards. Those who didn't have security clearance simply couldn't get in to look at files they weren't privy to.

Plus, the most important files, the ones that even Alé couldn't look through, were further encrypted with an algorithm that had been around for many years called RSA-4. This was the highest level of encryption known to man and it secured the top-secret files on the NASA cloud. They referred to anything encrypted with RSA-4 as a "black file."

After uploading the astrophysics data on the Delta, Alé opened up a tile on his holo-screen and pulled up the encryption program. The primary database holding the Diamond files flashed up on the holo-screen in front of him, each file denoted by a three-dimensional rotating folder icon. The database had about three thousand files in it, so he knew it would take him a while to find anything about Eta. So far, everything he'd found in the Project Diamond files had been per the norm.

He picked up where he'd left off the day before and began opening up files and sifting through their contents. It was a boring task. Most of the files were full of mathematical data, mechanical measurements, and schematic drawings. Specifically, he was looking for medical data or something involving human physiology related to Eta among the files. After about twenty minutes, Alé paused to take a sip of his coffee when a file name caught his eye.

On the edge of the holo-screen field, a folder named "ETA 18" hovered in and out of clarity, catching the light from the desk lamp. All the files in the database had this type of ambiguous name, full of letters and numbers. Some had full words included and others were merely a string of randomness that made no sense to anyone but the person who created them. But this file actually had Eta's name on it. Would they be so bold as to put her name on the file? He shrugged. Only one way to find out.

Alé lightly tapped the rotating file and a cloud of document icons materialized on the screen. There were at least a thousand documents in the file. He tapped the first one in the line named "11-8, Touchdown." August 11 was the day Eta landed. The file contained a detailed log of the Soyuz landing based on the ground crew's observations that day. Someone had uploaded it the night Eta was brought to the NASA facility at White Sands near Las Cruces, New Mexico.

As he continued to make his way through the folder, he found what he was looking for—Eta's medical reports. They were keeping track of everything from her blood pressure and bone density to her menstrual cycle and bowel movements. There were detailed psychological reports, again completed by Tess. Alé found surgical notes and radiological charts, including X-rays and full MRI reports showing Eta's brain function.

Not only had they been tracking her medical condition, they had been experimenting on her! He discovered notes about medications they had tested on her to see if they could increase her bone density faster. They had also purposely kept her from receiving appropriate physical therapy and had withheld certain vitamins from her diet to see if her muscles would atrophy further without the use of a controversial medication.

Alé continued to read for the next hour, opening each file and sifting through it before moving on to the next. Although he was angry at what he saw, he also saw hope in her medical records. According to Tess's own notes, Eta was healing at an alarmingly fast rate, a factor Tess could only attribute to the controversial stem cell treatments she'd received during her surgery. She was growing in strength every day. Her immune system was holding up. She had very little pain and the medical team had scaled back her pain medication to almost nothing. By all accounts, she seemed to be thriving, doing much better than astronauts of the past when it came to microgravity recovery.

It was obvious to Alé that they considered Eta the ultimate guinea pig to test best practices for improving physical health during long-term space missions. And nowhere in the files did he find anything stating they had obtained the proper waivers from Eta allowing these experiments to be done on her.

It was a file named "LT – Eta, PD" that stopped him. Could LT stand for "long-term"? Perhaps this was what he was looking for: some idea of what they ultimately had planned for Eta. As he lifted his index finger to tap the rotating file, he paused for a moment. This was the point of no return. If he opened this folder, he knew he could never unsee what was in there. If Patrick and the NASA Guard decided to look into who had been digging around the Diamond files, they would find him and realize he knew their plans. It would be a risk to both him and to Eta.

Alé took a deep breath and thought of her, all alone, not aware of what was happening. Scared. Hurt. Waiting for him. He clenched his eyes shut to push back the emotions welling up behind them. She might think he had abandoned her. She might hate him for it. That thought was more than he could handle. He gritted his teeth, opened his eyes, and touched the file.

To Alé's surprise, the file icon twisted into an error message and turned black before resuming its original shape and its gentle rotation along with the other files.

This was a black file.

Chapter 6

The tray table rattled against its latch as the airplane hit a patch of turbulence. Alé didn't notice the sound, although it was loud enough to briefly rouse Kane from his nap in the seat across the aisle.

Preoccupied, Alé thought about the conversation he'd had with Jade four hours earlier. She had called Alé into her office to confirm his seat on the NASA jet to New Mexico.

"Look, Alé," Jade said before he left her office, "I know how badly you want this. Hell, you've been asking me about it every other day for the last month. And, according to Tess, Eta's been asking to see you as well. So, I'm okay with you going.

You'll stay out there for a week. That's how long the jet will be there. During that time, you can work remotely and continue processing the Delta files. When you return, I'll expect you to be ready with your mission wrap-up, which should include the postlanding medical data. Patrick wants to see the completed presentation within the next two weeks. It's vital that they get the highlights of the Delta files before moving forward with Project Diamond. Will that work for you?"

"Yes." He nodded to confirm his obedience.

"Good. But hear me out." She leaned over her desk to put extra emphasis on the words. "I like you, Alé, and you know that. You're a smart kid and I appreciate smart people. Do yourself a favor and take this piece of advice: don't get too close to her. I mean it. Visit her a couple of times while you're out there, chat with her about her recovery, bring her a gift. But don't get too close. Get whatever feelings you've got out of your system and leave them in New Mexico... for your own good."

He steadied his gaze on her. "Is that a threat?"

"Not a threat." She shook her head. "Just a suggestion. Do you understand?"

He narrowed his eyes, slowly nodded, and turned to go. Jade stopped him at the doorway. "Oh, Alé, a heads-up—Kane will be going with you on this trip."

Now he *knew* it was a threat.

As he sat in the jet, ignoring the clank of the tray table, he played that conversation with Jade over and over in his mind, trying to make sense of it. Jade was conveying a pretty powerful message to him by sending Kane on the trip too. They would continue to monitor him closely. He wondered if they'd caught wind of the snooping around he'd been doing in the Diamond files.

No, he decided, there was no way they knew about that. He had been very careful, working diligently on the data processing project and only sneaking in time to look through Diamond files when he had finished his work each day. His encryption program was simple but highly effective and he was confident it would hide his activity. Plus, if they did know what he'd been up to, he certainly wouldn't be on a plane to New Mexico.

Alé glanced around at the other passengers on the small yet luxurious private jet. He was in the last seat on the left side of the jet. Across the aisle, Kane snored lightly. There were three rows with one seat on either side of the aisle ahead of him. All the seats were filled with some of the highest-ranking NASA officials, including John Patrick who sat in the front row.

As Alé had boarded the plane, Patrick, who was in the midst of a conversation with the woman sitting opposite him and sipping a cut crystal glass full of amber liquor, eyed him from head to toe and tipped the glass in Alé's direction, almost as if he were giving a toast. He gave Alé a sparkly smile and resumed his conversation. Alé had made his way to his seat as quickly as possible, avoiding eye contact with everyone else on board. He wasn't sure what was going on in New Mexico that involved so many of the most important members of NASA's elite, but he had an idea it had something to do with Eta and Project Diamond.

The NASA facility at White Sands was originally established as a missile range in the early 1960s. It was the primary rocket engine testing facility for many of NASA's rocket propulsion systems prior to the war. During the war, it became a pivotal base in the fight against the South Americans. They'd later revamped White Sands and built huge underground housing and training structures to house troops.

After the war ended, NASA turned the labyrinth of interconnected underground tunnels and housing structures into one of their primary research facilities. Much of the Project Diamond training was being done at White Sands because the underground facility lay far away from the prying eyes of the press and the public. They had taken over several large cave systems in the nearby Organ Mountains where the Project Diamond astronauts were training to live, work, and commercially mine on the Moon.

Alé didn't know the full scope of the White Sands facility—few people did—but he knew it was vast and had heard rumors there were miles of underground tunnels that went all the way up into the mountains. He had realized early in his digging that it wasn't a coincidence Eta's Soyuz capsule had landed in New Mexico.

The Soviets built the Soyuz during the 1960s. Unlike the US, the Soviet Union did not have easy access to water landing sites, so they designed their spacecraft to touch down on land, utilizing retrorockets to slow the capsule and dynamic cushioned pilot chairs to minimize bodily harm. Because of this, Alé had assumed that NASA leadership chose New Mexico as Eta's landing spot because it had vast open areas of desert and better odds of avoiding civilization. But in reality, they chose New Mexico because the White Sands facility was located there. They knew all along that they would bring Eta there after she landed, even though they told her they were taking her to a hospital near Albuquerque.

Alé peered out the tiny window of the private jet. They had taken off from the Thurgood Marshall Airport in Baltimore at 5:38 p.m. EST and they were four hours into a five-hour-and-twenty-minute flight which would take them directly to their destination. The White Sands facility was located on a dry lake bed that served as a runway for government flights and had even been a backup landing spot for the Space Shuttle many decades before.

Three nuclear bombs hit the Dallas-Fort Worth metroplex over the course of the war. Because of this, the pilot took care to fly north of the area as the radiation effects were still too intense for regular air travel. After Oklahoma City, there wasn't a single city under the air path to White Sands. People had virtually abandoned the Texas panhandle when the droughts set in due to nuclear fallout. Alé watched the darkened Oklahoma landscape slip by below him and noted not a single light in the area.

They must be getting close.

His thoughts turned to his meeting with Eta and the butterflies started to build in his belly. A flush of hot blood washed over his face and he thought of Jade's words to him: *Eta's been asking to see you as well.*

Was that true? Alé didn't know who or what to believe anymore. There was a time when he respected Jade and considered her a capable and worthy superior. But after reading Eta's medical logs, those days had passed and he'd lost trust in her. Still, there was a part of him, and he didn't realize until now how big that part was, that wanted to believe Jade. That wanted to believe Eta had been asking about him.

If what Jade said was true, and Eta was asking for him, then what must she have thought all these weeks when he didn't show up to see her? Certainly, they wouldn't have told her the truth, that they had held him back. No, they wouldn't have told her that. They probably told her he wasn't interested in seeing her. Maybe they made up a lie about him deciding she wasn't important. Eta might not even want him there now. He hadn't been there when she needed him most. Maybe she would send him away.

No, he wouldn't let himself think that. Not yet.

If the time came when Eta didn't want to see him, he would respect her wishes. But until she told him that herself, he wouldn't believe it. He trusted her. She was one of the only people he could trust.

And he longed to see her face for the first time.

***

The jet landed in White Sands at 9:05 p.m. after having gained two hours crossing time zones. Kane slept through the landing and the attendant had to shake him as they prepared to clear the plane. He glanced at Alé, emotionless, hardly fazed by the interruption to his sleep, and stood to remove his guard-issued duffel bag from the overhead compartment.

Alé reached for his own suitcase and followed behind as the managers filed out of the quiet plane. He climbed through the exit door and down the narrow stairway where three large NASA Guard vans waited to take them from the landing site to the living quarters at the White Sands facility. The landscape was pitch black except for the headlights of the vans as they drove over the dusty gravel roads leading to White Sands.

Thirty minutes later, they pulled into the small parking lot in front of the main building. During the day, the offices and laboratories sitting at surface level functioned like any other public building. People came and went, working their nine-to-five jobs. But the real work went on far below in the deeper levels of the facility. This was where hundreds of scientists and engineers lived and worked, preparing for the Project Diamond mission.

As they entered the main building, several NASA Guard members met the party at the door. Patrick and the rest of the managers chatted quietly as the guard led them down a hallway off to the right. Alé heard them discussing an upcoming meeting regarding funding the supply missions and he assumed that was where they were going. A short, stocky guard, whose name tag read *Nate* met Alé and Kane and escorted them to the elevator at the end of the building. Once inside, Nate pushed the button labeled "4."

"There are no upper floors," Nate explained. "Level four is four stories below ground." Alé noticed that this elevator went all the way down to level twelve.

Once on level four, they exited the elevator and walked down a series of narrow hallways until they reached a door marked "4-16." Nate motioned for Alé to open the door. "This is our visiting crew quarters and this is your room, Mr. Bakas." He then motioned Kane to the room next to Alé's. "This is your room, sir."

Kane nodded without saying a word and stepped into his room. Alé reached for the door handle and Nate stopped him. "Mr. Bakas, you're slated to meet with Ms. Shepard tomorrow at 0700. I'll be here to escort you. After your meeting, I'm directed to take you to the lab on level six to show you where you'll be working during your stay. Oh, and there's breakfast in the cafeteria starting at 0630. You'll find the cafeteria at the end of this hallway and to the right."

Alé nodded and opened the door to his room. It reminded him of a small hotel room. There was a double bed with a bedside table that held a clock and a desk lamp. A small bathroom to his right offered a toilet, sink, and shower. Across from the bed stood a desk with a holo-screen built into it. On the far wall, there was a window covered in blinds.

Alé knew the window was fake. After all, he was four stories below ground. When he lifted the blinds, a holo-screen glowed to life displaying a desert scene. At the bottom of the screen, there were small icons denoting different scenes he could choose from. The screen offered a forest view, mountain view, canyon view, and even a view from low-Earth orbit.

He figured this fake landscape must have to do with mental health. With so many people living and working underground, they must have these windows built into the rooms to ensure people didn't go stir crazy.

After dropping his suitcase on the bed, Alé slipped his personal holo-screen out of the front pocket and set it on the desk. With his encryption program running, he went through the process of signing into the cloud via the wireless ethernet. While on the flight, he'd had an idea.

Until this point, he wasn't sure if this was all in his head. The idea that NASA would rescue Eta from the Delta and keep her hidden away for research purposes was absurd, right?

Yes, they were working on a top-secret mission to start a mining operation on the Moon.

Yes, they'd purposely kept this mission from the public.

Yes, John Patrick ran the organization like his own secret club.

But were they really capable of doing what Alé thought they were doing? He had to be absolutely sure before he proceeded with his plan.

As the screen glowed to life, he flicked his finger through the index and pulled up a messaging program called Stax. It was a program that ran exclusively on the dark web, meaning it was virtually untraceable for anyone who wasn't adept at navigating the underground world of hackers. Alé wasn't exactly a hacker, but he knew enough about programming to access Stax.

Hackers around the world used it to communicate without fear of being targeted by increasingly paranoid governments. One of the first acts of the South Americans during the war was to use a collaborative network of cyberterrorists to hack into the world's satellite network and permanently disable the satellites.

This attack had taken years to set up and was incredibly complex, but the cyberterrorists had been wildly successful at disabling the rest of the world powers. Because of this, the world had to learn how to communicate all over again through different means. This very attack was what had disabled the Delta Space Station's ability to communicate with ground control, stranding Eta's mother on board.

What most people didn't know was that many of these master hackers lived normal lives, worked normal jobs, and took great care to blend in seamlessly with the rest of society.

Some of them even worked under the watchful eye of John Patrick himself.

Alé knew exactly who to contact to crack the black file.

***

Xander Kent settled back into the cushy depths of his faux fur, oversized beanbag chair, resting his head on it and allowing his curly mop of hair to fall down the back of the chair. He didn't have much furniture in his small apartment in Baltimore, but this chair was his pride and joy. After the war, beanbag chairs were hard to come by and he'd bought this one for a hefty price from a fellow dark web hacker living in Dusseldorf, Germany. Few things were as enjoyable as sinking into that chair after a hard day of work.

Gaming remote in hand, he waved a command at the sixty-inch holo-screen mounted to the wall a few feet in front of him and the screen bounced to life displaying the welcome portal of his gaming network. He'd had a long day and was looking forward to a beer (or three) and a few hours of gaming with his squad before hitting the hay.

He needed to decompress.

The orbital motions team at NASA, which Xander headed up, was part of the astrodynamics department at Johnson Space Center in Houston, Texas. The past few weeks had been brutal as NASA worked to analyze the data taken from the Delta's computers. Xander's team had received batches of data about the orbital maneuvers done over the last nineteen years on the Delta and they were in the process of sorting the information into useful packages. This data was critical for them to learn how Eta had kept the Delta in orbit all those years and it was a game changer for the upcoming Project Diamond mission.

When before they had been flying blind, creating an orbital plan full of computer-generated what-if scenarios, they now had a multidecade road map for how to keep a spacecraft in orbit under extreme circumstances. Xander had personally taken on the bulk of the data mining project and it meant long hours and many nights. He had even moved to Baltimore to be closer to the team working on the Delta project.

He was tired.

As he settled into the soft chair and prepared to start a round of Midnite, a first-person team shooter game, a notification dinged on his holo-screen.

It was a new Stax chat message.

This intrigued him because it had been many months since he'd been on the secure hacker chat program. Who could be contacting him now?

Standing, he walked to the screen and touched the pulsing blue envelope with his index finger. The envelope disappeared and the message popped up from user AKabob26.2. Xander was familiar with Alé's username as the two had been friends on the chat network long before either of them worked for NASA. The message read:

AKabob26.2: Bro, need a lift. You down?

Xander had been part of the hacker network since he was sixteen, almost two decades, so he was well aware of the underground language the hackers used to communicate. Asking for a "lift" meant you needed a favor, one that involved a particularly in-depth hack. It referred to "lifting" sensitive information. This was the type of service Xander usually charged top dollar for, but he and Alé had a long history and the request intrigued him. He tugged on the bottom of the holo-screen image to reveal the virtual keyboard and started his return message. He chuckled as his username, Dyn@moX1, popped up in the dialogue box. It was a nod to his role at the astrodynamics department at NASA.

Dyn@moX1: I'm intrigued. What u got?

AKabob26.2: Can't explain too much now. Might need a burner. Job's a deep dig on a black.

Xander's eyes opened wide. Alé was asking him to break into a black file in NASA's database. He'd never done it before, but he'd often thought about how he could go about it. The idea of actually doing it excited him. Alé's message also alluded to needing to use an old-style burner cell phone to communicate the information in the file once Xander hacked it.

Burner cell phones were extremely difficult to come by and Xander wasn't even sure his contact was in business anymore. But again, Alé's request was highly intriguing and Xander wouldn't let the burner issue get in his way. He had other contacts if need be.

Dyn@moX1: No prob on the burner. Send the black location and I'll get the shovel.

AKabob26.2: Thx. Sending location now.

"Get the shovel" meant Xander was up for the dig. He couldn't resist the prospect of successfully hacking into NASA's most confidential files. It was a challenge he would eagerly accept, no matter how tired he was. Alé sent a series of encrypted messages telling him exactly where he could find the black file in question.

His game now forgotten, Xander got to work.

Chapter 7

Nate collected Alé at the cafeteria the next morning and made him go through a thorough frisk search before they proceeded to Eta's room. "It's protocol," Nate said with a shrug.

Alé finished his cup of coffee and allowed the search of his person, but he was well aware that typical security protocol in most NASA facilities did not include this type of intrusion. After Nate seemed satisfied that Alé had nothing of interest on him, they left the cafeteria and headed down the hallway to the elevator.

Once on level six, Nate led Alé down a series of hallways and past several laboratories, moving through two passcodeprotected doors along the way. They were obviously moving deeper into the complex, hence the heightened security measures. Just past the second set of security doors, they stopped in front of a door that opened into a small office.

"Ms. Stanton requested that we provide you with a workspace while you're visiting. This is your office. Per Ms. Stanton's request, this workspace is located not far from Ms. Shepard. She knew you'd want to be close. You'll use your holo-watch to enter the doors. We've remotely programmed your watch for the access. Any questions?"

Alé shook his head and walked into the small room, noticing that it too had a fake window at the back. The window was switched off at the moment, but the holo-screen that controlled it glowed to life as he walked through the door— motion censored. He set his bag down on the small metal desk and went back out to the hallway.

Nate nodded and they set off again.

The hallway curved to the right before opening up into a large, open room filled with cubicles. This was the nurses' station, Nate informed him. It was the main workspace for the nurses and research assistants in charge of monitoring Eta.

A man and woman sat at a bank of desks along the wall inputting data into holo-screens. Each wore a white lab coat with the NASA Guard insignia sewn onto the left breast. They didn't look up as Nate and Alé passed them.

"Are they nurses or guard members?" Alé asked, puzzled by the lab coats.

"They are guard members but also nurses. The medical staff in this unit is a division of the NASA Guard."

"Wow." Alé shook his head in disbelief. "I had no idea the guard had a medical division. I thought their role was strictly security."

Nate nodded but didn't respond. Apparently, it was not his job to elaborate. Now that Alé thought about it, he hadn't seen anyone who *wasn't* wearing the guard insignia since he arrived. Even the handful of people eating breakfast in the cafeteria that morning had worn these lab coats.

They continued down the hall to a separate office at the back of the room. Tess stood in the doorway wearing a smart blue, striped pantsuit. He could tell it was her office from the array of paperwork and dirty coffee mugs lying in haphazard piles on the desk. Alé had worked with Tess for months during the rescue mission and knew that keeping her personal workspace clean was *not* one of her priorities.

"Good morning, Alé," Tess said as he and Nate approached, a tight smile drawn across her face. She nodded at Nate, who nodded back and turned to leave. "Let's go see her, shall we?"

Chapter 8

New Mexico

Time Since Touchdown: 35 Days

The door to Eta's room looked like every other door on level six of the White Sands facility: gray metal, no window, with a holo-screen locking mechanism surrounding the knob. Tess stood at the doorway and pressed a button on the holo-screen, which beeped in response.

"Eta, there's someone here to see you," Tess said into the screen, which beeped again.

A short moment later, Eta's voice came through the screen. "I'm awake, Tess. Come in." It sounded clear as a bell and exactly as Alé remembered from his many conversations with her while she was on board the Delta.

Lovely.

Tess glanced at Alé and waved her holo-watch in front of the locking mechanism. The door clicked, allowing her to twist the handle and enter the room. Once inside, she gestured for him to follow her.

Alé stepped into the room. He wasn't sure how he thought he might react to seeing Eta for the first time, but he never expected what actually happened.

She sat in the bed, propped up with pillows, holding a holo-screen. He had an idea of what she looked like based on conversations he'd had with her and, in many ways, she looked exactly how he imagined. But at the same time, she looked nothing like what he expected.

She had dark brown hair swept gently to the side of her neck, hanging down past her shoulder. In contrast to her hair, her skin was pale with a hint of freckles across her nose.

But it was her eyes that caught his attention. They were large and liquid, wide set on her face, with dark brown irises.

Eta looked up at him for only a moment before realization came over her face. Her breath hitched in her throat and the holo-screen dropped from her hands, landing on her lap. For a brief second, she closed her eyes. When she opened them again, a fat tear rolled down her cheek as her lips parted into a smile.

"I'll just step out and give you two a moment," Tess said, quietly leaving and allowing the door to click shut behind her.

Alé took a hesitant step toward the bed. He wanted so desperately to come closer to her, but his legs didn't seem to want to work. It was as though someone had shot him through the chest with a stun gun—electrical pulses paralyzing his limbs. His eyes widened and his throat became tight.

"Come here," Eta said, her voice steady despite the tears rolling down her cheeks.

He gulped and, willing his legs to move, took two steps, not taking his eyes off her face.

Then two more steps.

Then two more in short, jerky motions.

When he reached the edge of the bed, he sat, his eyes still fixed solely on her. The emotions seemed to hit him all at once. He'd longed to meet her in person for so many months, his mind couldn't seem to wrap around the fact that he was now here, looking right at her. Before he realized it, he was sobbing, holding his face in his hands.

"No... Please don't do that," Eta said, her chin trembling.

He choked back another sob and wiped his eyes before looking down and gently taking her hand. Her skin was so smooth, and he stroked the back of her hand with his fingertips, memorizing the sensation of it—warm and smooth and soft. She squeezed his fingers in return.

Her eyes were so large and warm, he felt like he could look into them forever, and if he got too close, maybe he could fall right into them and feel her warmth surround him. He released her hand and brought his fingers up to her face, gently cupping her cheek. She dropped her gaze and let her head fall into his hand, allowing him to support her. He ran his thumb across the smooth skin of her cheekbone.

"Alé, you saved my life." Her voice was calm and smooth.

He pulled her face closer to his, examining her lips. They were plump and pink and slightly parted. He wanted to memorize every millimeter of her skin.

"Eta, I have waited my whole life for you. There is so much I want to show you."

"Show me, Alé. I want to see everything."

Chapter 9

His hands cradle my face. Both of us are crying.

After several moments, he releases me. My body reacts to the sudden absence of his hands. My neck gives a little, and my head drops slightly. The movement is so sudden that my breath catches in my throat.

He must see the look of loss on my face because he smiles. A small, crooked little bit of a smile, but a smile, nonetheless. Then he tips his head to the side like he did when he first entered the room and the smile grows broader.

"How are you feeling?" he asks.

A polite question. As if the last few moments never happened. As if he didn't just tell me that he's waited his whole life to meet me. As if I am a child lying here in this hospital bed.

"Wonderful," I say.

And it's true. I feel better than I have for years. When I was on the Delta, I feared I would never adjust to the full gravity on the surface. I thought it might crush me—mind, body, and soul. I wondered if I would miss the weightlessness and the views of the freefall.

But I don't miss the Delta. The gravity has been difficult to battle, but I've done it. In a way, I'm more accomplished now than I ever have been.

"Wonderful," he repeats with that same crooked smile. I notice something in his eyes. That smile doesn't quite make it up that far. It curves out of his lips and pulls at the dimple on his right cheek, but it doesn't touch his eyes. They are dark brown, like mine, and there is something sad in them.

Something wary.

"Why haven't you been here to see me yet?" The words come out tight and strained. I try not to sound accusatory, but I can't hide the hurt. He was my lifeline for so many weeks and he—*we*—worked so hard to get me back here alive. It doesn't make sense that he would wait so long to see me when I finally got here.

"I tried…" he says, his voice trailing, his eyes falling to the floor. He sounds hurt and I feel terrible. I don't want him to hurt. He sits up a little and clears his throat. "I tried, Eta. But I didn't want to bother you while you were recovering."

"You would never bother me, Alé. I've been waiting. I mean, I wondered why you weren't here and I thought…" I don't know how to finish the sentence. I'm not sure what I thought, but it wasn't anything good. I wanted to believe he wanted to see me. But the longer he waited, the less I believed.

"You thought," he says. It's only a repeat of my words. He isn't asking me to elaborate. "It's complicated, Eta." Again, his voice trails. His face looked composed before, but it crumples once again and his eyes are full of pain. He takes my hand and this time, he brings it up to his cheek, pressing the insides of my fingers and palm to his skin. It is smooth, yet under the top layer, I detect the stubble of his beard, which will peek out to reveal a five-o'clock shadow within the next few hours.

My mother's skin felt like mine. It had an inherently female quality to it. Soft, smooth, and light to the touch, almost bouncy. Of course, during the last stages of her illness, her skin became tougher, thinner, and withered. I remember her holding me as a child though, when her skin wasn't dying with the rest of her body, my face pressed into her chest, her warm, womanly skin next to mine.

Alé's skin is nothing like that. It's delightfully rough and manly, and it's tight against his cheekbones. Yet the warmth from my hand makes it inviting. Immediately, I try to memorize its texture. He won't keep my hand there for long and I want to savor it. It's strange that the feel of his skin delights me, but apart from my mother's and my own, I've never felt another person's skin before.

Even the doctors and nurses wear gloves whenever they touch me. Tess's hands are always clasped together at her waist, her fingers pointed and bony. Alé's dark, rough skin might be the most exciting thing I've ever touched and I never want to forget what that's like.

To my terror and delight, he closes his eyes and leans his face into my palm, lightly kissing it.

His lips.

I don't even have the words to describe how they feel. They are heaven. After pausing for a fraction of a second with his lips on my palm, he slips my hand down from his face and cups it between his hands in his lap.

Breathless and elated, I feel *alive*.

I must have a strange expression on my face because he asks, "What are you thinking?"

Heat immediately rushes through me, the blood burning my cheeks like fire. With my blush, his face lightens some and that crooked smile returns to his lips, the lips he pressed against my palm seconds ago.

"I... I..." I try to get ahold of myself. "I'm just realizing that I've never felt another person's skin before. I mean, someone other than my mother. I've never touched a man's skin before."

I have spoken the truth, but I might die of embarrassment.

His smile widens and he nods slightly. He understands. Then he looks down at my hand, still cupped in his. He gently traces the lines of the veins on the back of my hand with his index finger. Again, I feel like my skin might burn under his touch. Electric shocks of delight shoot up my arm and a shiver rolls through my entire body.

Before I can catch my breath, he places my hand back on the bed next to me and stands. Looking down at me now, he says, "Eta—"

He's cut off by the door opening behind him and turns to look. I don't look at the door.

Only at him.

Tess pokes her head in. I know it's her at the door because I can see her dark red hair in my periphery. But it's only in the periphery. Alé takes front and center in my frame of vision.

"Alé, I need you to come out here. You have a call," she says with hesitation in her voice.

Alé nods to her and turns back to look at me. Again, his eyes have that pained look in them. He's furrowed his brow, a tight line running from his forehead down to the top of his nose.

Is he worried about something? Is that what I see in those dark eyes?

Tess does not leave the room this time. Instead, she watches his movement from the door. He lightly touches my arm, his fingers grazing the skin. But it's enough of a touch to send the hot blood shooting through my body again. "Eta, I need to take this. I'll be back to see you soon."

"No." My voice has been surprisingly calm, but it's starting to break. It wavers and the tone rises, bordering on the edge of panic. I gulp. "No. I don't want you to go. Stay… please." I beg with my eyes. I reach up and grab his arm with more strength than I thought possible from my own feeble hands. I hold on tight. Desperation rises in my throat. It tightens up and I have to swallow. "Please?"

His face instantly smooths and he smiles again. That delicious, crooked smile. He's trying to put me at ease. "Soon, Eta. I will be here again soon. I promise."

He takes my hand, the same hand that touched his face only moments before, and pulls it up to his lips, giving my fingertips one final kiss. He sets my hand back on the bed and turns to leave. Before I can recover, he is gone, slipping through the door behind Tess. The door clicks shut.

I am alone again.

After he leaves the room, strength flows out of me like air rapidly escaping a breach in a pressure hull. I slide back onto the bed and rely on the stiff mattress to fully support my head, neck, and shoulders. Rolling my head to one side, I stare blankly at the wall to my left.

It's painted a stark white. There are no pictures or decor, only the flat, matte surface of the wall. Mounted to it are two cabinets used to hold medical supplies and a bank of electrical outlets—all white.

Plugged into the outlets are numerous cords that run to the various machines that surround my bed, taking all sorts of measurements. Tess says every medical observation they make will go down as a titanic leap forward in the science of understanding how the human body works in space. With my eyes, I follow the thick, black power cords to the machines that sit right next to me. I follow the tubes and wires that protrude from those machines and wind their way to my head, neck, arms, stomach, and legs. There are electrodes taped all over my body taking constant measurements of my vital signs.

My eyelids become heavy with sleep and exhaustion. I think of Alé, right outside my door, yet not in the room with me. My final thought before I allow sleep to overcome me is that I don't know if I'll be able to wait until he visits again.

I must get stronger.

Chapter 10

New Mexico

Time Since Touchdown: 35 Days

Alé stood with Tess outside Eta's door, stunned. He had wept in front of this person whom he'd never seen before. Yet, it was as if they'd taken his heart from his body, folded it into a blanket, and laid it, still beating, on the bed.

Seeing Eta for the first time was like seeing a part of himself. His final piece. He'd spent his whole life feeling incomplete and now, she was there, the missing piece. The pain in her eyes when Tess had called him out of the room was almost more than he could take.

"Is there a call?" he asked, a roughness to his voice.

"No," Tess said, crossing her arms in front of her chest. "Things seemed to be getting a little too emotional in there. I don't want her getting upset."

Alé's face twisted into a look of disbelief, his mouth falling open.

"Wait. You called me out because she was getting too *emotional*?" He spat the last word, his heart pounding. "Let me back in!" As he reached for the door handle, Tess stepped in front of him.

"Alé, listen to me." She took a breath and reached up, grabbing his shoulders and looking him straight in the eye. "It's extremely important that you understand what I'm about to tell you. Eta is vital to our research. The things we'll learn from her are far more important to the future of space travel than any experiment we've ever done in the past. I can't risk *anything* upsetting that research. Do you understand?"

His jaw tightened and his fingers clenched into tight fists. "Tess, I get it, she's important. But for heaven's sake, she's been through hell! I was the first person she ever spoke to other than her mother. I laughed with her and kept her company when she was lonely. I worked with her for hours on end to ensure a safe rescue. I was there for her when she needed me. She needs me now! Didn't you see the pain on her face? She's struggling, Tess... and I can help her. Why would you want to prevent that?"

Tess nodded, her hands still planted firmly on Alé's shoulders. "Yes, you can help her. But you can also jeopardize the research. She's very fragile right now, physically and emotionally. This is one of the reasons I thought it best to keep you away from her during this time. I don't want any emotional reactions to derail her recovery."

Seething, Alé pushed Tess's hands away from him. He moved closer to her, his breath hot, and through clenched teeth, he said, "What does *she* want?"

Tess flinched slightly but didn't back away, jutting her chin defiantly. "That's none of your concern."

"What does *that* mean?" Suddenly, he couldn't bear the thought of standing so close to her. He feared what he might do. He turned to face the wall, resting his hands against the cold, painted concrete.

"It means, Alé, that you are not her doctor. I am. And her medical status is none of your concern."

He turned swiftly to face her. "You haven't even asked her, have you?" The words were barely audible as they escaped his clenched teeth. "All that time we spent—hours upon hours of sleepless nights—trying to rescue her. I thought you were on her side, Tess." His face twisted in anguish and he fought to keep the angry tears from escaping his eyes.

His harsh words weren't what she expected. She turned her eyes away uncomfortably and crossed her arms in front of her chest. "Yes, well, I *am* on her side. She'll come to understand that what she's doing is part of a groundbreaking move forward. She's a smart girl. When Project Diamond lifts off, she'll understand her role. I am confident of that."

"It sounds to me like what you're doing is illegal, keeping her here for 'research' without her consent."

Tess stepped forward, her face suddenly stone. "Are you threatening me, Alé?"

Her eyes had turned cold, and despite his anger, he knew he'd gone too far. If Tess or anyone else got the idea that he wasn't playing on the NASA team, he'd be out and there would be nothing he could do for Eta.

So, instead of spitting in her face like he wanted to do, he softened, allowing his shoulders to slump.

"No, of course not," he said, running his fingers through his curly hair. "Just promise me you'll ask her. Please? Do it for her, Tess. Ask her permission to do your research."

Tess nodded but remained silent. She looked away.

Alé sighed. "Can I at least see her once more before I leave?"

"Yes, of course. I'll arrange a final meeting for you on Friday. I believe that's the day before the jet goes back to Baltimore."

"Thank you."

Defeated and exhausted, Alé leaned against the wall and allowed his head to roll back on his neck, his eyes closed as Tess paged Nate over her holo-phone. Nate reappeared in less than a minute to escort Alé back to the small office where he was to begin his day of work. As he turned to leave, Tess put her hand on his shoulder. "Cheer up, Alé. I promise you this will turn out to be a good thing for everyone—including Eta."

He didn't look at her as he walked away.

Chapter 11

The night nurse is named Millie. She comes in at 9:30 p.m. every night to record my vitals, give me my medication, and ask if there's anything I need before I sleep.

It's like clockwork. No deviation. At 9:30 on the nose, she makes her way into my room.

Millie always plugs her portable holo-screen into the primary console that controls all the other medical monitoring machines and compiles the data. She uploads the data the machines have collected and clears the console before disconnecting her holo-screen. When she leaves the room, she always punches in a code that puts the primary console into sleep mode. The lights on it dim and the beeps it makes throughout the day are silent. I assume she does this so I can sleep without the machines waking me.

The morning nurse is named Nila. When she comes in, again, like clockwork at 8:30 a.m., the first thing she does is bring the primary console out of sleep mode. But Nila does not plug in her holo-screen.

This is important. It means they aren't monitoring me throughout the night. How could they? They stopped putting the electrodes on me during the night because I was having such an issue with nightmares. The cords would get tangled around me and I'd end up ripping the electrodes off my skin in my sleep.

I'm planning to teach myself how to walk again and I don't want them to know about it yet. Something about this place isn't sitting well with me. Although they're taking care of me, they don't seem interested in making me stronger or more independent. I have had only limited interaction with physical therapists and no one has prompted me to move much other than doing simple exercises in my bed to keep the bed sores at bay.

Well, with the exception of that one time they got me up to walk in front of all those nurses and doctors. But after thinking about that for a few weeks now, I know that exercise wasn't for my benefit. It had something to do with their research.

No, nothing they've done here has been much about me at all.

Tess comes to see me every day at least once. I ask her every time I see her when I'll get to leave the room and every time, she puts me off. She tells me to have patience, or to stop worrying and keep my mind on recovery, or she abruptly takes a call from her holo-phone.

It's not right.

When I ask the nurses, they act as if they have no idea what I'm talking about. Doctors come in from time to time too and they aren't any better, telling me the same things Tess does: concentrate on recovery and let us do the worrying for you.

Well, I'm tired of leaving things up to them. I'm going to get stronger on my own. I am absolutely determined that the next time Alé sees me, I'll be able to stand up next to him on equal ground. I'll be able to walk around without pain. I will show him that I'm getting better and hopefully he'll help me understand what's going on around here.

There is one flaw in my plan: the cameras. There are four, one in each corner of the room. At first, I wasn't sure if they actually were cameras because they're hidden behind opaque glass bubbles. But the longer I've looked at them, the more I believe they must be cameras.

I mean, why wouldn't they have cameras on me? They're monitoring everything else I do. What are the odds that they shut down the cameras, like the monitoring equipment, at night? Probably slim. But it's a risk I must take if I'm going to get stronger on my own. If they are watching me at night, and if they do have a problem with my exercise plans, I'll hear about it soon enough.

I start my plan the first night after Alé's visit. Millie puts the console into sleep mode and leaves the room. I lie awake for a few minutes listening in case anyone decides to come in. Then I begin my exercises.

First, I work on sitting up in bed. I've been lying in this bed now for weeks and pulling my torso away from it is no easy task, but I start with a little at a time. It takes me a few minutes, but I come to a seated position at the edge of the bed, my legs still supported by the mattress. I lean over the railing and stare down at the white tile floor. It seems almost menacing, daring me to push myself.

My abdominal muscles are weak and pathetic, and they need some serious work. After several minutes of staring down at the floor, daring myself to make the next move, I collapse back on the bed. Maybe I'll feel better about taking that first step if I do some leg exercises.

I start slow, lifting each leg and holding it at an angle until my muscles feel like they might split open. I work on this on and off for several hours, taking breaks when my legs feel like they're on fire and picking them back up after they've cooled off. I'm so exhausted, but I know I must keep trying. I can always sleep later. This—getting myself moving again—is too important. Seeing

Alé has reminded me of that. If I want any chance of getting out of here, I must do this for myself.

I scoot my butt to the end of the bed, gripping the railings with sweaty palms. It takes me several moments of grunting and sweating to get myself in the right position, but I do get there eventually, and I pause to wipe my hands on my hospital gown. My legs are now dangling over the edge of the bed, and the railings, which I have been relying on for support, are too far behind me now. I'll have to use the mattress to push my body up over my legs.

Planting my hands firmly into the mattress, I take a deep breath. I count backward from ten to get myself mentally ready to push my entire body weight up.

And then… I push. Hard.

Before I realize it, I'm standing. My bare feet have hit the cold floor with a thud and I'm supporting almost all of my body weight over my very own legs. To my amazement, it doesn't feel that bad, not like the first time I tried it and nearly collapsed from the effort.

My hands are still firmly on the mattress holding up some of my weight in case the load becomes too great. I don't want to fall on the floor. I'll never get back up.

After two or three seconds of standing, my knees give way and my butt falls down, thumping on the mattress. I'm so happy with this progress, that I immediately prepare to do it again, and this time, I'm able to stand on my legs for five seconds before they give out on me. Then ten. Then twenty. I count them off in my head, making a mental note of my progress.

I spend the next two nights practicing this, working on leg and abdominal exercises to make my muscles stronger, and standing at the end of the bed. Before the third night is over, I can stand for a full five minutes. I can lean from side to side and can even bend over and touch my knees.

Walking is different. It requires coordination.

By the fourth night, I'm ready to try. I'm not used to how I should pick up my legs and plant my feet. It feels so different from the way it did on the Delta where the gravity was so light. I learn that because my legs are so much heavier here, I can't take very long strides. If I do, my knees buckle; they're still weak. But if I keep my stride short and take little shuffling steps, I can actually walk all the way from the end of my bed to the door across the room, about two meters.

As my coordination and strength improve, I become more confident and start to do laps around the room, counting how many I can do at a time before I have to stop and rest. First two laps. Then five. Then fifteen. By the end of the fifth night, I realize I've spent the entire night walking around the room and only had to rest a few times.

I am standing behind the door to my room tonight when I hear some familiar voices outside. This is strange because it's the first time I've heard anything happening on the other side of the door. Though I've lost track of time, I know it's almost time for Nila's morning check. But curiosity takes over and I lean in closer to catch the clipped end of a sentence.

"…but she's getting stronger."

Inhaling, I place my hands lightly on the back of the door and press my ear directly on the metal surface. I recognize the voice on the other side.

It's Tess.

"Do you really think that's a good idea?" Her voice sounds muffled through the door. "I can perform the surgery, but it's going to put a halt on her recovery."

"I understand your concern," says another voice. This one's deeper, a man's voice. "But the amount of medical data we could obtain from an exploratory laparotomy would be invaluable. We may as well do it now before she makes any further progress. If we don't, we'll miss our window."

He's got my full attention now. A laparotomy is an abdominal surgery. I know this from my medical research when my mother was dying of breast cancer on the Delta. It's the type of surgery done when they need to examine the contents of the abdomen and determine the source of any bleeding or trauma. It's not something a doctor would do on someone healthy. Unless they were studying that person.

The realization that they're talking about me hits me like a fist to the chest and I instinctively flinch away from the door. Are they seriously planning to put me under the knife to study my internal organs? I press my ear to the door again as Tess begins to speak.

"Yes, I see your point. The stronger she gets, the harder it will be to convince her of the need for this."

"Look, the fact is, we don't need her permission. This is our research and this exploratory surgery is essential for further study of her anatomy. But, in the interest of saving face with her, at least for now, let's convince her that this is necessary. It will be easier that way. You can do that, right?"

"Sure, I don't see a problem with that. She's under our care here. Why would she question the need for an additional surgery?"

"That's the spirit." I hear a light slap, as if the man has slapped her on the shoulder, a gesture of good will. "Let's continue with the current plan to keep her mobility limited. How long do you think you'll need to get prepared for this? I don't want this rushed, Tess. Your research is vital to the coming mission and I want full documentation before, during, and after the procedure."

"Right. Of course. Give me a few days to put together a surgical team. We'll also need to set up the operating room for multicamera filming of the surgery. I'll need two holo-screens for surgical assistants to take notes and categorize photographs, and we'll need at least three full days with the lab to analyze tissue samples taken from the surgery once it's complete."

"Whatever you need. Email Jade with your list of necessities and recommendations. Keep it quiet with the medical staff until you can talk to the subject."

The "subject" is me, I realize. A sick feeling comes over me and my body starts to sway. I brace against the door to keep from falling over.

"I'll keep you posted," Tess says.

Before I can collect my thoughts, the door lock beeps and the handle clicks. Panic grips me. I do not want them to find me here, standing and walking around my room.

I push my body away from the door and spin around to face the bed. I've never shuffled so fast in my life, but I manage to make it to the bed without tumbling over just as the door cracks.

Fortunately, Tess is still talking to the man outside, wrapping up the tail end of their conversation, and she isn't paying attention to the door. This allows me time to scoot myself into bed and fling the bedsheet over myself. I lay my head to the side and close my eyes, counting the numbers down from ten to calm my breathing.

Ten, nine, eight, seven…

I peek through half-closed eyes to see Tess pushing the door open further, still preoccupied with her outside conversation.

Six, five, four, three, two, one…

She finishes speaking and pushes the door wide open, walking in with a big smile plastered across her face. She flicks on the light and directs her smile at me. Her teeth blaze behind orange lipstick. The sight only serves to worsen the ill feeling in my stomach, but I manage to get myself under control and play as if I've just woken from a long, peaceful sleep.

"Good morning, Eta. How did you sleep?"

Chapter 12

New Mexico

Time Since Touchdown: 39 Days

There was a sharp knock at the door.

"Come in."

Patrick looked up to see Tess standing in the doorway of his office at White Sands. Her red hair was wild around her face and she looked frazzled. Patrick noticed a coffee stain on the left breast pocket of her white lab coat. She'd been putting in twelve-hour days preparing for Eta's exploratory surgery, which was scheduled to happen in ten days. Apparently, it was taking a toll on her.

"I need a quick word with you. There's been a... development," she said, biting her lower lip.

Patrick motioned for Tess to take a seat in front of his desk. The office was much smaller and far less regal than his office in DC, although it was one of the nicer offices at the White Sands complex, set aside for the few times a year Patrick made the trip to the facility. The metal desk was small, which helped to make the room feel larger than it was. A large holo-screen meant to serve as a false window adorned the wall behind the desk with a picture of the New Mexico desert projected on it. A single chair made of wood and cheap vinyl stood across from Patrick's own leather chair to accommodate visitors. Aside from a large credenza on the far wall, which held a fake potted plant and an antique set of encyclopedias, the room had no other furnishing or wall embellishments.

Tess plopped into the chair and let out a sigh, setting a small holo-screen on her lap.

"What's going on?" Patrick asked.

"It might be easier if I show you." Tess set the holo-screen on Patrick's desk and flicked her finger across it to bring it to life. She maneuvered through the screen files and pulled up a video feed tile. She pinched the holographic image to widen it. Patrick saw it was a video of Eta sleeping in her bed. Tess flicked through a few frames and Patrick watched as Eta sat up and carefully scooted to the end of the bed.

She skipped ahead a few more frames to show Eta standing at the end of the bed before immediately collapsing. She skipped forward again to a frame showing Eta taking several tentative steps.

"When was this?" Patrick asked, his eyebrows drawing together.

"Three days ago. She's been doing this every night as soon as the night nurse clears her dinner tray and puts the monitoring equipment into sleep mode. She usually waits about ten minutes before she starts."

Patrick watched Eta move around the screen, his eyes fixed on her. "Fascinating. She's actually walking."

Tess nodded. "Yes, she's walking. And she's become quite good at it. We've been telling her that she needs time to heal and that we'll have her up and walking soon, but apparently, she's decided to take matters into her own hands. The stem cell caps that the surgeon implanted into her hip and thigh have helped to speed the healing and it appears she's walking with no pain."

Patrick touched the screen to pause the video. "Okay, so what's the problem?"

"No problem really. I thought maybe we should start getting her up during the day. Moving her around more. I don't see how it could hurt. Her door is locked and only those with a high-level security clearance can enter the room. Perhaps it's time."

He let out a thoughtful sigh. "Perhaps. For now, let's stick with the treatment protocol we've set up so far. The surgery is only a few days away. After she's recovered from it, we can start her physical therapy. Have you talked to her about the surgery yet?"

"No." Tess bit her lip. "I'm planning to wait a few more days. I'm still trying to work out how I want to broach the subject with her."

"Yes, well, time's running short. Figure it out soon."

"I will. Should we do anything about the walking at night?"

"Not now. Just keep an eye on it like you've been doing. If she starts to mess with the door at all, I want to hear about it immediately."

"I wouldn't worry about it. Unless the door lock is disabled, it will register if there's any movement on the knob from the inside. So far, we've had nothing except verified entries and exits."

Patrick nodded his approval. "Good. Anything else?"

"No, sir."

Tess stood to leave but he stopped her as she got to the door. "Tess, get some sleep tonight. You look like hell."

She nodded and left the office.

Chapter 13

New Mexico

Time Since Touchdown: 40 Days

Alé flipped the tiny silver phone around in his fingers, over and over. This was a very old flip-style cell phone, not anything new or fancy like the NASA-issued holo-phone he had in his pocket. The burner phone had arrived a day earlier via a courier named Scott.

Scott reminded Alé of Xander with his long, curly hair and rough beard. They were cut from the same cloth, no doubt. His security badge indicated he was a NASA courier with the lowest level of security clearance—essentially a gopher to bring mail to and from the people working at White Sands.

Scott had delivered a package to Alé containing some random files that were part of his data processing project. It was nothing Alé really needed, but he'd sent for them to allow Xander a way to get the burner cell phone to him. As Scott slipped the package out of his bag, he palmed the phone from his pocket, handing the package to Alé with the phone concealed underneath. Alé accepted, quickly slipping the phone into his own pocket, knowing they probably had security cameras hidden throughout the hallway.

Now, he waited for Xander to call with the details of what he'd found in the black file. They had chatted briefly about it on Stax using code words. Even though Stax was the most secure way for hackers to communicate, it, like all computer programs, was not immune to hacking if the right person tried. They'd decided it would be best to discuss the contents of the file with the burner phones Xander had obtained from his contact in Germany.

Alé waited for Xander's call outside the front doors of the main entrance to White Sands. There was a gift shop inside which, at one time, was intended for tourists. There were no longer tourists allowed at the facility, but many NASA employees spent time at the complex working on various projects. NASA had turned the shop into a convenience store where employees could get drinks and snacks at well above market prices, and the shelves still housed some small knickknacks and other odds and ends one would find in a gift shop.

The clerk behind the counter had a badge similar to Scott's—lowest security clearance. He watched Alé through the plate glass doors, no doubt wondering what this NASA employee was doing, sitting on a bench outside in the sweltering New Mexico heat.

Alé continued nervously flipping the phone around in his fingers, inspecting every surface of it, trying to keep his mind calm. His plan, which he'd formed before leaving Baltimore, involved a precise timeline and even he had doubts about whether it would work. As he was running through the timeline again, mentally piecing together everything that had to happen for it to work, the phone buzzed to life with a suddenness that caused him to jump. He snapped the phone open and placed it to his ear.

"Yeah."

"Hey. The lift is done." Xander's normal voice was calm and cool with a hint of hippie charm. But today, he sounded worried, his voice shaky and clipped.

"What did you learn?"

"Nothing good, man. First, that file took a shitload of time to decrypt. And now that I've gotten in there, I see why."

"Okay. What's in there?" Alé's patience was wearing thin. He was watching the store clerk behind the glass doors and he didn't want to be outside long and risk drawing attention.

"They're planning to send her back up," Xander said, his words quiet and almost inaudible.

"Excuse me?" Alé instinctively reached up and covered the ear not pressed against the phone to make sure he heard every word clearly.

"They're planning to send her back up," Xander repeated, then sighed. "Look, I'm sorry man, but that's the deal. And it's not something they've thrown together. That file was full of flight plans showing Eta as part of the crew for Project Diamond. I mean, they've spent some serious time planning this. They may have even been planning it when she was still on the Delta."

"You've got to be kidding."

"I wish I were. They don't seem to have any desire to ask her opinion on the matter either. As far as NASA's concerned, nobody outside of the small circle of engineers who helped with the rescue knows that Eta even exists. They know as long as they keep her a secret, nobody will ever question it—and that's their number one priority—keeping her a secret."

"Why?" Alé asked. "What reason could they possibly have to bring Eta back into space?"

"They want to use her as some sort of expert or consultant or something. Like when they took Ellen Ripley back to LV-426 in *Aliens*. They think she can teach the crew how to keep the spacecraft running long-term. She's the ultimate space station handywoman. Plus, they want to continue medical studies like they've been doing on the surface. They want to see how her body will react to another long-term trip."

Alé shook his head in disbelief, his jaw clenched tight. He had no words, only seething breath.

Xander seemed to sense Alé's frustration because he continued. "That's not all either. They're planning to do a series of exploratory surgeries on her starting in just a few days. They'll go into her body and take measurements and samples from all of her organs, joints, bones, connective tissues, you name it. They want Eta healed and ready to get to work by the time of the first Project Diamond launch."

"How far up does this go?" Alé asked the question, but he already knew the answer.

Xander paused. "John Patrick signed the orders for the surgeries a few days ago."

"Damn!" Alé said in a forceful whisper. He took a moment to calm himself, breathing deeply and clenching his eyes shut. "Thanks for doing that for me, Xander."

"Hey, no problem. Look, Alé, do you have a plan? If Eta's going to have any shot at a normal life here on the surface, you've got to get her out of there. Like, now."

"Yeah, I've got something in mind."

"Is she strong enough to leave? I mean, an escape won't do much good if she still can't walk... or run."

Alé nodded. "I've been keeping an eye on her medical logs. They say she's off the charts. Her bone density and muscle strength are up to ninety percent of a normal, healthy person. And she's improving with each day. Plus," he paused and pushed his hand through his hair, "she's been walking on her own."

"Oh yeah? They've got her up and walking already?"

Alé sneered, shaking his head. "No, *they* don't have her walking. She's been doing it on her own. I found security camera footage showing her doing laps around her room in the middle of the night. She's obviously decided to take it into her own hands."

"Wow." Xander's voice rose. He sounded truly surprised.

"Yeah, she's pretty unbelievable." Alé could feel his face flush thinking about Eta alone in her room, confined to her bed, taking it upon herself to learn how to walk in Earth's gravity. He meant the words—she *was* unbelievable. "Anyway, I think she's strong enough. Even if she still has some pain, she'll fight through it. I believe in her."

"Good. That's good, man." Xander paused and audibly inhaled and exhaled. "Is there anything I can do to help? I don't need to know your whole plan. In fact, the less I know, the better. But if there's anything I can do to make it easier for you, let me know."

"Yeah, actually, there is something you can do." Alé gave Xander a quick rundown of what he needed. "Will that be a problem? I know it's a lot, but I think this is the only way."

"No problem here. Compared to cracking that black file, this will be a piece of cake. Get to the big chicken in nine days. I'll have more intel for you then."

Alé nodded. "Thanks again, Xander."

"You got it."

Alé hadn't realized it, but he had started pacing. With the phone still at his ear, he turned to see the store clerk watching him. He ducked his head and walked along the sidewalk toward the parking lot. Once he reached the pavement, he took a sharp left and continued a few more steps until he was behind a small maintenance shed. He removed the phone from his ear and snapped it in half, dropping the pieces into a sewer grate behind the shed. He watched as they rattled down the metal pipe and disappeared.

Then he pulled out his holo-phone and quickly dialed his mother's number before walking out from behind the shed. As he made his way back to the front of the building, two NASA Guard members walked out the front doors. Alé noticed the store clerk was still there, still watching the happenings outside. One of the guards, a young guy with blond hair, held up his hands and said, "Mr. Bakas. Would you like to tell us what you're doing out here?"

Alé heard his mother's voice mail message play in his ear and reached down to disconnect the call. He flashed the guards a smile. "Just getting some fresh air while I make a phone call to my mom." He turned the holo-phone screen so they could easily see it. "See?"

The guards looked at each other and nodded, seemingly satisfied with his answer. The blond one said, "You'd better get back inside. They're serving supper in the dining hall in five minutes."

Alé nodded and they turned toward the glass doors. He tucked his hands in his pockets to conceal his shaking fingers.

Chapter 14

Is there really such a thing as "waiting patiently"?

The very act of waiting means you're in flux between one life event and another. Even if you're calm and collected, you still want the ensuing event to make its appearance sooner rather than later so you can stop waiting and get on with it.

That's what I'm doing now.

Waiting.

But I wouldn't describe this waiting as the patient variety. I'm jittery and I can't concentrate on anything except the door to my white room.

Alé is visiting me today—in three minutes, to be exact. Tess told me he'll be leaving on the NASA jet tomorrow morning and going back to Baltimore. I half-heartedly asked her why he only came to see me once on his visit and she gave me a half-hearted answer. "He's been busy working on an important project and simply hasn't had the time," she said.

I know she's lying. I saw the look in his eyes when he was here. He knows something isn't right here. And he wanted to be with me.

I must believe that!

I must trust the feeling I had when he touched my cheek and held my hand. When he cried into my fingers. I must remember it. Even if I never see Alé again after today, I must hang on to that memory to keep myself going.

My holo-screen is set up in my lap and it's open to page fifty-two of the book I'm reading. I've read page fifty-two at least three times over the last five minutes, but I couldn't tell you the first thing about what it says. My mind won't focus. Alé is visiting soon. He'll be here in two minutes... if he's on time.

Oh God, please let him be on time!

As I check the time on the screen for the thirteenth time in as many minutes, I hear the sharp click of the door handle twisting. The door cracks for a second, then swings wide open and Alé walks through, followed by Tess.

"Alé," I say.

The word escapes my lips like a sigh of relief. But I quickly suck my breath back when I see Tess slink over to the sofa and take a seat, crossing one short leg over the other. She's wearing her red hair in a bun at the base of her neck today, the curls harpooned into place by two long, green hairpins. As she perches on the edge of the sofa cushion, she watches Alé approach my bed. The look on her face confirms that she absolutely will not be leaving the room anytime soon. She takes out her holo-phone and begins scrolling, pretending not to notice our presence in the room.

"Eta, good evening," Alé says as he sits down on the edge of my bed. This time, he does not get too close. His eyes briefly pass over my face and his lips form a cool smile. "How are you feeling today?"

"Wonderful. Much stronger."

"Wonderful," he repeats, nodding, his smile broadening ever so slightly. "Good. I'm glad to hear that. Are they taking good care of you here?"

"Of course. Why wouldn't they?"

His eyebrow raises slightly at my question. He understands. "Yes, of course. They would only provide the best care for you. I am confident of that." His eyes dart to Tess, who continues to scroll, seemingly uninterested in our conversation. He turns his attention back to me. "I came here to bring you a gift before I leave on the jet tomorrow."

- 121 -

I hadn't noticed at first, but he has a small package wrapped in brown paper tucked under his arm. He slides it out and hands it to me.

The package is heavy and about the size of the small toolbox Nix carried with him when he went outside the Delta to do maintenance runs. Nix was the station robot. He helped me keep the Delta running and was my only friend after my mother died. He was programmed to provide companionship and the occasional comedic relief. But he was much more than that for me—he was my hero, my Iron Man. I say that only because his face looked like Iron Man's face mask and it used to make me laugh when I was a child.

Nix gave his life to save mine by cutting the Soyuz loose from the Delta after a seal malfunction prevented it from releasing on its own. As my thoughts flicker back to that moment, a tiny pain opens up in my chest. I haven't thought about Nix in so long, I didn't even realize that wound in my heart was still there. I breathe deep and straighten up in bed, bringing my attention back to the gift in my hands.

The paper is crisp and dry. I've never felt paper of this texture before. I take a moment to run my fingers over it.

"It's wrapping paper," he says, noticing my curiosity. "I'm sure you've never felt wrapping paper before. Honestly, it's all they had down at the gift shop. I guess I didn't think about it being your first experience with wrapping paper. I would have picked out something more… beautiful."

I smile. "It *is* beautiful." I carefully slide my finger under the small swatch of tape holding the package together and unfold the wrapping paper. Inside is a book bound in deep brown leather with the word *Journal* etched into the spine. I turn it over in my hands, examining it and memorizing the feel of the leather.

It's smooth and the surface gives ever so slightly when I press my fingers into it. I bring it up close to my face and close my eyes, taking a long, deep breath. It smells like the soil in the garden on the Delta. Inside the journal, there's blank, cream-colored writing paper. I slide my thumb along the edge, letting the pages fan out under my skin.

"It's really nothing special," he says. "They had it in the gift shop and I thought… well, I thought maybe you'd like it."

"It's the most beautiful thing I've ever seen." Tears prick at my eyelids. That's almost true. It's the most beautiful thing I've ever seen aside from him walking through my door.

He smiles and his eyes seem to cloud up a bit too. Tess, sensing the emotion in the room, makes a small "tsk" sound through her teeth. A look of frustration comes over Alé's face, but he quickly composes himself. "Well, I'm glad you like it."

"I'll cherish it. Thank you."

He nods. "You're welcome. It was wonderful to see you again, Eta. I hope…" He pauses and glances over at Tess. "I hope we can see each other again soon."

The tears have left my eyes and are flowing freely down my face. I make no move to stop them. The thought of him leaving again is almost more than I can bear. I want to show him how hard I've worked teaching myself to walk again. I want to hold him in my arms and tell him how grateful I am that he saved my life on the Delta. I want to run away with him and see everything there is to see on this beautiful planet.

But I realize that's not in the cards. I won't be leaving with him on the jet. I won't be seeing the world with him. I may not be on the Delta any longer, but I am still alone.

"Please don't cry." He takes my hands in his and leans forward. Very gently, he presses his lips to my cheek. More tears stream down and I'm sure he can taste them. His head tilts slightly so his lips are right next to my ear. He whispers, "Check the inside binding."

He pulls away from me and his eyes dart to the camera in the corner of the room above my bed and then back to my eyes. He winks, flashing me that handsome, sideways smile he flashed me when I first met him. It takes me only a second to realize what he's done and I replace the confused look on my face with a solemn mask. He lifts my hand and gives me one more peck on the back of my fingers before standing and clearing his throat. Tess looks up from her holo-phone, nods, and stands to go.

She hasn't noticed a thing.

Chapter 15

Again, I must be patient. I feel like the suspense might kill me though.

A few moments after Alé leaves my room, Tess comes back in. She does her normal routine, sitting on the edge of the sofa, chatting about this and that, nothing meaningful or even noteworthy. She bids me farewell as the nurse brings me my supper.

Today's menu is potatoes sauteed with bell peppers, onions, and black beans. On the side, they've included a small salad with oil and spices drizzled over it.

Over the last forty-one days since touchdown, they have fed me strictly food that I would have had in the garden on the Delta. My mother had worked on the garden tirelessly when she was alive and it became a large, thriving part of the old space station. I continued to keep it up after she died, not only because it provided me with my only source of food and oxygen, but because it made me happy to work on it. The plants were the closest things I had to companions, aside from Nix.

So, yes, I loved the garden. When I was on the Delta, I became quite good at cooking the various foods the garden provided. But I'm not there anymore and I would like to try some other foods. I've never tasted meat or eggs or milk. I've never smelled barbecue or orange juice or tuna casserole. I've never experienced the texture of raw oysters or coconut flakes or freshly baked bread slathered in butter.

I want to try new things!

But so far, all I've gotten are the same old fruits, vegetables, grains, and herbs I had on the Delta.

I asked Tess about this and she assured me they planned to work new foods into my diet. She gave me an elaborate spiel about their dietary plan and how bringing in new foods too soon would cause serious digestive tract issues and could even lead to the development of allergies and food intolerances.

I think she's full of it.

For some reason, they want to keep me eating only the foods I've grown up with—only foods that can be planted in a space station garden.

I sigh as they bring in the familiar meal. Whoever made it didn't cook it long enough because the potatoes are still crisp on the inside. I push it around with my fork for a few minutes after the nurse drops it off.

When I'm sure she won't come back in, I reach for the journal tucked under my bedsheet and open it, flipping the blank pages back and forth against my thumb. I slide it under the tray table so it's sitting on top of my legs but out of view of the camera watching me from over my head and continue to push food around on my plate. I'm fairly certain that from the other cameras in the room, it looks like I'm just eating.

After taking a few more bites, I slide my finger along the edge of the back cover of the journal. Indeed, there is a thin gap between the leather and the actual cover of the book. I slip my finger into the gap and feel a piece of paper tucked into the space. I pause to take another bite of my food and a sip of water before delicately sliding the piece of paper out of the journal.

Again, I pause to take a bite of food so, if they are watching me, they won't notice anything suspicious. I spread the note out on top of the journal so I can read it by glancing at it under my tray table. In tiny, neat handwriting it says:

Eta,

You are in danger here. I can't explain everything now, but I will as soon as it's safe.

Do you trust me?

I have a plan. At exactly 2:15 a.m., the nurses will change shifts. That's your chance to get away. Leave your room. The door is not locked; I've already ensured that, and go down the hallway to the left. You'll come to an intersection of another hallway. Take a right. The second door on the left is a linen closet. Go inside and wait for me. I'll be there to get you shortly after 2:15 a.m.

If you don't want to take this risk, I understand. You've been through so much. If you decide not to come, I will make my way back to my room and nobody will know anything of this. But I hope you'll come with me.

I want to show you everything.

Be safe, Miss Coco-naut,
Alé

My breath catches in my throat and tears sting my eyes. He called me a "coco-naut" in an email the night before I left the Delta. He was teasing me, of course, but I still remember it as one of those funny, sweet, magical connections we made while I was still in orbit.

My heart pounds and my fingers shake as I lift my fork to take another bite of potatoes. I close my eyes and take a deep breath, forcing the tears to retreat back into my body so I won't give anything away for the watchful eyes behind the cameras.

With the note still on top of the journal, I close the pages, tucking the note safely inside. I contemplate leaving the rest of my supper on the plate, but decide it's not a good idea. I'll need my strength and I quickly gobble down the rest of my meal. I push the tray table to the side and slide the journal under my bedsheet again. Then I grab my holo-screen and return to page fifty-two of the book I'm reading.

The nurse comes a few minutes later to clear away my tray and asks me if there's anything else she can do for me before bedtime. I tell her that I'm fine and to turn the lights off when she leaves, which she does.

As soon as she's gone, I curl up in a fetal position under my sheets and wrap my arms around the journal, bringing it close to me. The leather touches the skin of my chest, cool at first, then warming to match the temperature of my body.

In the note, he asked me if I trusted him. It's a shame he even needed to ask. I'll make sure he knows the answer.

I close my eyes but instead of willing sleep to come, I turn on my imagination and a smile spreads across my lips as I think about his words.

I want to show you everything.

A shiver runs through my body. Again, I find myself waiting. This time though, I'm not nervous or scared.

I've never been as confident about anything in my life.

Chapter 16

I'm standing behind the door of my white room moments after two o'clock, my fingers resting gently on the cold metal knob, their tips tingling with anticipation. I remove them from the knob and wipe my sweaty palms on my cloth pants.

I wish I had some other clothing, but the light blue scrubs they've given me are all I've got. Immediately after touchdown, I had to wear a god-awful gown with a big slit up the back and thick Velcro strips holding it shut. That was the worst. I asked several times for something else to wear and they finally gave me the same medical scrubs the nurses wear. I have no shoes, only a thick pair of socks with antislip rubber pads on the bottoms. And despite the fact that the slate floor is cold as ice, my feet are sweating in anticipation of the next few minutes. I have Alé's journal cinched into the waistband of my pants. I want to have this with me. I'm willing to leave everything else behind but not the journal.

I'm watching the shaft of light under the door. Usually, if anyone walks up to the door from the hallway outside, their footsteps make the light dance. But now, there's nobody coming. It's a solid beam.

There's no window in this door. Most nights, I'm happy about this, but tonight I kind of wish there was a window. The thought of opening the door to the unknown that lurks on the other side is making my stomach flutter. Again, I bring my trembling fingers to the door handle.

The clock on the wall ticks with the turn of the minute: 2:05 a.m. I have an internal battle going on in my mind. If I leave the room too early, I risk running into the nurse before the shift change. I have no idea what the configuration of the hallway is outside my door, so I won't be able to avoid the nurse's station if it's in sight of my door. If I leave the room too late, I might miss Alé, and the thought of him leaving me here because I didn't get to the closet on time makes my mouth run dry.

I decide to take one final walk around my room before I open the door. It's not a very big room—perhaps five meters square—with a small bathroom attached. I can walk from the door to the fake window opposite the door in twelve steps. Then it's another twelve steps to the back of the room where the small bathroom is. I walk past the sofa where Tess always sits to give me her reports. Stepping behind my bed, I carefully avoid the monitoring equipment that surrounds it. I let my fingertips graze the mattress and think of all the time I've spent in this bed.

On the final side of the room is built-in cabinetry—all white—with a countertop and a small sink built into it. I run my fingers over the metal faucet. It reminds me of the small sink in the bathroom on the Delta, compact yet functional, the type of thing NASA would implement.

I take my final few steps and I'm back at the door. The clock ticks again: 2:12 a.m.

It's time.

With a deep breath, I grasp the door handle and twist. The handle is surprisingly easy to turn, and, as Alé promised in his note, it is unlocked.

I wonder how he pulled that off?

The door opens easily and I peek out into the hallway. I see the source of the light streaming under the doorway is an open room to my right. There are several desks and cubicles in the room. This must be the nurse's station. I don't see or hear anything coming from there, so I slip out the door and close it behind me, flinching as the latch clicks into place. It seemed very loud to me and I immediately look up and jerk my head from side to side, inspecting the hallways, making sure nobody heard it.

To the left of me is a longer hallway and I see the intersection he mentioned in his note. It's darker down there, which eases my mind slightly.

Suddenly, I hear a rustle coming from the direction of the nurse's station. Someone has stood from a chair and is wheeling it back into place.

I turn toward my left and run on the tips of my toes down the hallway. Behind me, I can hear two women speaking to each other. I can't make out what they're saying, but I don't think they've noticed me yet. Fortunately, my socks are silent on the tile flooring. When I reach the hallway intersection, I duck to the right and spread my back up against the wall, finally out of view of the nurse's station.

For a few seconds, I can actually hear my heart hammering in my ears. That's the type of thing I would read about in thriller novels saved on the Delta's archives when I was in space, but it's not the type of thing you ever expect to experience.

It's then that I realize this is the first time I've run since I left the Delta. I used to run for hours on the circular track to keep my body strong in the limited gravity. It was an activity I genuinely enjoyed. And the feeling now of the blood pumping through my veins has me reinvigorated. A smile comes over my lips as I quietly try to catch my breath.

I wait here for several more seconds, listening to the ladies at the end of the hallway. They're continuing their conversation and don't seem alarmed in any way. I turn to see that this hallway is much longer than the last one. The only light is coming from an open door about halfway down. I can hear a man inside talking on a phone.

I close my eyes and draw in a breath to calm my heart and my mind; then I carefully tiptoe across the hall to the second door on the left of the intersection. This door has a small window in it, but it's pitch black inside the room. I turn the door handle and it makes a sickening squeal that sends me into a panic.

The man on the phone down the hall hears it too. I hear him say, "Hold on for a sec. I need to check something out."

I quickly pull the door open wide enough for me to squirm my body through the opening and allow it to click shut behind me. I have no time to survey the room before I hear the man's footsteps coming down the hallway toward me.

Did he see me go into this room?

I duck away from the window and cower into a ball on the floor behind the door, making myself as small as possible in case he does open the door. Each footstep in the hallway sends my heart into a frenzy, but I manage to keep my breathing as low and quiet as possible. Eventually, he reaches my door and continues on past.

He did not see me come in here. I let out a huge breath of relief.

The room is very dark and it takes a few moments for my eyes to adjust enough to make out anything but inky blackness. It's a small room, more of a closet. Floor-to-ceiling shelving surrounds the walls. There are cleaning supplies and stacks of linens filling the shelves. On the floor next to me are several buckets, mops, and brooms, hastily pushed into the corner. In the center of the small room is a rolling laundry bin. I've seen them push these bins into my room before when they're changing the bedding. Inside this bin are piles of used sheets and towels. Above the bin is a chute, about a half meter square that goes up into blackness.

As I'm making my way around the laundry bin, I hear the familiar squeal of the door handle. I immediately drop to the ground and crawl behind the bin thinking the man from the office must have come back. But two seconds go by with no noise or light.

Surely the man would turn the light on if he were inspecting the room, wouldn't he?

Another second passes and my heart skips a beat when I hear a whispered voice.

"Eta? Are you here?"

Chapter 17

New Mexico

Time Since Touchdown: 42 Days, 2:16 a.m. MST

It takes me only a moment to recognize the voice, yet I still feel like I might pass out from shock.

"Alé, my God…" I gasp and brace myself against the wall, holding my hand over my chest to contain my racing heart. He closes the door quietly behind him and moves to my side, taking my hand in his. This gesture does nothing to calm my heart rate.

"Sorry," he whispers. "I didn't mean to frighten you. But what can you expect from a man lurking around inside a dark laundry room?" Through the darkness, I catch him smile.

I blush, thankful for the darkened room, and clasp his hand tighter. As my eyes adjust to the darkness, I can make out a vague outline of his facial features. His lips are pursed together and his eyebrows are pulled toward the center of his face in a look of tight worry. He smells like peppermint and sage.

"What's going on? How do you plan to get out of here?" I ask.

"I'll explain everything in detail later, but you're not safe here. They're planning to study you and use you as part of their Moon-mining expedition."

"Wait, you can't be serious." The realization hits me in the chest like a meteorite and my mouth drops open as I try to process this information. "How do they plan to 'use' me?"

"They're planning to send you back up."

"Back into space?" The words escape my mouth with a hiss and I blink in utter disbelief.

"Looks that way. Shhh…" He puts his index finger to his lips and jerks his head around, glancing at the small window in the door. He pulls me to the floor and we wiggle our way around the laundry bin to a hidden spot in the corner. We've just made it out of sight of the door when suddenly, the handle spins and the door swings open. Someone steps inside and turns on the overhead light.

The sudden presence of intense LED light shocks my system and a small gasp escapes my lips. Alé gently clasps his hand over my mouth. His fingers are hot on my face. My eyes are wide and my body's shaking with fear.

Alé's face is intense as he peers around the edge of the laundry basket. I can see only the feet of the person in the room with us now. Whoever it is wears heavy black boots. Alé turns to me, gives me a small nod, his eyes hard and serious, and slowly takes his hand away from my mouth. I return the nod and sit absolutely still, taking in only a slight, faint breath and holding it.

After what seems like an eternity, although probably only a few seconds, the person shuts the light off and closes the door.

We both release our breath at the same time and Alé peers around the laundry bin and nods, confirming whoever it was is now gone.

"NASA Guard," he whispers. "Come on, we need to get out of here now. It will only be a matter of time before they notice you're gone."

He takes a small pair of scissors out of his pocket. They look like a pair of metal snips I had in my toolkit on board the Delta. He holds my hand and gestures toward my wrist. The ID band glows faintly in the darkness. "I need to cut that band off your wrist."

"It won't set off an alarm?"

"No. This is simply for identification purposes. I've looked through your medical files. They're keeping them off the

- 140 -

NASA cloud, only accessible on a CPU in this building, but I've got a friend who's pretty good at hacking this type of stuff. So far, they haven't implanted any kind of tracker in you, which is good news for us. You've made amazing progress over the last few weeks—off the charts really. They know all about how you've been walking around your room at night and how well you're moving around."

I curse under my breath. I was trying so hard to keep my nighttime movements a secret. Of course, they were watching all along.

"Okay, cut it off," I say.

He snips the metal band and it gives the scissors no more hassle than a piece of paper might. They must be sharp snips. Then he tosses the band into the laundry basket and tucks the scissors back into his pocket.

He points at the chute over the laundry basket. "We're going up there."

"What? How?" The chute goes straight up into the ceiling and I can't imagine how we'll pull ourselves up into it.

"Do you trust me?" he asks, standing and offering me his hand.

He says there's danger here. He says they're going to send me back into space. I can't imagine ever going back into orbit. I spent the last eighteen years of my life trying to reach the surface and I haven't even been outside this building. I haven't felt the sunshine hot on my face. I haven't smelled the soil or tasted fresh water from a stream.

It's because of Alé that I'm alive now. Of course I trust him. I take his hand and squeeze it, standing up from my crouch. This is when I realize how short I am compared to him. He's at least one head taller than I am.

He pulls himself up onto the edge of the large laundry bin, balancing precariously as he stretches his hand up to the chute. After searching around for a moment, a thick rope drops down from the chute and makes a thud as it hits the floor. I touch the rope and realize it's a rope ladder with rungs in it.

"You first," he says, dropping back down to the floor and holding the rope ladder at the bottom to make it more stable for me to climb on. "When you get to the top, there's a chute that goes off to the left. It's a conveyor system that brings soiled linens from other areas of the complex and dumps them here. It runs all the way through the facility. We're going to follow the conveyor to the far northwest corner of this level. Once we get to the end, there's a maintenance shaft that goes up to the surface and comes out in a small maintenance shed just outside the complex. That's how we get out of the building."

"Then what?"

"I've got it taken care of. Don't worry about it. Just get yourself up the rope and into that chute, okay?"

I nod and focus my attention on the rope ladder. I place my foot on the first rung and feel it fold around my foot as it supports my weight. The whole ladder swings slightly when I lift my other foot off the floor but Alé does his best to steady it. A brief wave of nausea comes over me as I focus on getting my bearings and climbing to the next rung. I'm still weak and this swinging ladder isn't doing my body any favors. But I force myself to focus on moving one rung at a time.

It's a strange feeling, climbing up in surface gravity. In a way, it reminds me of when I would climb from the partial gravity in the G Module of the Delta into the center Node which had no gravity. It always made me dizzy and nauseous. But the higher I climb on this rope, the stronger I feel. And it's nice to have Alé there to hold the bottom for me.

I reach the ceiling and pull myself up into the laundry chute. The rope is secured to a thick steel handle on the left where the conveyor tunnel is. I grab the handle and after some grunting, I pull myself into the tunnel, beads of sweat forming on my brow. The ordeal makes me realize how pathetically weak my arms are—I need to work on building up my strength.

Alé begins to climb the ladder behind me and reaches the top of the chute much faster than I did. He pulls himself easily into the tunnel and drags the rope ladder up behind him, pulling the knot loose from the handle and coiling the rope up into a bundle. He slips the bundle through the back of his belt and gestures with his hand for me to follow him through the conveyor tunnel.

The tunnel isn't very big—only wide enough for one of us to fit through at a time and we have to crawl on our elbows and knees. Alé goes first and I follow close behind. It's very dark in the tunnel and I keep reaching out to touch his feet to make sure he's still in front of me. The conveyor is made of thick rubber, like the running track on the Delta where I ran endless circles to keep my body conditioned in the limited gravity. It's difficult to move along the rubber conveyor and before long, I'm panting from exertion. My legs are sore from the stopped crawl. The skin on my knees is becoming raw from the pull of the rubber through the thin fabric of my pants.

After a few minutes, Alé stops and whispers, "How are you doing?"

I take a moment to catch my breath, wiping the now-trickling sweat from my face. It's hot inside the tunnel and not well ventilated. The air is thick and heavy.

"I'm okay. Let's keep going so we can get out of here."

He doesn't reply but starts moving forward again. Every few meters, there's another chute leading down into the conveyor from the rooms above us. We crawl for what seems like an eternity. When I'm certain my legs might give out on me, the muscles in my thighs exhausted, Alé stops and I bump into his feet.

"This is it," he says.

He pulls himself up into the chute directly above us. It's so dark I can't see a thing until he pushes open the small door leading out of the laundry chute. Blue light floods into the tunnel.

"Come on. Follow me," he says, standing and hoisting himself through the small door at the top of the chute. I follow his lead and stand up in the vertical chute. It's much too high for me to reach the door so he leans over the edge and pulls me up with a swift jerk. I land in a heap on the floor inside a small room full of garbage bins and cleaning supplies. That's when I realize the light is coming from a machine. I'm not familiar with the type of machine, but it has pictures of Coke bottles on it.

"It's a vending machine," he says, spying the confusion on my face. "This is a utility room that services level five. The main laundry facility is on level six, where we were. This is where people on level five deposit their garbage and laundry. They also have these vending machines that sell drinks and snacks for those who work down here full-time."

"Hmm." I nod and take in the small room. It's cramped and smells like soap. I don't like it. "Let's keep going."

He nods and takes my hand. Sparks of energy fly up my arm and I'm struck again by the strange feeling of his skin on mine. Carefully he opens the door to the room and pokes his head out before turning to me and motioning that it's okay to go forward. We step into a long hallway. Alé opens a door to our left and we enter a stairwell.

"Are we taking the stairs?" I ask.

"No." He shakes his head. "Behind this wall is a maintenance shaft. It's used to service plumbing and electrical running down to the lower levels on this side of the complex. We'll use the shaft instead. It takes us outside the building."

"But where is the entrance to the shaft?" I stare at the white wall in front of us. It doesn't appear to be anything other than a wall—no door, no chute—simply a wall.

Alé smiles and drops my hand. He spreads his fingers out in front of him and drags his hands over the wall, searching for the exact spot. He stares at it, his brow furrowed in concentration. After a few moments of feeling around the wall, he pushes on something and, as if it were a magic trick, a panel opens up.

"That's amazing," I whisper, my mouth hanging open. I examine the edges of the access panel. "How did they hide it so well in the wall?"

"It's called active-seam camouflaging. It's a construction method used to conceal access points like this within buildings. Takes someone with real talent to install them correctly. There are hundreds of these hidden panels down here, hiding everything from maintenance shafts to secret labs. If you look close enough and use your hands to feel around the walls, you can find the edges. You just have to know what to look for." He closes the panel and, as if it were a magical portal, it blends right back into the wall and disappears. He takes my hand and places it palm-side down on the wall, dragging it over the edge of the panel and, sure enough, I feel a slight divot where the edge of the panel was. I can't see it, but I can feel it.

"Wow," I say.

He winks at me and presses on the panel again. The panel makes a soft click and he swings it open to reveal a shaft about a meter square behind the panel. Running along the walls of the shaft are cords, bundles of wire and cables, ventilation tubes, and pipes. I glance up through the shaft and see the faintest light at the top, many meters up from where we now stand.

"There's a ladder to your right. It goes all the way to the top of the shaft. Grab onto it and hold tight. It's a thirty-meter drop from here if you fall. I'll follow behind you."

I reach around the edge and find a thick, metal rung sticking out of the concrete wall. It feels solid. I grab it and pull myself through the panel. I loop my elbow through the metal rung and feel around to get a footing on the rung below my feet.

Once I'm satisfied that my feet are secure on the ladder rung, I unhook my arm and hold on with my hands. I take hold of the next rung up and pull my body toward it. I do this twice more until there's enough room on the ladder for Alé to grab onto it too. He pulls the panel door shut and the shaft immediately goes dark, the only light a pale glow from the exit many meters above.

For a second, panic rises in my throat. I'm suddenly hyperaware of how sweaty my hands are and they feel like they might slip right off the metal rungs.

"Alé... I'm having... I'm feeling... I don't know. I'm really nervous here," I say, struggling to find my breath.

"Listen to me, Eta, you've got this." His voice is calm, patient. "It's no different from climbing the ladders in and out of the G Module on the Delta. Don't think about the depth of the shaft." I take in each word, closing my eyes and willing my breath to slow. "You survived reentry. You can climb out of this shaft. I know you can. I believe in you, Eta."

I nod, knowing he can't see me, but doing it anyway to convince myself. He believes in me; that's good enough for me. I wipe my sweating palm on my pant leg and reach up for the next rung.

Slowly, we make our way out of the shaft. The light at the top of the tunnel becomes clearer as we move. I listen for Alé's breathing behind me in the darkness, relying on the faint swish of air in and out of his lungs as a way to keep myself calm.

At last, we reach the top of the shaft and I realize the light I'm seeing is coming from outside the facility. It looks almost like moonlight. There's a large metal grate covering the hole.

"Alé, why would there be a grate over this maintenance shaft? Don't they worry about water getting in here?"

"The grate is there because they also use this shaft as a ventilation duct, bringing air to the lower levels of the facility. That grate has a dynamic cover that automatically closes when rain hits it, which is not very often out here in the desert. There's a latch on the left side there. Unhook it and push it open. It will be heavy, but I know you can do it."

I feel around the edge of the grate, unclick the latch, and push with all my might. It barely budges.

"Uh-oh," I say.

"You can do it, Eta. I know you can. Now, put your foot on the next rung up so you can get more leverage. Hook your elbow around the top rung to steady yourself. Then push your shoulder into the grate using the full force of your legs."

He sounds so confident. I try not to let the worry overtake me.

What if I can't open this stupid thing?

I follow his instructions and brace my shoulder against the rough metal of the grate. I release all the air in my lungs and count down from three in my head.

Three... Two... One... Push!

The grate swings open with such force that I fly out of the tunnel and topple over onto the ground next to it. Heavy breaths suck in and out of my lungs from the exertion.

Quickly, I roll over and see Alé's head poking out of the hole as he pulls himself through. Once outside the tunnel, he picks up the grate cover and carefully lays it back into place, the latch clicking as it closes. He walks over to me and pulls me to my feet.

"See? I knew you could do it," he says. His lips twist into a sideways smile illuminated by the moonlight. For a moment, I am struck by how beautiful he looks, his curly hair hanging over his forehead.

I'm so overcome with relief that it takes me a few moments to realize that I'm standing outside the complex. I'm standing in the desert night air with Alé.

For the first time in my life, I am standing outside on the surface of the Earth.

Chapter 18

New Mexico

Time Since Touchdown: 42 Days, 3:22 a.m. MST

I reach down and touch the sand beneath my feet, letting the grains run through my fingers. When I was on the Delta, I used to daydream about what sand might feel like. I've only ever felt soil before. But this… this is far different from what I expected.

The grains roll easily through my fingers and fall delicately back down to the ground. It's nothing like the soil on the Delta. That soil was always moist and thick and it would stick to your fingers and coat them in a fine black grit. The sand isn't sticky at all and when it's finished flowing and my hand is empty, my fingers feel as clean as they did when I first touched it. It's the strangest sensation and I smile and reach for another handful, carefully letting the grains sprinkle out of one palm and onto the other.

"Uh, I hate to interrupt this… but we're kind of pressed for time," Alé says, gently touching my shoulder.

"Oh, yeah, right. Sorry about that. It's just so strange. I've never felt it before. The sand, I mean." I stand and brush the remaining sand from my palms. My eyes have now adjusted to the scenery around me. There is a walkway in front of us with plants on either side of it. I can't make out what they are for sure, but they look like some sort of cactus.

The Moon is almost full and it shines a surprisingly bright, yet haunting light over the land. It looks much like it does in space, although I can see how the atmosphere warps it slightly. The edges of the giant orb hanging in the sky are dimmer and I can barely make out the pockmarks and craters on the surface. I could see them in much greater detail from the Delta.

Alé grabs my hand and points in the direction of the parking lot. There's a huge building next to it. "That's the parking garage," he says, his voice hushed. "We're going to have to run." He pauses to stare up at the Moon. "I didn't think about the Moon being so bright. We run the risk of being seen if we don't make it fast. It's a hundred meters or so. Do you think you can make it that far?"

My body stiffens at the thought of running all that way. Can I actually run that far? I only got the strength to walk a few days ago. In the moonlight, his face is tight with fear. I must at least try to do this. Looking him in the eye, I nod.

He nods back and, still holding my hand, looks both ways up and down the walkway before saying, "Go!" in a hushed whisper.

Before I realize what's happening, he's pulled my arm nearly out of its socket and we're off, running down the walkway. My feet are so clumsy that it takes me several meters to work up any real rhythm in my stride. But surprisingly, once I get my legs working properly, the instinct I've always had as a runner takes over and I feel strong and free.

The night air is cool and it whips around my face and arms so fast, it's as if there are tiny sparks running up and down my skin. I've never experienced anything as exhilarating. As we run along the walkway, I keep pace with Alé until we hit the pavement of the parking lot beyond. He glances back several times while we run to make sure there's nobody following us.

I thought for sure the gravity on the surface would make me feel thick and heavy, but that's not the case. I'm lighter, springier now that I'm running.

We make it across the parking lot much quicker than I expected, and as we enter the dark parking garage, it's clear I might have overestimated my abilities. I grab onto the stone wall beside me and clasp my chest, sucking in one breath after another, trying to make my heart stop pounding in my ears. For a moment, I'm sure I might collapse, but Alé grabs my arms and helps me sit down on the ground. The floor of the parking garage is cold cement and its texture is rough outside the thin cotton scrub pants I'm wearing.

The air is thick and it takes me several more breaths, but eventually, I'm able to stand again. Alé helps me up and we continue walking. He takes me up a narrow stairway to the second floor. There, parked in a neat, single-file line are ten cars. I can't make out the color of them in the dark but they are all exactly the same. Alé pulls a tiny scrap of paper out of his pocket and I see there's a number jotted down on it: a license plate number.

He motions for me to follow him and we walk down the line of cars before he stops at the third one from the end.

"This is the one," he says. He walks around to the driver's side and waves me to the passenger side as he types in a code to unlock the vehicle. A dim, yellow light glows to life inside the car. I touch the outside of the door, looking for a handle but feel nothing.

"Tap twice on the long panel to open the door," he says.

I feel around on the cold surface of the door until I reach a small oblong panel which I tap twice with my index finger. Like magic, the door gently pops open and I take my seat. He slips in next to me and presses a large button on the dash. The engine hums to life and he clicks off the headlights before typing in some coordinates on the holo-screen embedded into the dash. The cabin light fades to black and we're left in the dark.

He must know what he's doing, because he backs the car up in complete darkness and drives out of the parking garage. When we're in the moonlight, he looks over at me. I must have a look of utter confusion on my face because he says, "I had a friend of mine hack into this one and turn the tracking off. I came out here last night and memorized the layout of the garage so I'd know how to get out of here without having to use headlights. They'll eventually catch on to us and turn the tracking back on, but I'm hoping we can get at least through the night before we have to ditch it."

I nod, my eyes wide. I still can't believe what just happened.

"How do you feel? Do you need anything? There are some water bottles on the floor in the back and a few granola bars," he says.

"I'm okay." I realize that I'm still breathing hard and fast. I close my eyes and focus on calming myself. My hands are shaking and my fingers are ice cold. I slip them under my legs to warm them. Alé must see my body shaking so he punches in a command to the holo-screen and warm air begins to flow from the vents in front of me. I didn't realize how cold I was until now.

He follows the road around the complex and I realize we are probably fortunate that the Moon is so bright because it's not difficult to see the road even with the headlights off. After a few looping turns, he makes a sharp right onto a much bumpier road. Rocks and gravel fly up around the car as he pushes forward, eyes straight, forehead rumpled with concentration.

"We can't take the main road out of here," he says. "There's a checkpoint with guards at the exit. But this is a service road and it leads to a back exit. It's not one that's used very often because it's quite a way from the main campus. I don't think there will be a problem getting through the gate at the end."

He glances in my direction and I can tell he's not entirely sure if the gate at the end of this road will be unlocked. I stare ahead. The stars glide past the windshield and I lean forward to get a better look. The light from the Moon gives the sky a bluish-purple glow—a color I've never quite seen before. It's stunning.

Mountains surround us. We must be in some sort of basin, perhaps an ancient lake bed between the mountains. The land is flat right up until it meets the mountains many kilometers away. Sand and short, rough-looking plants, cacti, and thorny bushes cover the ground.

We continue to drive for another twenty minutes before we approach a fence with two tall metal gates standing in the moonlight. There's a chain twisted around the gates holding them together. Alé gets out of the car and walks up to the gate. He fiddles with the chain then walks back to the car and gets in.

"Well, it's locked." He sighs and runs his fingers through his hair.

I swallow hard. "What can we do?"

He stares ahead at the gate for a moment, his brow furrowed in thought. "I think we can make it."

"What do you mean, make it?"

"I think we can make it through if we crash into the center of the gates. That chain isn't very thick. This car has enough power to break it." He glances at me and adds, "I think."

I nod. "Let's do it."

He smiles that crooked, sideways smile and reaches over me, pulling the seatbelt down across my body and latching it. He puts the car into gear. "Hold on."

I brace my arms against the armrests and stare forward. Alé slams his foot down on the accelerator and the car shoots forward, dust flying high on either side of the vehicle.

The gate gets closer… thirty meters… twenty meters… ten meters. I close my eyes as the car makes contact with the gate, knocking the breath out of me as my body slams into the cross-body belt. My head lurches forward and my spine momentarily stings with pain before my head flings back, stopped by the neck support on the seat.

I open my eyes and look at Alé. He's smiling. I turn to see the gate standing open behind us.

It worked. We made it through.

Part II

After Escape

Chapter 19

The city of Dalhart, TX has a population of a little under ten thousand people according to the faded green population sign hanging onto its metal support post by a single screw as Highway 54 rolls into town. At least, that was the population before the great war. From the looks of it now, there isn't a soul left.

As we make our way through the dusty, abandoned streets, I'm struck by how ramshackle the place is. Signs hang precariously from broken chains outside of old stores. Shards of glass from windows busted many years before lie untouched on the sidewalks. Abandoned cars still sit in the streets, thick layers of dirt coating their bodies.

The most unfortunate part is we've already passed through several towns much like Dalhart. Long-forgotten and broken with age. I asked Alé what happened here and he told me that the nuclear strikes in the Dallas area caused radiation fallout throughout West Texas.

"The fallout really wreaked havoc on the weather patterns, causing a severe drought. You'll notice it's almost October, yet it's still hot as hell out here. But the weather can swing at the drop of a hat. Two years ago, they recorded sixteen inches of snow south of here in the middle of July. With the combination of the fallout and the drought, there wasn't much sense in people coming back here after the war ended. The economy was dependent on agriculture. Without the crops, there's no money. The leftover towns are few and far between."

"Okay, so why are we here?"

Alé chuckles. "Well, you can't really get out of New Mexico to the east unless you drive through West Texas. Plus, there's someone here who can help us. Dalhart is a bit out of the way, but it's a necessary stop. And it might slow them down if they're looking for us. They probably won't guess that we'll make a detour out here."

"Where in the east are we going?"

"There's a cabin in the mountains outside of Baltimore. It was where my mother took me during the war. We stayed there for four years after my father left to fight."

"He died in the war, right?" I remember Alé telling me about how much he loved his father and how difficult it was when he left to fight, never to return.

He sighs and his shoulders droop slightly. "Yes."

"I'm sorry. I shouldn't have brought it up."

"No, it's okay." He flashes me a reassuring smile. "It was years ago. Anyway, the cabin is very remote, right in the middle of the Appalachian Mountains. When we left Baltimore during the mandatory evacuations, we didn't have anywhere to go. We traveled around a bit at first, but my mother decided it would be better for us to find a place in the wilderness that we could make our own instead of going to a relocation camp. That's how we found the cabin. It's only accessible by hike and it's very rustic."

"And that's where we're going?"

He glances at me and clears his throat. "Um, yeah, is that okay? I mean, it's only a temporary solution. I figure we can go there for a while and hide out until some of the heat dies down. I don't think anyone knows it's there except for my family and me. It was built long ago and it's now on public land in the national forest. I doubt anybody even dares to venture out that far these days. Eventually they'll stop looking for you and then you can go wherever you want. But in the meantime, I think it's best to stay off the radar for a while."

"Hmm." I stare ahead and watch the dusty blacktop roll out below the car.

"Are you okay with that?" he asks again.

"Yes, I think it's a good idea. Actually, I'm quite excited to see the forest and the mountains."

He smiles and his eyes relax. "Good. I mean, it's really rustic. But it's beautiful too. You'll see." He focuses back on the road and after a few more minutes of driving says, "Here it is."

On the right side of the road is a rusty steel building with an old sign out front that reads "Shirley's Autobody." Alé turns the car into the small parking lot and honks the horn. To my surprise, the huge steel door that takes up half the front of the building creaks open and a man steps out.

This building, like the rest of the town, looks abandoned, yet here's another human being emerging from the depths of this old body shop.

He's an older man, wearing denim overalls with grease stains and ripped knees over a yellowed undershirt. The grease stains on the overalls match the ones all over his hands and he wipes a mop of equally greasy black hair out of his eyes to get a better look at us. He's chewing something, but I'm not sure what. The man walks over to the car and Alé rolls down the window.

"I reckon you're the NASA kid," the man says, spitting on the ground, narrowly missing the car door.

"That's right. And you're Buster?" Alé says.

"That's right," Buster replies before spitting again. His voice is gruff and low, and his words drawl. "Xander mentioned you'd be comin' by, but I wasn't expectin' ya till later this mornin'."

"Well, we made good time. I'm Alexandros, but you can call me Alé and this is Eta."

"Buster Shirley, pleased to meet ya. Well, I reckon we better get this car into the shop. Would hate to draw attention." Buster slowly glances around as if he expects someone to actually drive by. I almost tell him that I can't imagine it will be a problem, but I guess he knows better than I do.

Buster turns around and walks back to the shop door. He has his hands in his pockets and doesn't seem in any real hurry. He struggles to pull the heavy sliding door to the side and as he does, I hear the pinched whine of metal grating against metal. It's so loud, I have to hold my hands over my ears. I've never heard anything like that in my life and I hope to never hear it again. Eventually, Buster gets the door all the way open and waves Alé to drive forward into the dark shop. After we park inside, I press my palms to my ears until Buster has closed the big door.

It's pitch black inside the shop until Buster turns on the overhead light. That's when I see it truly is a working auto shop full of tools, gadgets, random car parts, and dirty rags. Alé steps out of the car and gestures for me to do the same. I'm still wearing my sticky footed socks and hospital scrubs and I'm suddenly self-conscious about my attire... although I'm not sure why. Buster certainly isn't concerned with it.

"Xander mentioned that you could help us out with a ride in exchange for this car," Alé says.

- 165 -

Buster nods. "Yep. This here'll make for a good scrapper. Top-dollar parts."

"Good. Make sure you scrap it right away. They'll be looking for it. And don't forget to destroy the tracker. The sooner the better."

Buster chuckles. "This ain't my first rodeo, son."

He reaches into the car and types a code into the holo-screen. The hood pops up and Buster fiddles with something around the engine. After a few moments, he produces a bundle of frayed wires and a small device for Alé to see.

"This here's the primary trackin' mechanism. Although, they prolly have some trackin' built into that screen too. I'll have to get that disabled. But this is what they'll rely on first and, as you can see, it's no longer a problem."

Alé inspects the device and nods. "That's great. Thanks, Buster. We should be on our way though."

Buster nods and waves for us to follow. We walk through a door in the back and I see several vehicles parked on the uneven dirt behind the shop. Buster points at a boxy black vehicle with huge tires and two doors. The word "Jeep" is printed across the back where a spare tire hangs, attached to the back window.

Alé's eyebrows raise. "It runs on gas? This won't work. We won't encounter a gas station for five hundred miles. We need something electric. Solar-powered would be best."

Buster shrugs. "It's all I got. You'll have to bring along these here jerricans." He points to three large metal containers sitting on the ground next to the Jeep. "I can fill 'em up for ya. After you pass Oklahoma, you should be fine. They still got gas stations pretty regular east of there."

Alé bites his lip, still unconvinced. Buster shrugs again. "Like I said, it's all I got. Besides"—he spits on the ground next to the Jeep's back tire— "you wanted somethin' they couldn't track. Well, this is the best option. Anythin' electric'd have a beacon in the operatin' system. Too hard to disable unless you're scrappin' it."

"Yes, that's a good point." Alé rubs his jaw and continues to look the Jeep up and down. "It runs okay?"

"Oh yeah. Built it myself. It'll get ya where you're goin'."

"Okay."

Alé shakes Buster's hand.

"Keys're up in the visor there. If you can make it up to Little Rock tonight, you shouldn't have a problem findin' a motel. But there won't be much in between 'cept Oklahoma City. Just a heads-up."

Before we leave, Buster fills up our gas cans and loads them into the back of the Jeep. He also lets us into the small apartment attached to the shop where he brings us three big sacks of clothes and two paper bags full of sandwiches along with several jugs of water. There are lots of different items of clothing in the sacks and I'm able to go through them and pick what I want.

"Xander mentioned ya might need some clothes and that you're a little bit of a thing. Wasn't sure what you'd like so I gathered up what I could."

"Thank you," I say.

He nods. "Take as much as you want. I ain't got no need for women's clothes."

I choose a pair of worn jeans, a purple shirt with buttons down the front, and a pair of black sandals. There are several other pairs of shoes in the bags, but I like the sandals. They have a thick sole and straps that cross over the tops of my feet. Alé says they're outdoor sandals, so they're suitable for hiking and even running if I choose. I can't imagine running in them, but I do get a shiver of excitement at owning my first pair of shoes.

The clothes are used, but surprisingly, they're in good shape and they fit me pretty well, although I do have to roll up the legs on the jeans. The shirt is a shade of purple I've never seen before and it makes my skin look less pale. The second I put it on, I feel beautiful.

The shoes are a different story. They're not exactly heavy, but they throw off my sense of balance. Whenever I lift my feet, they don't weigh what I'd expect them to weigh. My gait is so awkward, I have to slow down and concentrate on every step. Alé chuckles at me and tells me I'm waddling like a duck. This comment, although meant as a lighthearted joke, makes me more determined to master the walk and I keep at it, getting better with each step.

Buster bids us farewell with a nod, a wave, and a spit on the ground.

As we drive out of town in the Jeep, I'm more relaxed. Something about the vehicle makes me feel more comfortable than the fancy NASA car. It has a rugged appeal to it. Thick gray fabric, worn soft with age, covers the seats. The dash houses no fancy holo-screen but a touchscreen radio, which Alé says used to be in all vehicles before the invention of holo-screens.

"Can you believe that?" he says. "That old fellow living out here literally in the middle of nowhere is one of the most talented computer hackers in the country… possibly the world."

"Really?"

"Absolutely." He chuckles, shaking his head in disbelief. "That's how my friend Xander knows him. They're part of the same hacker network or something. He chooses to live out here in the sticks to keep a low profile, but in reality, he's running millions of dollars through various counterfeit operations over the dark web."

"Wow."

Alé tries to turn on the radio but it picks up nothing but static so he flips it off. Dalhart slips away behind us and we're left looking over the same flat, blank fields and endless blacktop for miles on end.

Exhausted, I rest my head on the side of the Jeep's door and watch the fields fly by, taking in every bit of it. Eventually, I can't force my eyes to stay open any longer and I fall into a deep sleep.

Chapter 20

Arkansas

Time Since Touchdown: 43 Days, 1:32 a.m. CST

Alé drives all day and into the night. We stop from time to time for bathroom breaks and to eat a sandwich or two. The sandwiches consist of soft white bread and canned chicken salad. Alé tells me that because Buster has connections all over the web, he has provisions shipped to him, which is how he's able to live in such a remote area. He mentions that although it looked like Dalhart was totally abandoned, there are a few other people out there, but not many. They all rely on Buster to get them what they need to survive.

The loud hiss of the air rushing outside the Jeep puts me into a daze. The wasted fields of West Texas give way to rolling plains through Oklahoma and eventually, we roll into the deep green forests of Arkansas.

Alé stares forward stoically even though he must be exhausted from driving all day. From time to time, we speak. He tells me more about Xander and the files they uncovered in the NASA database. He tells me what he knows about Project Diamond and how he believes John Patrick never had any intention of allowing me to live my life. He mentions that NASA never made the public aware of the existence of the Delta or my rescue.

We talk about the war and he answers my questions about what has happened in the world since my mother was marooned on the Delta. He talks about the devastation the nuclear attacks had on certain areas of the country.

The initial bombs took out parts of New York City and Los Angeles, but many other bombs were dropped throughout the course of the war. The US military set up strategic positions near large cities to cut off bombs headed for those cities, but without satellite communications, it was almost like shooting in the dark.

Eventually the military devised ways to track airborne missiles without the use of satellites and got much better at cutting off the bombs before they reached large metropolitan areas. But it was several months into the war before they could do this, and by then, the bombs had hit many areas multiple times, as was the case with Dallas and Fort Worth. Alé mentioned that people still weren't allowed inside the radiation zone around the cities.

They successfully cut off bombs headed to Chicago, San Francisco, and Philadelphia, but Minneapolis, Detroit, and Seattle weren't as lucky. Miami and the entire southern half of Florida are completely inhabitable. And even when they were able to intercept bombs headed toward cities, they often had to detonate them over other areas of the country, such as rural farming areas that would suffer the radiation effects for many years to come.

Alé tells me about the mass evacuation of major metropolitan areas and how they had to build huge bunkers to house displaced people. Many of these bunkers were underground to help shield people from nighttime bombings and radiation. This explains why my mother and I never saw much activity on the surface of the Earth, particularly at night. Power grids failed throughout the war, causing the government to enforce mass production mandates on solar power systems. Even so, most of the bombings took place at night and people were careful to keep nighttime light to a minimum to reduce the risk of being bombed.

During this time, many people fled to rural areas to avoid the crowded, dirty relocation camps. That's how Alé and his family found the cabin in the woods. They hiked and camped for many weeks through the Appalachian Mountains, foraging and fishing to keep themselves fed. His mother, an avid outdoorswoman, had stocked up on camping supplies and outdoor survival tools before they left Baltimore.

They eventually found the cabin and took up residence. It had an old power generation system, including a water wheel that reaped power from a nearby stream. They continued to fish and hunt while Alé's mother tended a large garden. As he tells me about the cabin, his voice becomes lighter and he makes gestures with his arms, all while smiling, his eyes shining. I can tell it was a happy place for his family to await the end of the war.

Talking with Alé brings me some peace, now knowing what was happening on the surface all those years while I was on the Delta. But the atrocities of the war can't be denied and I'm soon overcome by exhaustion. I drift in and out of sleep throughout the rest of the day.

I'm awoken by the feel of the Jeep slowing down, the wind noise waning. It's totally dark outside now and a bright service light shines into the car. We're in a parking lot next to a long building lined with doors and windows. The sign in the lot says "The Starlight Motel."

"Where are we?" I ask.

"Just outside of Little Rock. This place looks as good as any. I'm beat. I need to get some rest."

Alé tells me to wait in the Jeep while he goes in and gets us two rooms. After a few minutes, he comes out of the lobby and grabs the bags of clothes we got from Buster from the back of the Jeep. Then he gestures for me to follow him. We walk down the lighted walkway to the very end of the building. Stopping in front of a door marked "12," he hands me a thin piece of plastic.

"They have the old-fashioned kind of locks here—keycards," he says. "Wave this over that sensor on the door there and it will unlock the door."

I do as he says and the door handle makes a loud click. I'm not sure what to do next. Alé smiles and pushes the handle down, opening the door and allowing me to walk in first. He sets the bags down on the bed and I walk around the room taking it in.

It's a small room, but it's about twice the size of the little white hospital room. There's one bed in the center of the room, which Alé mentions is a full-size bed flanked by two bed tables. A small sofa sits on the wall next to the bed and a small table with two chairs is right across from it. Directly in front of the bed, there's a large holo-screen mounted to the wall. To the left of the room's entrance, there's a bathroom with a sink, toilet, shower, and bathtub.

"Our rooms are adjoining. See? This door opens into the room next to it, which is where I'll stay." He leaves my room and a few moments later, he knocks on the adjoining door. I unlatch the bolt and open it to see him standing in a room identical to mine.

"Well, I guess it's time to hit the hay," he says.

"Hit the hay?"

"Oh, yeah, it's an expression. It means 'go to sleep.' Actually, it doesn't make any sense. I'm not sure where it comes from, but people haven't slept on hay for hundreds of years." He shrugs and clears his throat before picking at his fingernails. "Yeah, so, anyway, I guess it's time for bed."

I smile and nod. "Good night, Alé."

"Good night, Eta."

***

In the bathroom, I run my fingers over the big brass knobs that control hot and cold water in the bathtub. I've seen bathtubs before in movies, but I've never actually taken a bath. At the New Mexico facility, they allowed me to take showers. Of course, I've taken many showers in my lifetime. But I've never actually submerged myself in water. They didn't build the Delta with the idea of such luxuries like taking a bath.

Now's as good a time as any.

I grip the knobs and twist. They squeal at first but then turn easily and water begins to flow out of the nozzle. I jump back in surprise at the noise and the volume of water rushing out but quickly giggle at my own silliness. The knobs are labeled "H" and "C" for hot and cold, so I fiddle with them until the stream of water is the right temperature. It takes the bathtub only a minute to fill completely.

After I undress, I stick one foot into the water. It's quite hot, but my skin quickly gets used to it. The feeling of wiggling my toes around in the water is something I've never felt. I take the plunge and fully submerge my body. It's warm and comforting and reminds me of when I was a small child and my mother would wrap her down blanket around my entire body and snuggle up to me as if I were a baby. The bathwater feels like soft, warm arms wrapping around every centimeter of my skin.

I allow my head to sink while my body floats, submerging my eyes so only the tip of my nose and mouth are out. My arms float beside me and the feeling is so nostalgic, it brings tears to my eyes.

Submerging in water *does* feel like being in microgravity.

I've always known that the only way people could simulate microgravity on the surface was to submerge astronauts in big pools of water to train them. I never believed that being submerged in water would actually feel like microgravity though. Which is why it's so shocking for me to feel my arms floating at my sides. I never thought I would have that feeling again, yet here it is.

I stay in the bath for almost an hour before the water becomes so tepid it's no longer comfortable. When I stand to get out, I feel heavy, almost like I won't be able to push my body out of the water. But I eventually do stand and the water rushes off my body in big waves, making me instantly lighter.

After my bath, I brush my teeth using the toothbrush the motel supplied and run my fingers through my hair. I rummage through the sacks of clothes and find a soft green T-shirt with a matching pair of shorts. After I'm dressed, I drop into bed, exhausted. The mattress is surprisingly comfortable and I pull the white sheets up around my chin, falling asleep in a matter of seconds.

***

I awake to pounding.

At first, I thought it was part of my dream—a steady thump, thump, thump keeping pace with me as I ran the running track on the Delta. I'm not sure what I was running away from, but whatever it was must have been terrifying because when I finally wake up, I am soaked in sweat and breathing heavily. My head pounding, I press my palms into my eyeballs to try to dampen the pain. The pounding continues and I hear a muffled voice. "Eta! Are you okay?"

It dawns on me that Alé must be pounding on the adjoining door. I turn on my lamp and open the door. He's standing on the other side; the light from the lamp casts a pale glow over his face. He looks terrified.

"What's wrong?" I say, wiping the grogginess from my eyes.

"Eta, you were screaming. I thought you were being attacked." He puts his hand to his heart and releases a sigh of breath he was holding.

"Oh, sorry." I shake my head, trying to get the dream out of my mind. "I have nightmares sometimes."

"Yeah, that must have been one hell of a nightmare. Are you sure you're okay?"

I nod. "Yes, yes, I'm fine. Really. I can't even remember why it was so scary. Something about the Delta. I was running around the track on the Delta. And something was chasing me. But I can't remember what."

"Is this normal? I mean, do you have these nightmares every night?"

I shrug. "Yeah, I guess so. That's why they couldn't put monitoring equipment on me at night when I was at the facility. I would scream and pull at the cords. They eventually gave up."

"Okay, well, if you're sure you're okay. It's about three in the morning, so I guess we'd better go back to sleep."

I nod and smile at him. He moves to close the adjoining door, but I stop him. "Maybe we could leave it open for now," I say. "Just in case."

He nods, lets the door swing wide open, and walks back to his bed in the other room.

I lie back in bed, my head still pounding from the ferocity of the dream. This one was particularly bad. I remember feeling alone and terrified. After a few minutes, unable to fall back asleep, I stand and walk to the door to Alé's room.

"Alé" I say. "Would you mind lying next to me for a few minutes? I think it might help me get back to sleep."

He stares at me for a moment, his eyes wide before he nods and stutters, "Sh-sh-sure."

I lie back down, facing the center of the bed, and he lies beside me, facing me. It's not a very big bed, so we're close and I can smell his skin—it's unlike any smell I've ever encountered. Almost like a mix between rosemary and mint, but not quite. There's something muskier about it.

He moves closer to me and gently drapes his arm over my waist, his hand resting on the small of my back. I snuggle into his shoulder, the top of my head tucked under his chin. I thought the bath was wonderful, but this might be the most amazing feeling I've ever had. He's soft yet firm at the same time. I press my cheek against the strong muscles of his chest. My skin tingles where his fingers press into my back, pulling me closer to him.

His soft breath flutters my hair. I'm so close to him, I can hear his heart beating and I pray he can't hear mine because I feel as though it might beat right out of my chest.

I open my eyes and look up at his face. He has the most peaceful look, a slight, crooked smile on his lips.

"Thank you," I whisper.

He squeezes me tighter.

I'm not sure when I fell asleep, but I know there were no more bad dreams that night.

Chapter 21

Nila Pecos scanned her NASA-issued holo-watch across the sensor at the door. The time stamp flashed on the watch: 2:32 a.m.

Damn, two minutes late.

It was the fourth time she'd been late this week. Tess would certainly have her panties in a twist over it.

She sighed. The new shift she'd been assigned was taking its toll. Never in her six years as a NASA Guard member had Nila worked night shifts before. Her four-year-old daughter Lina didn't take kindly to the new routine. Nila had to wake Lina up each night before her shift at White Sands to deliver the child to her grandmother's house. The two were on completely opposite schedules and Nila was lucky if she got to spend two hours with Lina each day. Lina had recently started throwing temper tantrums when Nila dropped her off, making Nila late for clock-in more often than not.

Unfortunately, they didn't have much choice in the matter. When the "girl from space" finally made her entrance into the atmosphere, it was all hands on deck to get the medical unit of the NASA Guard ready for her. Nila was a registered nurse and had been with the guard since it was first assembled after the war. She and her family moved to White Sands to work with the Project Diamond crew members and for the first few years, she had enjoyed a relatively easy schedule of day shifts monitoring the weekday astronaut nutrition schedule.

After they brought Eta to White Sands, Tess called Nila in and notified her that her duties were changing. She would now work the early morning shift as part of Eta's care team, and since Eta was now their highest priority, her care team would remain on call twenty-four hours a day.

In the span of five minutes, Nila's whole life changed and there was nothing she could do about it. The NASA Guard was a bona fide branch of the military and military rules applied. You went where they told you.

Nila's husband Drago also worked for NASA as a long-haul truck driver. He had a twice-weekly route bringing food and supplies to White Sands from the West Coast. Especially with Project Diamond ramping up over the last year, he had been working nonstop. She couldn't remember the last time she and Drago had taken a vacation. The few nights he was home, he dropped into bed like a sack of potatoes before she left for work and was gone by the time Nila's shift ended.

Nila closed the big steel door behind her and hurried down the hallway, taking care to walk as quietly as possible to avoid being seen coming in two minutes late. She bit down on the quick of her fingernail, a nervous habit she'd had since she was a toddler, and made her way into the nurse's station.

Millie, the evening nurse, sat at her desk, earbuds in, making notes on her holo-screen. Nila slid into her desk chair and flicked her finger across her own holo-screen, watching as it flashed to life.

"It's about time." The sound of Millie's voice made Nila jump.

"Jeez, Millie, you scared the crap out of me," she said, holding her hand to her chest.

Millie turned to look at her, a wad of gum tucked into her cheek as a smirk crossed her face. "Tess is going to have a shit fit if she decides to check your time card this week. What's the story anyway? Lina throwing fits again?"

"Yeah, something like that."

Millie smacked her gum and turned her attention back to her holo-screen before saying, "That's the shits."

"Anything new I should know about?"

"Nah, it's been quiet. She had a visitor today—some guy. I feel kinda bad for her, you know? She was all sad and quiet when I came to get her dinner tray."

Nila nodded. "Yeah, I know what you mean. She keeps asking about when she can leave her room. I hate having to brush her off."

The truth was, Nila didn't know when the NASA Guard would allow Eta to leave. She knew they were planning a surgery in two weeks, but Nila wasn't a surgical nurse, so she hadn't received any details. The only information she got was on a need-to-know basis. Nila didn't understand why they wouldn't let Eta out of her room, at least to walk around the facility and get a bit of exercise.

"Well, I'm outta here," Millie said, flicking off her holo-screen and bouncing out of her desk chair, her thick, dark hair woven into a braid that ran halfway down her back. "I've got plans." She winked at Nila and slung her bag over her shoulder.

"Plans? At 2:30 in the morning? You can't be serious."

Millie laughed and patted Nila on the shoulder as she walked past her, undoing the braid and shaking her head to release her hair from the grip of work. "Not all of us are tied down to the old ball and chain."

Nila couldn't help but smile. "Have fun. Don't do anything I wouldn't do."

"Yeah right. What fun would that be? See you tomorrow." Millie winked at her again and took off down the hallway.

Nila turned back to her holo-screen and finished logging in. She pulled up a tile that showed the video feed from the camera in Eta's room. Nila always checked the camera whenever she came on shift. It wasn't uncommon to see Eta in there practicing walking in the middle of the night. But tonight, she was in bed. Nila could make out the sleeping lump under the blankets Eta had pulled over her head.

Millie mentioned that Eta had had a visitor, the same man who visited her a week earlier. She wondered what the story was with him. Perhaps that was why Eta was sleeping tonight instead of walking around her room.

With a shrug, she flicked her finger across the holo-screen tile, minimizing it. She brought up Millie's report from earlier in the night and started entering data, a yawn escaping her lips.

She definitely needed coffee.

***

Four hours later, Nila walked back into the nurse's station, her third mug of coffee in hand. She plopped down at her desk and waved the data entry tile away, minimizing it to the bottom corner of the holo-screen. Again, she pulled up the tile with the video feed into Eta's room. There was the familiar lump under the blanket.

She was about to flick the tile away again, when she stopped and peered closer at the screen, her eyes narrowing. She pulled at the edges of the tile, enlarging the view so that it took up the entire width of the holo-screen.

Something wasn't right.

She tapped the tile lightly and spread it with her fingers, zooming in on the sleeping subject. There she was, Eta lying on her bed, blanket pulled over her head, sleeping in the same position she had been an hour earlier when Nila last looked at the camera feed.

That was the problem. Eta hadn't moved. Not a centimeter in the hour since Nila last looked at her. This wasn't normal for Eta. She usually moved around restlessly all night. She had a tendency to have nightmares and often woke screaming and thrashing, her blankets wadded up around her. Yet tonight, she'd slept soundly in the same exact position for hours.

"Hmm..." Nila pursed her lips and shook her head slightly, trying to make sense of what she was seeing. It was against protocol to go into Eta's room during the night unless she needed medical attention or a sedative for the nightmares, but

Nila decided she'd better go have a look. Something looked off and she couldn't shake it.

She stood from her desk and walked down the hallway to Eta's door. The locking mechanism flashed a dim, blue light, illuminating the darkened hallway. Nila waved her holo-watch over the lock and waited for the sound of the lock clicking open. But no sound came. She waved her watch over it again and again: still, no click. Nila tried the handle. It opened.

The door was unlocked.

The door to Eta's room was *never* unlocked.

There must have been a malfunction. She pushed the door open and walked into the room, tiptoeing so as not to wake Eta. When she reached the bed, Nila gently laid her hand on Eta's back expecting to feel her firm body breathing through the blanket.

Instead, she felt only softness.

She grabbed the top of the blanket and pulled it down to the end of the bed revealing not a sleeping girl, but a mound of pillows and wadded-up sheets.

Her mouth fell open and for a moment, she couldn't move, staring down at the white bedding and the otherwise empty bed. She grabbed the pillows and tossed them off the bed, making sure she wasn't missing something before running to the lighting panel to turn the lights on. A thick knot suddenly formed in her stomach as she looked around the empty room. She ran to the small bathroom and flung the door open to find it too was empty.

"Oh my God," she said, her voice small and tense.

Nila ran out of the room and down to the nurse's station. She picked up the holo-phone at her desk and typed in a number before putting the phone to her ear.

It rang only twice.

"This better be good," came the groggy voice on the other end of the line.

"Tess! We've got a serious problem here!"

Chapter 22

I wake with a start the next morning, briefly forgetting where I am. It feels like I've been asleep for days. As I look around the darkened hotel room, realization dawns on me.

I'm no longer in the white room. I'm no longer in New Mexico. I'm actually out in the real world. I am free.

Immediately, I look around for Alé. The memory of the night before floods back into my mind and almost topples me over. The feel of his arms, the smell of his skin, the sight of that slight, crooked smile on his lips. A shudder runs through my body.

The bed next to me is cold as I run my fingers over the sheet. He must have gotten up much earlier than I did. What time is it? The clock on the nightstand reads 8:36 a.m.

The door lock clicks open and my throat tightens in panic but quickly releases when I see that it's Alé. He's balancing two cups in one hand and has something round and yellow on a napkin in the other hand. When he sees me, he smiles.

"I'm glad you're awake. We should probably get moving soon," he says. He sits on the bed next to me and sets the cups on the bedside table, handing me the napkin.

"This is a doughnut," I say.

He chuckles. "Very good! I thought you might like something a little different. And this"—he points to the cup on the table— "is coffee. Black. Might as well learn how to drink the real stuff." He winks and hands me the cup.

The cup is made out of some sort of paper, although it's very thick and sturdy, and has a plastic lid. It's warm to the touch. The warmth of it surprises me and I almost let go, but Alé grabs it before it can slip out of my hand.

"Maybe we'll let it cool down a bit first. Go ahead, try the doughnut."

I inspect the pastry sitting in my hand. It surprises me how light it is. It's not really yellow, but more like a bright tan that's lighter around the edges and darker toward the middle. The doughnut is covered in a thick, shiny glaze that drips down the sides. I bring it close to my face and close my eyes so I can smell it. The scent is sweet like a melon—I had a honeydew melon vine on the Delta. I touch the top of it with my fingertip and the glaze spreads apart and sticks to my finger. It's warm and fluffy. I bring it to my mouth and take a bite.

The texture is totally different from anything I've ever had before. It's light and airy and my teeth cut through it much easier than I thought they would. As soon as the sugary glaze hits my tongue, it causes my cheeks to pinch together and I have to close my eyes. It's so sweet I almost can't swallow it.

Alé, who's been watching me curiously, lets out a big belly laugh and throws his head back. "You should see the look on your face!"

I manage to swallow the bite and fan my face with my free hand to bring it back to some semblance of composure. I'm sure my skin is as red as a tomato.

Alé must realize he's embarrassed me because he says, "No, no, don't be embarrassed. I'm sorry. I shouldn't laugh. You were just so cute though! I guess everything you try is going to be new and different so I'd better get used to it. Here." He hands me the coffee cup again. "Try this. It help cut the sweetness of the doughnut. Just be careful, it's very hot. Tip it back slowly."

I do as he says, tipping it back slowly until the dark liquid reaches my lips. He's right. It's *very* hot. But I allow only a few drops to cross my lips and find that it does help with the overwhelming sweetness of the doughnut. The coffee is bitter and it leaves my tongue tingling. The combination of the sweet doughnut and the bitter coffee actually tastes good in my mouth and I take another bite of the doughnut followed by a small swig of coffee.

"See, you're getting the hang of it," he says, winking.

I smile, my mouth full of doughnut, and feel the blush rise up in my cheeks again. It doesn't take me long to finish it and I even lick the extra glaze off my fingers. I'm smiling ear to ear.

Alé downs the last of his coffee and tosses the cup in the wastebasket. "We should hit the road. I want to try to make it to Virginia today. Xander has arranged a pack of supplies for us to pick up just outside of Roanoke. We'll have to spend one more night in a hotel before we set out for the cabin. It's a good six-hour hike to get to it and I want us to be rested."

I nod and stand. My feet and legs feel much stronger today than they did a week ago, even after sitting in the car most of yesterday. The more I walk, the stronger I get, and I like the feeling of being able to carry my own weight.

We pack up the few things we brought with us and head out to the Jeep. The sun is out and bright as can be. It amazes me how different it looks on the surface than it does from space. The idea of the sun is the same, a fireball in the sky—but the actual look of it couldn't be more different. On the Delta, the sun was always stark against a background of pure black. Here on the surface, the blue sky mutes it and makes it look less violent and exposed.

Alé puts the Jeep in gear and pulls out of the parking lot. As we drive, he explains what certain things are. He tells me about the road system and how the interstates connect the corners of the country. He describes how many of the highway systems around major cities were destroyed during the nuclear attacks and had to be rebuilt.

We pass by buildings made of all different types of materials: steel, brick, concrete, wood. Alé explains how water handling works when we pass by huge, gray water towers. When we pass an old, dilapidated post office, he explains how the country abandoned mail service in the years prior to the war in favor of more economical ways of communication. During the war, when the South Americans took out the communications satellites, they had to revert to the old postal system to deliver information. Until they rebuilt the cell networks, the postal service was the only means for people to communicate if they didn't have access to a wired telephone line. Eventually, they were able to bring back prewar technologies like holo-screens and holo-phones, and again, like a tattered piece of clothing, the postal service was tossed out in favor of advanced technology.

I watch in fascination as the miles tick by us and Alé tells me everything he can about the world around me. We must keep a wide berth around Memphis because it, like Dallas, was hit by a nuclear strike that left a trail of destructive radiation in its place. The dense forests eventually give way to the rolling hills outside Nashville.

Alé points out the huge gouges dug into certain hillsides near the city where underground bunkers were built. Hundreds of meters of solar panel fields flank the hillside gorges. He explains that nearly a million people lived in the underground complex we passed. They came out only to cultivate food from the hills and maintain the vast solar power plants. Many more bunkers like the one we saw existed all over the world, where people tried to hide out from the South Americans.

The people in the Nashville bunker were lucky. They had enough food and water, and the infrastructure of the bunker was good enough to keep clean air flowing and remove waste and sewage. Others weren't so fortunate. Alé told a story of a bunker near New York City that was discovered by the South Americans and targeted with missiles. Nearly two hundred thousand people died in the attack and the rest had to be relocated for fear of future attacks on the bunker.

The story brings on a sadness so deep, I think I might fall into it forever. I stare out the window and allow the tears to roll down my cheeks. The beautiful surface of the Earth slides by and I wonder how anyone with regular access to so much beauty could consider fighting over it.

A moment later, Alé's hand gently touches the top of my hand. I turn to look at him and he gives me a slight smile. He winds his fingers around mine and gives my hand a squeeze. Through the tears, I smile and lean over to rest my head on his shoulder, breathing in his scent.

Chapter 23

New Mexico

Time Since Touchdown: 42 Days, 11:16 a.m. MST

Patrick leaned back in the leather desk chair behind Tess's desk and watched her pace from one end of the small office to the next, wringing her hands and shaking her head. His gaze followed her and he tilted his head to the side. Kane sat in a chair in front of the desk, one ankle crossed over the knee, his thick black hair swept back from his forehead. There was no panic in his eyes.

It never ceased to amaze Patrick how easily his fellow humans could fool each other. Or how fast they could go from having their situation orderly and by the book to completely out of control.

That's where they stood now—out of control—and Patrick had a pretty good idea why. He knew the secret to having things go your way was to take care of them yourself. If you trusted others to do the job for you, you were screwed.

"I just... I can't believe it!" Tess said, her face tight. "I'm completely floored by this." She seemed on the verge of tears. Her hair was in an even more ragged state of disarray than it had been when he'd spoken with her a few days earlier, and she was clasping her hands together so tight that her pale fingers were turning purple.

"Yes, we have made a mess of this, haven't we?" Patrick said, tapping his fingertips on the desktop. He raised his other hand to his jawbone, rubbing it lightly. "Tess, quit pacing, please. Have a seat and let's go over what we know."

Nodding, she took her seat in the chair next to Kane, which would normally be reserved for visitors to her office. She had clearly been removed from her perch atop the medical department and replaced with someone of much higher importance who now sat in her $900 desk chair. She continued to wring her hands.

"The night nurse, Nila, called me at approximately 6:50 this morning and said she checked on Eta at 2:30 when she arrived. Actually," Tess snorted out the word, "she was late. I checked the time card and it was 2:32 when she punched in. Anyway, she noticed Eta hadn't moved after she checked her earlier in the night, and this isn't normal. Eta has nightmares and she's usually all over the bed. Recently, she's been practicing her walking at night. So, Nila decided to check the room in person and found that Eta wadded up her sheets and pillows under her blanket to make it look like she was sleeping."

Patrick nodded and motioned for her to continue.

"I called in Kane and the guard members who were on security duty. There weren't many of them in the vicinity, but the ones who had been patrolling the floor didn't see anything."

"Cameras?" Patrick asked.

Kane sat forward in his chair, planting both feet firmly on the ground. "Yes, we pulled up all the security footage we had and saw that the subject did leave her room at approximately 2:10 this morning."

Patrick held up his hand. "Now, explain to me how that happened. You told me the doors were always locked and only those with security badge clearance could open the door. How did she just walk out?"

Tess bit her bottom lip. "Nila mentioned that as well. She found the door unlocked when she went in there. She didn't need her holo-watch to open the locking mechanism."

"So, the door was just... open?" Patrick said, his eyes wide with disbelief.

"It appears so," Tess said, dropping her eyes to the floor.

"I'll ask again. How does that happen?"

"It must have been unlocked through the system," Kane said. "All the doors in this wing are connected through the same security server. Someone must have hacked into it and unlocked it."

"Any idea who?" Patrick asked.

Kane nodded and activated a holo-screen on his lap before setting it on the desk so Patrick could see it. He pulled up a tile showing video footage outside of Alé's room on the fourth level. The video showed Alé leaving his room at 1:47 a.m. to walk down the hallway. He entered a room at the end marked "Vending."

"This is Alé Bakas," Kane said. "He's an engineer with…"

"I know who he is," Patrick interrupted.

"Well, we show him going into the vending machine room, but we have no footage of him leaving it."

"Is there not a camera in the vending room?"

"There is, but it wasn't filming that night."

Patrick clenched his jaw. He was pretty good at containing his anger, but the longer he listened, the harder it got. "And why not?"

The pointed question didn't faze Kane. "Apparently," he said, his eyebrow lifting, "it was disabled during the recent software upgrade. I checked it myself. There was no footage."

"You've got to be kidding." Patrick shook his head in disgust. "Okay, so the kid went into the vending room and never came out. He's not still in there, right? He must have gone somewhere."

Kane nodded. "We believe he went through the laundry chute. It's the only way out of the room. Level four is the crew and visiting quarters. Laundry is on level six. There are chutes located at the end of each hallway in the vending rooms where the housekeeping staff deposits soiled laundry. There's a conveyor system between the levels that carries soiled linens from the deposit site down to the laundry bins. We believe he crawled through the conveyor into one of the laundry rooms on level six."

"Do we have footage of Eta after she left the room?"

"Yes," Tess chimed in. "We caught her on footage in the hallway just outside the nurses' station. She went into one of the laundry rooms. We found her ID band in a laundry bin. Looks like someone cut it off."

Patrick shook his head and tugged at the collar of his shirt. "I *knew* we should have put a tracking device on her. I let you talk me out of it." His icy blue eyes landed on Tess, who seemed to wilt under his gaze.

"Yes," she said, "well, you were right. I didn't think it was a necessary precaution at the time."

Patrick rolled his eyes and waved his hand around in a circle, urging her to continue.

Tess cleared her throat and gathered a breath. "Unfortunately, the camera in that laundry room is not night vision equipped. The room was dark and the footage is too grainy to tell where she went. Kane believes she met with Alé there and they exited through the laundry chute again. The shitty part is, one of the guards actually went in there moments after Eta did and turned on the light. But he didn't bother to investigate any further than a cursory look around." She shot Kane an accusatory glance. "We could have caught her right then and there if he'd been doing his job correctly."

Kane was unfazed by the accusation. He refused to even look in Tess's direction. "The two of them showed up again on the stairwell on level four, right outside the vending room," he said. "They accessed the hidden panel to the maintenance shaft. There are no cameras in that shaft, but it's pretty clear they climbed up and escaped the facility that way. The shaft leads to an air vent on ground level."

Patrick continued to tap his fingers on the desk. "Then what? How did they leave?" he asked.

Kane pulled up more footage on the holo-screen of a vehicle leaving the parking garage. "They left in one of the NASA cars stored on level one. They didn't just steal any car though—this one had been hacked. We know this because the transmitter was disabled somehow."

"Well, surely there's a backup transmitter on those cars, right?"

"Yes. The cars come standard with a transmitter built into the dashboard holo-screen and they also have a separate, independent transmitter built into the engine. Both of them were disabled. Neither has pinged on our boards yet."

"Well, hell…" Patrick let out a sigh and pounded his fist on the desk.

"Not all is lost though," Kane said, one eyebrow arching toward the ceiling.

"Oh? And why is that?"

"There was a third transmitter on the vehicle that they weren't aware of. Inside the trunk of each of the cars parked in the garage is a survival kit that contains a variety of emergency tools and supplies. The kit has a transmitter in it in case of a power loss on the vehicle. We implemented this as standard procedure a few months back after that courier got lost in the desert. Now all NASA vehicles come with the survival kit. So, whoever hacked into the car either didn't know about the kit or didn't have the ability to disable it."

Patrick sat up and leaned forward, elbows on the desk. "Great! So where is it?"

Kane pulled up a new tile on the holo-screen showing a map of New Mexico and Texas. He used his fingers to zoom in on an area of West Texas where a tiny red dot blinked in and out. "Dalhart, Texas."

"What the hell would they be doing there?"

"My guess is they took the car there to junk it," Kane said, shrugging. "I'm betting he knew we'd find some way to track that car."

"Maybe they're still there!" Tess said, jumping up from her chair. "Maybe we could go out there now and find them!"

Kane shook his head. "No, I don't think they're still there, but whoever they gave the car to *is* still there. So that's where we need to go first."

"Good work," Patrick said. "You've been surveilling this guy for a while now. Any idea where he might be taking her?"

Kane flicked his finger across the holo-screen shutting it off and settled back into his seat, elbows resting on the armrest, fingers tented in front of his face. "I have an idea, but I'm not ready to commit to it yet. I need to gather some more information first. Either way, I think Dalhart is the place to start."

Patrick nodded. "Take a team with you. Call in whoever you need. I want this treated as top priority." He stood from Tess's chair and smoothed his suit jacket with his hands, pausing to straighten his tie before walking toward the door.

Before he left, he turned to Kane. "This kid stole NASA property. I want my research subject back. And I want him to pay for the damage he's caused."

Chapter 24

The sun is beginning to touch the edge of the horizon when we pull into the town of Blacksburg. Alé tells me this town used to be a famous college town, but when Virginia Tech University closed up for good after the war, the population pretty much drained out of Blacksburg.

As we drive through the streets, I see, much like Dalhart, dilapidated buildings, boarded-up homes, and abandoned vehicles. This town is a bit livelier than Dalhart though. There is still a grocery store open near downtown and we find a small motel snuggled up to a grove of trees. It's nothing more than a single-story row of rooms flanked by a parking lot and an office.

Blacksburg is also much more beautiful than Dalhart. Rather than the drought-savaged, dusty streets of West Texas, Blacksburg has actual trees and a backdrop of mountains. Much more pleasing to the eye.

Alé parks the Jeep in front of the hotel. "Should I get two rooms?" His ears turn red and I smile.

"No, I would feel better if we stayed in the same room. If that's okay with you."

"Sure," he says, nodding. "Well, I'll be right back then."

When he returns with the room key, I ask, "How are you paying for these rooms?"

He flashes me a crooked smile. "Cash. It's not very common these days to have cash, but I was able to get my hands on enough to get us through the trip. I've been using fake names too."

I nod. He parks the Jeep and we take our few bags into the room. It's a much smaller room than the ones we had in Little Rock. The decor is old and it smells musty, but the bed is comfortable and I flop down on it, giving the mattress a try.

Alé sets his bag down but does not take a seat on the bed. "Since the grocery store downtown is still open, I'd like to buy some supplies," he says. "We've got a long hike in front of us tomorrow and I want to make sure we have some provisions."

"That's a good idea. I'm kind of tired of those sandwiches Buster made for us anyway."

Alé laughs and pulls the Jeep keys out of his pocket. "I'll only be a little bit. Maybe thirty minutes max."

"I'm okay. I promise," I say, and flash a smile to reassure him. His shoulders loosen a bit and he smiles back before leaving. He tells me to lock the door behind him, which I do.

I inspect the small room for a moment and turn on the holo-screen to find a movie to watch. This holo-screen is old and it works like the ones on the Delta, so I'm able to navigate the channels fairly easily. I settle on a classic movie channel playing *The Wizard of Oz* and prop myself up on pillows against the headboard. I used to watch this movie with my mother when I was a small child—it was part of the Delta archives. I haven't watched it in many years though and I realize, as Glinda sends the Wicked Witch away in a plume of red smoke, that this movie should have been terrifying to a young child. Not to me though. I loved it, wanted to watch it over and over again. The memories of my mother and my childhood flood over me and soon, fat tears roll down my cheeks.

When Alé returns, he drops some packages onto the small table and rushes to my side. "What's the matter?" He asks, his face drawn with worry.

I shake my head and grab a tissue from the nightstand. "It's nothing. Really. Just some old memories."

"You used to watch *The Wizard of Oz*? So did I." He stares at the screen. It's the moment Dorothy and the Scarecrow come across the Tin Man and they're trying to decipher the word "oilcan". A smile crosses his face and he sits on the bed, mesmerized by the film. "I loved this movie. Couldn't get enough of it."

"Me too," I say.

We watch in silence for a few more moments before Alé suddenly stands. "Oh, I almost forgot. I brought you something."

He reaches for a brown paper bag and hands it to me. The bag is heavy and warm. I squeeze it lightly with my fingers. Whatever's in it feels soft.

"Open it," he says, smiling.

I pull the top of the bag apart and look inside. Immediately a smell hits my nose. I'm not sure what the smell reminds me of, but it's delicious. My mouth waters.

Onions! That's what the smell reminds me of. I used to make peanut oil using an oil press on the Delta and my mother would use it to sauté onions. That's what this bag smells like. But there's another smell too—potatoes maybe.

"It's a hamburger and french fries," Alé says. He has a bag too and sits down at the small table to unwrap his burger.

I pull mine out of the bag. When I open the white paper wrapped around it, the hamburger is big and soft, almost fluffy under my fingers. I squeeze it and turn it over in my hand, unwrapping the paper to reveal a deep brown bun with tiny seeds lodged in it. The burger has lettuce, tomato, and mayonnaise on it and the meat is charred almost black around the edges.

I hold it between my hands and take a big bite. An array of flavors hits my senses and the rush of it is so exhilarating, I close my eyes to make sense of it all. The bun is sweet and the meat is tangy. My cheeks pinch together as I chew my very first bite of burger.

When I open my eyes, I must have a strange look on my face because Alé, who also has a mouthful of burger, bends over in a full-blown belly laugh, spitting his bite out into a napkin. A few moments later, we are both laughing, all red-faced and runny-nosed.

We finish our meal and stay awake late into the night, laughing, telling stories, and watching classic movies. When it's time to go to sleep, Alé offers to sleep on the ragged and impossibly small sofa next to the bed.

I think about this for a moment and shake my head. "Will you sleep next to me again? I have these awful nightmares and I think it helps to have you here."

He smiles and lies down next to me.

"Good night, Eta."

"Good night, Alé."

His hand wraps around mine and he gives it a reassuring squeeze. I sleep better that night than I ever have in my life.

Chapter 25

Buster wasn't surprised to see the boxy NASA Guard vans pull into the driveway of his shop. He was, however, surprised at how quickly they'd made it there.

"Dammit all to hell," he muttered to himself as he watched the fourth and final van park. An extremely tall man with jet black hair, dressed head to toe in black combat gear, a pistol strapped to his waistband, stepped out of the passenger side. As the man walked toward Buster, he lifted his hand and removed his wire-rimmed sunglasses, tucking them into the pocket of his shirt. Buster spat and a wad of chewing tobacco landed a mere centimeter from the man's shiny steel-toed boot.

Whoever he was, he wasn't fazed by the gesture. He didn't even look down.

"Excuse me. Are you Buster Shirley?" The man had a tight jaw that hardly moved while he spoke.

"I reckon you already know the answer to that question," Buster said, spitting again, this time hitting his mark with the spit wad landing on the man's boot tip. Two more men dressed in the same gear walked out of the car and stood behind the man. "Who's askin'?"

"My name is Carter Kane. I'm looking for a couple of people who I believe came through Dalhart not more than twenty-four hours ago."

"What kinda agency ya with?" Buster had found in his many dealings with governmental officials that it was often best to play dumb.

Kane ignored the question. "Have you seen these people?" He held up a holo-phone to Buster's face; pictures of Alé and Eta flashed on the screen.

Buster rubbed the three months of beard growth under his chin. "Don't look familiar. I'll ask ya again, what kinda agency ya with?"

Kane tucked the holo-phone back into his pocket and turned his attention to Buster's shop, eyeing the worn, steel building up and down. "I think you know the answer to that Mr. Shirley. In fact, I think if I were to look through your parts inventory, I'd find a few pieces that were formerly attached to a NASA-owned vehicle." Kane turned back to Buster and looked him square in the eye.

"You want the parts back?" He figured there was no sense in pretending. He also cursed himself for not running a bug finder over that vehicle. He'd assumed he got the only two tracking devices on it, but apparently, he'd been wrong.

"No, you can keep the parts. I want to know where those two people went after they dropped off the car here with you."

"Can't say as I know what yer talkin' 'bout." Buster spat again on the dirt, this time aiming for the toe of one of Kane's guard members. The man jumped back, a look of disgust on his face. "I picked up that car abandoned on the highway outside'a town. I'll show ya where if ya like."

Kane took a step closer to Buster. "That won't be necessary. Mind if we have a look around?" Kane's face split into a slow grin and he added, "We usually find out what we need to know, Mr. Shirley. No matter the cost."

Buster spat once again on the ground and made a gesture with one hand toward the building. As Kane turned his head to look, Buster took the heel of his other hand and jammed it fast and hard into Kane's nose. The movement was so quick, Kane wasn't sure anything had actually happened until he reached up and felt the blood running from his nose and the thick split in his upper lip.

Before any of the guard members could react, Buster, who was much more agile than he looked, sprinted to the side of the shop and out of sight.

"Get him!" Kane screamed.

Buster revved the gas on the motorcycle and raced around the corner of the building, nearly knocking the other two men over. With the cycle on full throttle, he was out of the driveway and a block down the road before anyone could catch him.

Three shots rang out, one hitting Buster's right ankle. The bullet didn't stop him though, and he pressed forward with the bike, winding in and out of the abandoned streets of Dalhart, hoping to lose the guard members he was sure would be on their way inside their black vans.

When he reached the edge of town, he kept going at full speed before turning down a narrow dirt road that led into what seemed like a dead end in the middle of an old cotton field. As he'd feared, a black van was not far behind him, kicking up clouds of dust on the old road.

Buster neared the end of the road and swerved, avoiding the skeletal remains of a long-gone cotton crop leading to the edge of a cavern below. He zoomed to a spot beneath the lip of a cliff and slowed down to a stop, straddling the bike with the engine still purring. As he watched, the van with the two men, going at least sixty miles per hour, went headfirst over the steep cliff and took a nosedive four stories down into the cavernous hole below.

Standing, Buster gave the bike some gas and drove it back up a small ramp to the top of the cliff. He punched a code into the holo-screen mounted to the bike handles and, as if it had never been there, the cavern in the ground disappeared.

Active camouflaging was Buster Shirley's specialty and he'd done a thorough job of ensuring the old mining site in the middle of the cotton field was only known to him. He used it as a dumping ground and storage site for various illegal commodities he dealt.

After dusting himself off, he examined his ankle. Fortunately, the bullet had only grazed the skin, but it was bleeding a fair amount and he shook his head and groaned. He'd been very lucky. A guy like Kane was sure to be a good shot and he could have easily hit Buster square in the back. He wrapped a handkerchief around his ankle and knotted it up tight to quell the bleeding before he left the cotton field.

***

Back in town, Kane stood in the doorway of the tiny, dingy office at the back of Shirley's Autobody. He pressed a stem cell patch to his busted upper lip. The patch deposited stem cells directly into the wound, helping it to heal much faster than it would naturally. He'd shoved a wad of medical gauze into his left nostril which had taken the brunt of Buster's palm. The broken nose was already turning purple and the bruising had seeped up into the skin under his eyes, giving him the distinctive look of a man who'd come out on the wrong end of a bar fight.

He walked around the cluttered desk and sat on the faux leather swivel chair pockmarked with spots of missing leather. Another guard member, a man named Strickland, walked into the office. "We did a preliminary search of premises, sir. No sign of either subject," he said. "We didn't find a single part from the car, although we haven't checked the lower level yet. He may have stashed them there."

"I can't believe you idiots let him get away," Kane said, his words muffled under the patch. "Have you found Mason and Klein yet?" The two guard members had gone in one of the vans to find Buster Shirley after he maimed Kane's face with the heel of his hand.

Strickland lowered his eyes to the floor and shook his head. "No, sir. It's like they disappeared. They won't answer their radio either. I sent Lieutenants Jackson and Lamont out to find them but they've had no luck. No luck finding Mr. Shirley either."

"No." Kane shook his head. "He'll be long gone by now."

"We'll continue our search of the facility, sir. I can't imagine he could have taken a whole car's worth of scrapped parts far in one day's time."

"I don't give a damn about the car parts." Kane winced slightly as he pulled the patch from his split lip and set it on the desk. "Continue the search. Bring me anything that looks out of the ordinary. I know they were here and I'm not leaving until I find something that can help me figure out where they went."

"Yes, sir," Strickland said and exited the room leaving Kane alone.

Kane stared out the murky, dust-covered panes of the small window next to the desk. He could see the back alley through the window. He inched closer to it and used the palm of his hand to wipe away years of grime from the windowpane. As he peered out the semiclean circle in the window, he noticed cars parked behind the building. He counted three of them, each in a different state of disarray.

Junkers, he thought.

An idea came to him. He turned his attention to the desk in front of him. There were three stacked drawers on either side of the desk. He opened the first drawer and started routing through the contents: half-used erasers, old paper pads with only a few sheets of paper still on them, broken pencils, dead pens, staples and bent paper clips. Not what he was looking for.

He opened the next drawer. Same. All six drawers were soon standing open in front of him. He turned his attention to the stacks of paperwork scattered haphazardly around the desktop, picking them up and flipping through each stack. Still nothing.

He sat back in the old chair and crossed his arms over his chest, his eyebrows drawn together and his lips pursed. Again, he turned to look out the small window.

Kane didn't know much about Shirley, but he did know that a scrapper who deals in stolen car parts would never leave stolen or illegal vehicles on his property. And it was apparent by his clever escape that Shirley was perhaps a bit smarter than your run-of-the-mill scrapper. So, Kane figured, it must mean that Shirley had the proper title work for the three vehicles in the back alley.

Where would Shirley keep vehicle titles? Scanning the office again, he stood and walked around. There were no other drawers or cabinets in the office. He touched the fake wood paneling that adorned the walls and allowed his fingers to drag across the smooth surface. When he lifted his fingers, they were black from years of built-up dirt. He grimaced in disgust.

Kane continued to walk around the perimeter of the room, running his fingers over the walls, not quite sure what he was looking for, when suddenly, he felt a click. He stopped and pressed on the wall again. This time, seemingly out of nowhere, a panel sprang from the wall.

"I'll be damned," he murmured out loud. This hillbilly who didn't appear to have the sense God gave a goose had a perfectly hidden, active-seam camouflaging this panel. Kane had seen plenty of these types of hidden doors at White Sands, but he'd never seen a civilian engineer one that blended in so perfectly.

He swung the door open to reveal a safe behind the wall panel. He tried the handle. Locked. He let out a long, low sigh. How would he open that? Then he had another idea.

"Strickland!" he called. A moment later, Strickland walked through the door.

"Yes, sir?"

"Do we still have that portable welding kit in the back of the van?"

"Um, yeah, I believe so. Unless it was in the van Mason and Klein took. I'll check."

As Strickland left to check the van, Kane grabbed the edges of the safe and started to shimmy it out of the hole in the wall. Fortunately, it wasn't bolted into place, only pushed into the small compartment. It was a small safe but still quite heavy. He set it down on the desk as Strickland walked in holding a yellow welding machine about the size of a suitcase.

"Here you go, sir." He set the welder on the desk and pointed to the safe. "Do we need to open that?"

Kane nodded and within a few minutes, Strickland had cut through the metal hinges of the safe, sliding the door off. There wasn't much inside. A few personal documents, a small bag of gold coins, an old army service medal. At the back of the safe was a folder. Kane pulled the folder out and flipped it open. A smile spread across his lips and he turned and walked out of the office heading for the back door of the building. Strickland followed.

"What did you find, sir?"

Kane pointed at the document on top. It was a vehicle title for a Chevrolet pickup truck. He walked to a pickup parked at the back of the alley and pulled open the door to check the VIN, which matched the VIN on the title in his hand.

Kane grinned at Strickland and said, "There's one."

He did this again two more times with the other two vehicles in the lot. Both vehicles had matching titles in the folder. None of the titles were actually in Buster Shirley's name, but Kane assumed he hadn't registered them yet, likely because he had dealer status.

Kane pulled one final title out of the folder and held it up. "This one's missing," he said, his grin growing bigger. Strickland looked at the vehicle title Kane held in his hand.

It was for an old model black Jeep with a gasoline engine.

Chapter 26

Virginia

Time Since Touchdown: 44 Days, 10:48 a.m. EST

I feel bad. We're hiking through this forest and Alé's carrying almost all of our supplies in a large hiking backpack we picked up at a drop point a few kilometers outside of Blacksburg. He said his friend Xander arranged to leave the bag there so we would have plenty of supplies to last us a few weeks at the cabin.

He's grunting under the weight of the backpack as we climb up a steep trail that's leading us deeper into the mountains. I'm carrying only a small pack with the few clothes I brought from Buster's and my water bottle.

"Are you sure I can't help you carry that?" I ask.

"No, I'm good," he says, turning to flash me his signature crooked smile. Beads of sweat cling to his forehead.

"Really though, I feel bad. I can at least strap those blankets onto this bag I'm carrying. To take a little weight off. I don't mind."

He stops and turns around with a look on his face that says *No, and stop asking.* I'm about to offer up my next argument about why I should help, but his eyes soften and his forehead wrinkles in thought. He unstraps the backpack and sets it on the ground next to a big boulder.

"You know, it might be a good idea."

"What, for me to carry more of the load?"

"Yeah. I mean, it's fine. I've done many backpacking trips over the years, so I'm used to carrying these heavy packs. But it might be a good idea to have you work on your strength by carrying a little more. Do you really think you can handle it?"

I nod, happy he's given me the opportunity to help. He begins to rearrange items in the backpack and before long, my pack is bulked up and he's helping me sling it over my shoulders. The extra weight makes me a little off balance at first, but after a few meters, I'm able to get my bearings and the walk feels more natural.

It's getting easier for me to adapt my gait to different situations the more time I spend on the surface. The pack is heavy on my back and feels like it's dragging me back down the mountain trail. But I keep putting one foot in front of the other and eventually I get used to the weight. My back feels stronger and I make a conscious effort to pull in my ribs and stabilize my stomach muscles. After another ten minutes or so, he turns around to check on me.

"How are you doing? Want me to take some of it back?"

Although I'm breathing heavily, I feel good. "No, I think I'm okay." A puzzled look comes over his face. "What?" I ask.

"Nothing." He shakes his head. "I'm just amazed. That's all."

"Amazed by what?"

"By you."

I blush so hard I think my face might explode. "Why? Because I can carry a few blankets on my back?"

His lips curl up slightly and he narrows his eyes as if examining me. "No, not because of that. I just don't understand how you're able to do this. It's only been, what, maybe six weeks since you landed? How are you able to hike up a mountain trail carrying a backpack after such a short time? Honestly, it's unheard of. Astronauts used to be laid up for months after they landed and very few of them actually had injuries. You broke your pelvis and leg and several ribs... yet here you are." He shakes his head again and continues to give me that strange stare.

"Great. One more reason I'm strange and unusual," I grumble, kicking the dirt with my hiking sandal.

"I didn't mean it like that. It's only... well, maybe there was something to your routine."

"My routine?"

"Yeah. When you were on the Delta, you had a strict routine, right? Every day you did the same thing. You ate a vegan diet because it's all you had, and you included like an hour and a half of exercise in your routine every day."

"That's right. So?"

He shakes his head and chuckles a bit. "It's funny that we humans have been trying to figure out ways to live longer, get stronger, be healthier. Maybe the answer has been right in front of us all along—eat a plant-based diet and get lots of exercise. I mean, look at you." He waves his hand in my direction.

I'm not sure how to take his gesture. I stare down at my skinny legs.

"You're doing it. You're the healthiest version of a person there is. You lived most of your life in a simulated gravity environment, so your bones and joints and ligaments haven't been under the stress the rest of us face in Earth's gravity."

"Well, I didn't do the healing myself. You said something about stem cells. That's why my body healed so quickly after the crash."

He nods. "Yeah, the stem cell capsules probably did help the bones heal quicker. That technology came around during the war as a way to treat wounded soldiers easier in the field. I'm sure they gave you the best stem cells money could buy. But as a whole, you're doing so much better than anyone thought you would. I guess I see why they want to study you so badly. They need to know how to replicate your success if they want to put people in space for many years." He shrugs. "And, I suppose it explains why they want you to go back up too. They want to see how well you adapt to it a second time around."

I decide that I'm tired of this conversation and walk past him up the trail. "That may be, but I have no intention of going back into space. Let's keep moving. I'm ready to see this cabin."

He laughs and takes off behind me. The trail is barely more than a footpath and less than a half meter wide. We parked the Jeep on an abandoned national forest road a good way from the main highway and had to hike through raw forest for a few hundred meters before we came to the footpath, which Alé knew was in the woods near the Jeep. We hid the Jeep in a grove of trees so no one would spot it. Alé said he'll have to come back to it at some point to meet up with Xander and get us fresh supplies.

We've been hiking for about two hours and I decide that I made a good decision in choosing these sandals as my footwear. The soles are thick yet springy. The straps fit perfectly to my feet and make it easy to bend and move them around. Plus, they allow my skin to breathe, which is nice because it's quite warm in the woods today. I know I won't be able to wear them in the winter, but I plan to wear them as long as I possibly can. They feel like part of my foot now.

We stop and have some lunch. Alé shows me how Xander included a bunch of prepared meals vacuum-packed into tiny packages that we add water to. They're all plant-based, he says, since it's hard to prepare animal products this way. But he tells me he plans to do some hunting and fishing for us after we get to the cabin. There's a stream next to the cabin that leads to a lake, which is full of fish. He tells me there was a large garden there too when his family lived there and he thinks he might be able to get it cleaned up and growing again. He made sure Xander included a variety of seeds in our supplies.

The idea of tending a garden again makes me shiver with excitement. The garden was the only real thing I enjoyed about the Delta. It kept me busy. It gave me food and oxygen. It was because of the garden that I was able to remain sane all those years, especially after my mother died.

While hiking, I've been taking a mental inventory of the trees and plants we pass. We have a holo-screen, which Alé has stocked with books and survival manuals. We can't hook up to the cloud because they would be able to track it, but we can at least use it to look up things we need and keep ourselves occupied. He says there is an electricity source at the cabin, so we shouldn't have an issue charging it. I want to look up these plants as soon as we get there. I know there's a book about foliage on the screen.

The smell of the forest is what really amazes me. In a way, it smells like my garden on the Delta. It's the smell of wet dirt and thriving plant life. But in other ways, it smells totally different. I didn't have any trees in the garden and the smells of the evergreens are delightfully tangy and delicious. The feel of their needles is so strange too. Some of the trees have long, spiky needles that prick your skin and others have soft, silky needles that bend with your fingers.

Four hours into the hike, Alé stops and puts his finger to his lips. He points to a clearing a few hundred meters away. I peer through the trees and see three deer standing there, each bending over to eat the soft grass on the meadow floor. I gasp and put my hand over my mouth, my eyes wide. The noise causes all three deer to pop their heads up, their ears perked and alert. They stare in our direction. They have the biggest eyes I've ever seen.

Alé smiles and then, out of nowhere he yells, "Hi deer!" and he waves his arms up over his head. As soon as they hear it, they scamper off with big bounding leaps into the cover of the trees and we watch them until we can't see them any longer. I find myself doubled over laughing at Alé's silliness.

The sun is beginning to sink over the top of the mountain when we enter a large meadow and see the cabin nestled in the forest on the other side. It's small, with only a few rooms, and has walls made from rough logs stacked on top of each other and crossed at the corners. The roof is peaked and made from sheets of metal covered in big black solar panels. A set of stairs leads up to the small front porch.

"Were the solar panels always there?" I ask, confused by how they got solar panels so deep into the woods.

He nods. "The cabin is very old, maybe even over a hundred years. I'm guessing it may have even been here before the national forest was set up around it. Along the way, someone came up here and added these modern features to it. Those solar panels are older, perhaps thirty years old, but the last time I was here was last summer. My brother and I came up here for a few weeks. Everything still worked at that time. Whoever remodeled it did it right. That's why we were able to stay here for so long. Not only is there a complete solar setup with panels, batteries, and an inverter system, but there's also a water wheel set up in the stream that runs behind the cabin. If we need to, we can use water instead of the sun to provide us with power."

"Wow." I realize my mouth is hanging open. "Who would leave a place like this?"

He shrugs. "I guess whoever it was didn't have a need to come back after a while. Maybe they died and nobody even realized they had done this. Like I said, I believe the cabin predates the national forest because you couldn't build a cabin on government land in the years building up to the war. Whoever it was probably never owned the land."

We walk up to the cabin and I can see the remnants of the garden. "That must have been a huge garden!" I can't hide the excitement in my voice.

Alé smiles. "Yes, it was. My mother loved taking care of it. It provided us with so much food during those years. We would stock up the storage cellar with root vegetables for the winter." He points to the other end of the meadow. "There's an apple tree grove a few hundred meters into the woods that way. We would pick apples and store them in the cellar as well."

We climb up the stairs to the front porch. Despite the age of the cabin, the wood feels solid beneath my feet. Alé opens the door and we walk inside. The front room has a stone fireplace on one side and a big picture window on the other. Two windows flank the door as well. A handmade sofa sits in front of the fireplace with thick cushions.

In the back of the room, there's a small kitchen with an island and three stools in front of it. The kitchen has an electric stove, sink, and a bank of cabinets along the back wall. A hallway in the back leads to two bedrooms, each with a bed and a small table, and a small washroom with a sink and a bathtub.

"There's no toilet," I say.

Alé shakes his head. "No, whoever upgraded this place didn't add plumbing. There's an outhouse out back and there are two big water tanks behind the cabin that should be full of rainwater. If not, we can bring in water from the stream and boil it to make sure it's clean. We'll have to bring in buckets of water to use in the sink and bathtub. They drain right out into the woods."

I nod and walk around the tiny cabin, running my fingers over the rough wooden walls.

"So, what do you think?" Alé asks, shoving his hands into his pockets and looking tentatively in my direction.

"I think…" I keep walking, taking in every bit of the cabin. I close my eyes and inhale the musty smell of it. "I think it's wonderful."

He lets out a long sigh and smiles. "Good. I was worried you might think it was too… rustic."

"It's wonderful," I repeat and turn to him, smiling. "Perfect."

Chapter 27

The road rumbled under the van as it cruised northeast, kicking up the thin layer of dust that settled on the highway. There hadn't been a road crew out to repair these roads in many years as was evident by the buckled pavement and deep potholes.

Kane sat in the back of the van with Strickland at his side. The inside of the van was about as high-tech as one could get. Holo-screens lined the interior walls, each set to a different monitoring program. The van had satellite communication capabilities and was linked with NASA's brand-new tracking and data relay satellites or TDRS, launched a mere six months earlier. There was no cell service out in this area of the country and there hadn't been for many years, but the new satellites gave the NASA Guard crew an edge—they now had capabilities for constant communication.

"Pull that one up there," Kane told Strickland, pointing at a highway map on the screen. They were looking through surveillance camera feeds located on several of the major highways between Texas and Baltimore. "They wouldn't have gone south—it's too far out of the way. They would be headed due east. Probably through Arkansas."

"Yes, sir."

Kane's holo-phone rang at his belt, also connected directly to the satellites. He lifted it up and saw it was Patrick.

"This is Kane."

"Tell me. What happened?"

Kane relayed the story of what happened at Shirley's Autobody, leaving out the part where he got his nose broken and his lip split by the heel of Buster's palm. He also neglected to mention that he'd lost two of his crew members and a van in the chase to catch Buster. He wasn't sure what became of them, but he had left two of his guard team behind with one of the vans to keep searching for them. He was confident they would turn up eventually.

"We believe they're headed east in a black Jeep, gasoline engine, twenty-two years old, last four of VIN 2437."

"What makes you think they're headed east?" Kane knew Patrick wasn't a fan of flying by the seat of his pants: he liked working with facts, numbers, and hard truths.

"He's from Baltimore, sir. I assume he'll go back to what's familiar to him. From my prior research, we know he and his family disappeared into the mountains west of Baltimore during the war. I think that's where he'll take her."

"To the mountains? Like camping? Can they survive for long out there?"

"He's a trail rat. Takes hiking trips out to the mountains all the time. I believe they can survive. Plus, I think they have a destination in mind. He and his family lived in the woods for years. They probably have a place there—a cave or a cabin where they can hole up for a while."

"Right. What makes you think you can find the Jeep? I mean, those old gas vehicles aren't common anymore, but they certainly aren't defunct either. There's got to be hundreds of them out on the road."

"The plate number was written on the title: Texas plates, VST 6224. We're planning to utilize surveillance camera feeds on the highway system. Once they get east of Oklahoma, highway cameras are much more common. We can tap into any feed we need using the TDRS by intercepting the feeds as they're relayed back to their highway patrol stations. It won't be hard to find them." Kane had an air of assuredness in his voice that even Patrick admired.

"Good. Where are you now?"

"Oklahoma, sir. We'll be passing through Oklahoma City in less than an hour. We're working our way east based on the path I believe they took."

"Okay, keep me posted."

"Yes, sir."

Kane ended the call and tucked the phone back into its holder on his belt. He turned to Strickland. "That's the main highway going into Arkansas. I want you to look at every vehicle that crossed the state line starting twenty-four hours ago."

Strickland nodded. "Yes, sir."

Kane sat back in his seat and lifted his arms over his head, stretching, a smile growing on his face. He never enjoyed a road trip. But a hunt… that was another thing.

He always enjoyed a hunt.

Chapter 28

I wake up to a strange smell and the sound of something hissing or sizzling. It takes me a moment to remember where I am. My first night in the cabin was surreal. We arrived shortly before dusk and Alé showed me the outhouse and stream. The water in the stream shimmered over smooth, round pebbles and it looked like something you might find in a fairy tale.

After that, we ate meals Xander packed for us, adding water from the storage tanks out back. As the chill of the night air invaded the space, Alé brought out blankets stored in one of the closets. They smelled musty, but they were dry and the warmth they provided was inviting.

"We can't build a fire," he said. "They might be able to see the smoke. Tomorrow I'll get the electrical system up and running and check on the furnace. It's a small one, doesn't heat the whole space on really cold nights. But it's better than nothing."

I was so exhausted; I fell asleep on the small sofa almost immediately after Alé tucked the blankets around me. At some point, he must have carried me to one of the bedrooms because that is where I now find myself.

The bed linens we brought with us are already on the bed and the room is chilly, so I snuggle back down into the blankets, curling my legs up next to my chest. I don't really want to leave the bed, but I'd like to know what it is that's making the delicious smell, so I pull the blankets aside and step out of bed and into the hallway.

In the kitchen, Alé is standing over the electric stove where he's frying something in a pan and I quickly realize this is the source of the sizzling sound. Alé turns around to see me standing there and his face spreads into a wide smile.

"Good morning. I got the electrical system up and running. The batteries have lost some of their juice, but not much. They were almost completely charged. I went up to the roof and cleaned off the solar panels to make sure we're getting as much light as possible. So far, everything's working as it should."

"Great," I say. "What is that smell?"

"Bacon! Xander included several packages of cured meats in our pack. I went through everything we have and made an inventory of supplies. Today we'll plan to hike around the cabin so you can get a feel for the land. I want to show you the lake too. We'll have to check out the garden as well and make a list of what we need to do to get it going again. There are only a couple of months left in the growing season."

I walk to Alé's side and look at the pan of bacon. The smell is sweet and salty at the same time and it makes my mouth water. Leaning closer, I close my eyes to get a better whiff but jump back in surprise when the bacon suddenly pops in the pan.

Alé laughs. "Be careful! It has a tendency to do that."

I walk to the kitchen island and take a seat on one of the stools tucked under it. Sitting on the island is a bowl of fresh berries. "Where did these come from?"

He points the spatula at the kitchen window. "There's a grove of wild raspberry bushes along that tree line. It's a little late in the year for them, but there are still plenty on those bushes. We'll have raspberries for several more weeks if the weather holds up."

I pick up a berry and study it, rolling it around between my fingers before popping it into my mouth. It's plump and explodes as I bite down on it. The tangy sweetness of it is so surprising, my cheeks pucker and my eyes water. Eventually, my taste buds get used to the flavor and I pop another into my mouth. "These are delicious!"

Alé nods and clicks off the burner on the stove, removing the sizzling bacon pan from the heat. I take a seat on the sofa. A few moments later, Alé brings me a plate of bacon and eggs and a mug of coffee and sits down beside me on the sofa with his own plate. The eggs are rehydrated from the food packs and the coffee is instant, made from hot water and a mix, he tells me.

I bite down on the bacon and am immediately surprised by the texture. It's soft, yet crisp at the same time. And so salty! Again, my mouth puckers, but I eventually get used to the taste and before I even realize it, I've eaten the entire plate.

"This might be the best meal I've ever had." I smile as I set the plate down on the table next to the sofa.

"I'm glad I could prepare your favorite meal, my lady," Alé says and winks at me, finishing off his last piece of bacon.

"How long do you think we'll stay here?"

His expression turns serious and he gazes out the window. "I don't know the answer to that." After a long pause, he continues, "I believe they'll look for us, but I'm not yet sure how *hard* they'll look. Does that make sense?"

I shake my head.

"They've spent a lot of time and money on you—bringing you down from the Delta, medical expenses after the crash landing, research, and so on. I know they consider you an important asset. I'm hoping that when they don't succeed in finding us initially, they'll give up the search and move on... although, if I know anything about John Patrick, that's probably not the case."

"And what if they don't move on?"

He gives me a half-hearted smile. "We'll have to see how it goes. I'm planning to lay low here for the next week. Then I have an arranged meeting with Xander. He's leaving a burner phone for me along with another pack of supplies at a chicken restaurant about a kilometer from the parking spot of the Jeep. I'll know more after I talk to him. He's keeping an eye on things at NASA for me."

"A chicken restaurant?" I crinkle up my nose.

He drops his head back and laughs. "Yeah. It's not actually open anymore. Now, it's an abandoned building, but it has an unlocked storeroom at the back. I guess the hacker network often uses it to make drops when they're trying to evade the government. Plus, there's a giant chicken statue perched on top of the building. Apparently, you can't miss it. Anyway, he plans to leave the burner phone there along with the pack. I'll be able to talk to him on the phone undetected."

"I see. Turn left at the giant chicken, right?" I giggle.

"That's right." He's laughing too.

"So, after you talk to him, we'll be able to make a better plan?"

"Hopefully. We'll be able to evaluate our situation better." He turns and looks me in the eye, a curious expression on his face. "How long do *you* want to stay?"

"That's a good question," I say. "Nobody's really asked me yet what I want to do. I want to see the world… but I think, for now, I like it here. It's the perfect place for me at this moment."

He nods. "Good. I'm glad. Besides, you'll have plenty of time to think about it."

I stand up and stretch my arms over my head, already feeling invigorated from the food and the conversation. "So, what should we do today? I'm ready to explore!"

He laughs and stands. "Let's start in the woods. I'll show you some of the trails we made in the woods around the cabin. Then we can go to the lake."

***

We spend the rest of the morning hiking up the side of the mountain. There are a few rough trails cut into the area, but not many, and we end up making our own way through the trees. We bring the holo-screen with us and use it to look up various types of plants and trees. Alé tells me what he knows of them and shows me plants and berries that are acceptable to eat and others that are poisonous to the touch.

For lunch, we sit on a rocky outcropping overlooking the valley below. Alé brought a small backpack on our hike and he fishes out two lunch packets, sweet high-calorie protein bars, and fruit. The sun beats down on us and it actually gets hot on the rock. I see the cabin far below us at the base of the mountain and the trail where we hiked in on the other side of the meadow. The breeze is light and fragrant with the smell of the pine trees surrounding us and I eventually feel like I might fall asleep on that warm rock.

Alé grabs my hand and pulls me up. It's time to hike back. He tells me again how happy he is to see how strong I've gotten and how amazed he is that I can hike around in these woods only a few short weeks after I landed in the Soyuz. All of this makes me blush, of course.

As we come down the mountain, we eventually meet up with the stream meandering its way through the woods and it leads us back to the cabin. Once we're back, Alé grabs us fresh water from the holding tanks and we follow the stream deeper into the woods. After about ten minutes of hiking next to it, we see a break in the trees ahead.

Alé grins. "That's Fairy Lake."

"Fairy Lake? I didn't realize it had a name."

He shrugs. "I guess it's technically not a named lake. But that's what I've always called it. At night in the summer, this lake has millions of fireflies on it. I always thought they looked like fairies prancing around on the surface."

I close my eyes and try to imagine it. I can't. We keep walking until the forest splits open and the lake sits in front of us, shining in the afternoon sun. There's a gentle breeze causing small ripples in the surface. Lazy rapids mark the spot where the stream runs into the lake and I can see tiny fish swimming in the clear water. I kneel down on the sandy shore and reach into the water, trying to grab one, but it's much too fast for me and they shoot away from my hand in all different directions. They must not have a very good memory because all I need to do is let my hand sit in the water, still for a few moments, before they meander back, poking their little lips into the sandy bottom.

Alé kneels next to me and points to the areas of rapids where the stream flows into the lake. "We have a small, collapsible fish trap that we can set up in the stream over there. It's part of the survival supplies Xander sent. I'll get it set up tonight and hopefully, by tomorrow, we'll have some fish to clean and eat."

The water is cold but it feels good in the warm sunshine. "Can we swim in it?" I ask.

"Sure. But we must be very careful at first. You don't know how to swim."

I don't know what comes over me, but I suddenly want nothing more than to be in the water. I rip off my sandals and take off my light jacket, tossing them onto the shore so I'm only wearing a pair of black leggings and a tank top. I take off at full speed and splash right into the clear, cold water. I keep wading until I'm waist deep. Sucking in a deep breath, I plug my nose with my fingers and plunge my head into the lake.

Underwater, I open my eyes to see a totally foreign world. It looks like something straight out of a science fiction novel. The water is green and murky in all directions. My ears fill with water and a strange muffled sensation comes over me. Beams of sunlight shoot through the waves from above. The feeling of limited gravity that I felt in the bathtub back in Little Rock comes back to me, but now, with my entire body submerged, it's a whole different sensation. My feet lift off the pebbled lake bed and I wiggle my toes in front of me. I see my hair waving around me exactly like it used to when I was in microgravity. I wave my hand in front of my face.

Suddenly, strong arms wrap around my waist from behind. Before I realize what's happened, Alé has dragged my head out of the water and pulled me to shore. We're both out of breath as we topple over onto the sandy beach.

He grabs my shoulders. "What the hell are you doing? You could have drowned!" I'm stunned and look at him, my mouth hanging open. With his eyebrows drawn together, he stares at me, breathing hard. His hands are shaking. "Eta, you really scared me. You could have drowned."

"I… I just wanted to know what it felt like."

He releases a long sigh and pulls me into his chest, hugging me tight. My face presses against his wet T-shirt and he wraps his arms around my body. "Are you okay?" His voice sounds shaky. He releases me from the hug and cups my face in his hands, staring into my eyes. "Are you okay?" he repeats.

I nod, so overcome that I can't speak. The excitement of the cool water surrounding my body. The sensation of weightlessness. The terrified look on Alé's face. The embrace. It's all so much. A hot tear runs down my cheek. He's so close to me, I can feel his breath on my skin. And the gentle touch of his fingers on my face is sending waves of heat through my body.

His face softens and his lips part slightly. He pulls my face closer to his, still staring into my eyes. We are only a few centimeters apart. I realize I'm clutching his shirt in my hands, pulling his body closer to mine.

Then, he kisses me.

His lips are soft and wet and the breath catches in my throat. The kiss is delicate and gentle at first, but after a moment, his fingers wind into my hair and I sense a hunger emanating from him as his lips press harder into mine. He pulls me closer to him and I reciprocate, sliding my hands around his waist. When he peels his lips away from mine and opens his eyes, there are tears in them. He runs his thumb across my cheek.

"I'm sorry… I don't know what came over me," he says, dropping his eyes.

"No. Don't be sorry," I say, meeting his gaze.

This time, I kiss him and pull him tighter against me. When the kiss ends, he wraps his arms around me and I tuck my head against his chest at the base of his neck. We sit in this embrace for what feels like a long time, staring out at the lake. He holds me tight and rubs my back. After a while, he lets go and stands up. He pulls his wet T-shirt off so he's only clothed in the shorts he wore on our hike. His skin is smooth and dark and he's surprisingly muscular. Gazing at the water, he offers me his hand.

"Come on," he says, flashing that beautiful, crooked smile. "If you're truly determined to swim, you should have some lessons."

I smile and take his hand as we walk back out into the water.

Chapter 29

Virginia

Time Since Touchdown: 44 Days, 7:50 p.m. EST

Kane eyed the tree line where the old national park maintenance road disappeared into the forest. From where he stood, on the edge of the pavement, it looked like the perfect place to hide a vehicle. He squatted down, chewing methodically on a piece of gum, to get a better look at the gravel where the road turned off from the highway.

"You think this is where they came?" Strickland asked as he waved the second van to a stop next to the highway.

"Fresh tracks." Kane gestured toward a rut in the gravel about a meter in front of them. "I can't imagine there's any need for people to be on this road. I'd venture to guess most people don't even know it's here. Looks like a dead end from the road. But you can see it actually goes quite a way back into the forest."

Strickland nodded, then yawned, a big, openmouthed whiny kind of yawn. The search crew had had a rough couple of days. Kane kept them on the move nonstop to try to keep up the search. As they'd made their way east, they'd searched hundreds, if not thousands, of hours of highway camera footage and Kane had been right—they were able to track the Jeep down.

First, they'd spotted the Jeep entering Arkansas on I-40 and tracked it to a dive called the Starlight Motel outside of Little Rock. The owner confirmed the two had stayed in the hotel two days before. They'd gone around Memphis because of the fallout, but they'd been lucky to find that Alé had joined right back up with I-40 after the detour. They managed to find the Jeep on six different cameras between Little Rock and the junction with I-81 outside of Knoxville.

From there, they tracked the Jeep on almost to Roanoke but weren't able to pick up any footage of it after that. Kane had the team concentrate their efforts on the area of I-81 southwest of Roanoke and, sure enough, they caught the Jeep exiting toward Blacksburg. At that point, Kane called in additional help from NASA. On orders from Patrick, a team of mapping engineers used the satellites to get updated photography of every road in the general area of Blacksburg. Along with some additional highway camera footage, they were able to find the last sighting of the Jeep leaving Blacksburg to the west on Highway 460. The roads after that were rural and they weren't able to pull much footage, but from what they could pull, the Jeep never emerged from the national forest.

After investigating several trailheads and service roads, the old maintenance road had popped up on their satellite aerials. Kane brought Strickland and six other men in two vans to check it out.

Strickland yawn again. "Want us to drive down there and check it out?"

"You and I can go on foot. I want to follow these tracks and I don't want our vans or a bunch of guard boots destroying them."

Strickland nodded and gestured for the other members of their guard crew to wait in the van before he and Kane took off, Kane leading the way. As he walked, Kane paid special interest to the tire marks in the gravel. The set he was following was light, as if someone had driven through several days prior, yet deep enough for Kane to know it was recent. Many years spent tracking in the jungles of South America had taught him how to follow even the slightest of tracks.

They made their way to the tree line where the road seemingly disappeared and Kane gestured off to their left, showing where it veered into the forest. To most people, it would look only like a short driveway from the road, but Kane knew better. They continued on the road for another ten minutes with Kane stopping every few feet to feel the track in the ground. As they went deeper into the woods, the old gravel got more worn as it was overtaken by the forest around it. Tree roots grew up in the center of the road and a thin film of moss was starting to take hold on the road. Kane imagined that within a few more years, the road would be more like a path: less manmade and more a part of the forest itself.

Eventually, they hit the end—or so it seemed. "Looks like we lost it," Strickland said, scratching the back of his neck.

Kane ignored him and knelt to touch the road again. He pointed to a patch of moss. "See that spot there? It's been driven on. Recently. You can tell by the way the moss seems to be flattened toward the forest. Whoever drove on this road kept going."

"But where? Looks like it ends here," Strickland said, scratching his neck again.

"There!" Kane jumped up so suddenly, it caused Strickland to teeter back for a moment. Kane pointed to a thicket of Virginia Pines off to their left. The evergreens ranged in size from three to four meters high and looked younger than the old-growth forest that surrounded them, as if someone had planted them only a few years earlier. Kane walked over to the thicket and started pushing the thick branches aside, making his way deeper into the woods.

After a few moments, he yelled, "Strickland, over here!"

"Well, I'll be damned," Strickland said, shaking his head once he caught up to him.

There, parked in the freshly cleared center of the thicket, was the black Jeep they'd been seeking for the last three days.

Kane pointed at the broken limbs beneath the vehicle. "Looks like he was able to run over most of the new growth. But a few of these bigger trees have been cut with a saw. I suppose he scouted out the best spot and cut out what he could to make it fit."

Strickland's mouth hung open. "Well, it's a damn good hiding spot. I couldn't see it at all from the road."

Kane shook his head. "Not so good. I spotted the wheels as soon as I knelt down to examine the turf."

"What do we do now, boss?"

Kane pulled on the driver door handle and the door popped open. He looked around the inside, noticing some used sandwich bags and empty water bottles. In the back there were three jerrycans. "That's how they got through West Texas in a gas vehicle. They brought it with them. Let's call the other guys down here. I want to set up a surveillance spot near the Jeep so we can keep a watch on it. I'm betting they'll be back when they need supplies. Why else would they go to the trouble of hiding the Jeep? When they do come back, I want to follow them out."

"What for?"

"To see who's helping them."

"What makes you think someone's helping them?"

Kane slammed the door and continued walking around the vehicle, inspecting the underside as he went. "Because they couldn't have made it this far without help."

"Buster Shirley?"

"Maybe. But I'm betting it's an inside job."

"You mean someone at NASA?"

Kane nodded. "Whoever it is, they're damn good. I had my top security guys go through the code on that door, the one to the girl's room that was unlocked the night she escaped. They couldn't pin it. Whoever hacked into that door knew what they were doing and hid their tracks well. Shirley's involved with them somehow, but I don't think he's the mastermind."

"So where do you think they are? Bakas and the girl?"

Kane finished his walk around the car and made his way back to the road. Strickland followed suit. Kane pointed into the trees. "They're out there somewhere."

"They couldn't have gone far."

"Don't be too sure. According to the doctors, she was stronger than she looked—had been walking on her own for a week when she escaped—and he's a hiker. He and his family lived in these woods for years during the war. I'd suggest they hiked for half a day after they abandoned the Jeep."

Strickland smiled. "Great, we can go after them then."

"We can try." Kane shrugged and pulled out his holo-phone. "First step is to set up surveillance of that Jeep. Then we'll organize teams to head into the woods." As he walked, he pulled out his phone and dialed. Patrick answered after one ring.

"Yes. What's the news?"

"We found the Jeep, sir."

Chapter 30

The last week has been a blur of new sights, sounds, smells, tastes, and feelings. I didn't understand how much I missed gardening until I returned to it. The garden at the cabin is large and was in rough shape when we started working on it on our second day here.

We spent a full day clearing out unwanted growth and weeds before we could see what we had to work with. The garden still had healthy beds of asparagus and broccoli. Onions and sweet potatoes were in pretty good shape too and I think they will flourish now that we've cleaned them up. The small herb garden outside the back door of the cabin still had chives, rosemary, lavender, and basil, and I think we can bring the mint back with some time and pruning.

Alé had Xander include seeds in our supply pack and we spent the better part of day three planting pumpkins, several varieties of lettuce, tomatoes, carrots, and cucumbers. There was even a grapevine complete with big ripe bunches of purple grapes that reminded me of the grapevine I tended on the Delta.

After we got the garden under control, Alé worked with me on swimming lessons. I found a bathing suit in the clothing Buster gave me, and we've been going to the lake every afternoon to cool off after working in the garden. He says I'm a natural swimmer, which surprises me—a girl who's never been submerged in water can be a natural swimmer?

Being in the water brings me a sense of calm and familiarity. It's so similar to microgravity yet not the same at all. I've learned how to tread water and hold my breath and I'm working on my swimming stroke. I still have some trouble getting my feet to move with my arms, but Alé tells me I'm not far off.

Swimming has also made me stronger. I could tell the difference almost immediately: my arms feel lighter at my sides and my legs can carry me on steeper hikes. The pain from my injuries has passed completely and I feel as though I could conquer the world.

I even started running again. I used to run almost every day on the Delta, going around and around the centrifugal force module, watching the Earth spin around. Running on the surface is so much more fun! I ran around the meadow six times yesterday, which Alé believes is about three kilometers. I felt light and free, springing on my sandals in the tall grass, my lungs pumping the fresh air in and out of my body.

On our third day at the cabin, it rained—a proper thunderstorm complete with wind and lightning and drenching rain. At first, it was terrifying. When I was on the Delta, I never would have understood how loud a thunderclap can be. And the rain pounded on the metal roof, echoing like a drum through the tiny cabin. I was scared the roof would give way, but Alé only smiled and told me not to worry, that it rains all the time and the cabin is still standing. After that, we went out on the porch to watch the storm.

"I want to know what it feels like," I told him.

He laughed and took off into the yard in front of the porch. He stood there, arms outstretched, drenched from head to toe, turning slowly and looking up at the sky with his mouth open, smiling. He looked so beautiful with the lightning flashing over him. I ran to him and threw my arms around him, feeling the raindrops beat on my skin for the very first time. We stood there laughing and spinning until the rain slowed to a drizzle and we were too cold to stay out any longer.

Alé set up the fish trap and we ate trout for the first time. He seasoned it with rosemary and a tiny bottle of lemon juice, brought in our supply pack, before grilling it along with asparagus from the garden. It might have been the most delicious thing I've ever tasted. He showed me how to work the trap and we moved it around a couple of times throughout the week to find the best place for it in the stream. Every day, we pull up two or three fish.

I've been studying the survival guides on the holo-screen and learning about the various kinds of fish we're catching in the lake. We've reviewed the different types of plants in the forest and are working on learning what plants are safe to eat. Alé knows some of them, but even he has benefited from the holo-screen guide.

He showed me how the electrical system at the cabin works and we clean off the solar panels every few days to ensure they pick up as much sun as possible. Surprisingly, the battery bank and power cells are similar to the technology on the Delta. When I was in space, I spent the better part of each day making repairs, cleaning, maintaining, and figuring my way out of problems. In comparison to the things I had to do on the Delta, troubleshooting the electrical system at the cabin should be a piece of cake.

We spend our evenings relaxing in the cabin, talking about everything under the sun. Alé makes me laugh with stories about bar hopping in Washington DC and workplace shenanigans at NASA. He lies with me at night and holds me tight so I won't wake from the nightmares. I find myself smiling all the time and I catch him smiling too.

Tonight, we wrap blankets around ourselves and take two chairs out onto the front porch so we can look up at the stars. We set the chairs right next to each other and sit close. I lean on his shoulder and sit back to view the sky. I've seen the stars plenty of times in my life, but there's nothing quite like watching them here. In space, the stars are sharper, clearer, more vibrant. On the surface, I can see the haze of the atmosphere dimming their edges. It's a totally different night sky but it's just as beautiful.

I'm staring up into the sky looking for all the visible constellations when Alé takes my hand. I turn and see that he's watching me, smiling. He laces his fingers in mine and squeezes. After a moment, he brings his other hand up to my face and cups my cheek. Heat shoots through my skin where he's touched me. As is usually the case when he touches me, I lose my ability to breathe and my heartbeat speeds up to a light flutter.

Gently he draws my face close to his and kisses my cheek, my jawline, my lips. A moan escapes me as I let my cheek rest in his hand and allow him to draw me closer to him. To my surprise and dismay, he lets go after a few seconds and my body protests. I want to be as close to him as possible. I never want to let go.

"Eta," he says. His voice is only a whisper but it sends shivers through my body. He takes my hand in his and brings it up to his cheek. I feel the beautiful rough texture of his skin beneath my fingers. He closes his eyes and leans his face into my hand, gently kissing my palm, my fingers. "I need to tell you something," he says.

I nod, unable to speak.

"I..." He pauses and closes his eyes again, as if he's working up the courage to continue. "I love you, Eta."

The magnitude of the moment doesn't sink in right away and I must have the most confused look on my face because his eyebrows knit together and he says, "Is that wrong?"

"No!" The word escapes my lips so quickly and fiercely it causes him to jump. I stumble over my thoughts, trying to connect one word with two, and two words with four, trying to form a sentence. "It's... No... I'm sorry, I can't seem to breathe." I pause and focus on taking a deep breath before continuing. "No, that's not wrong. It's the most wonderful thing I've ever heard."

His lips part and he lets out a long, slow sigh as if he's also been holding his breath. He's still holding my hand and I clasp it with my other hand. I'm trembling. Tears spill out of my eyes. I smile and say, "I love you too."

He kisses me again. Long and slow and passionate. The perfect night. I never want this feeling to end.

Part III

After Freedom

Chapter 31

Alé pressed on through the forest using the walking stick he brought along with him to push aside branches. It had been seven days since he and Eta arrived at the cabin and he'd never been happier, but he knew as well as anyone that they were still in danger. He had to get back to the Jeep and find the burner phone at Xander's drop point.

The fact that he had no idea what was going on at NASA weighed on him. He would love to dig his head into the sand and spend the rest of his life at the cabin with Eta, tucked away in the woods, unseen from the rest of the world. But they couldn't stay there forever. Eventually, John Patrick would catch up to them and he had to be prepared when that happened. Xander was his best ally.

The six-hour one-way hike out of the forest from the cabin would take its toll on him today, that was for sure. Especially because he planned to be back before the sun set that night. He had left before it rose that morning, knowing he would need every second of daylight to make the round trip.

That morning, they had breakfast together. As he left the cabin, Eta handed him the small backpack stuffed with food, water, and survival tools. She had tears in her eyes as she hugged him tighter than she'd ever done so before. She told him she didn't want him to leave and said she loved him more than life itself. He assured her he would come back to her. Though he'd put on a smile and a brave face to quell her worries, he hated to leave her and he had hiked hard the first few hours trying to shave as much time off this trip as he could.

The hard hiking had taken its toll on him and now he had to lean heavily on the walking stick to keep moving forward. He checked his holo-watch. Soon he'd be approaching the area where he'd hidden the Jeep. Though he stopped to take a few swigs from his water bottle, he didn't linger long.

After another half hour of hiking, he came to the abandoned maintenance road and quickly found the thicket of pines. There stood the Jeep, just as he'd left it. He breathed a deep sigh of relief to see it. The drop point was not more than a kilometer away and he easily could have walked there rather than coming back to the Jeep. But he wanted so badly to get back to

Eta as quickly as possible. It would shave an hour off his time if he drove the Jeep.

He climbed in and pushed the key into the ignition, listening as the engine buzzed to life. He put the car in gear and backed out of the thicket, taking his time to make sure none of the bushes and trees got caught in the underbelly of the Jeep, before taking off down the rugged maintenance road. As he pulled onto Highway 460 going toward Blacksburg, he never noticed the black van as it pulled out behind him.

***

Jack's Chicken Shack sat just off the highway, a tiny cutout in the forest that surrounded it. It had been shut down for more than five years, a casualty of the soft economy that took its time sputtering to life after the war ended. In reality, nobody knew who "Jack" was, but everyone in the town of Blacksburg and the nearby communities knew of the chicken shack because of the eight-foot plaster chicken that stood atop the roof. The chicken had seen better days—peeling paint, cracks, and general weathering adorned it, same as the building on which it was perched.

As Alé pulled into the parking lot, he wondered how on earth a man who was smart enough to put a giant chicken on his chicken shack could possibly have gone out of business. He parked the Jeep in the back where it would be out of the way of prying eyes and walked up to the building. Just as Xander had promised, the handle of the back door twisted easily and he opened the door to the back room.

He grimaced as he stepped inside. A foul odor invaded his nose. Garbage of all kinds filled the room: dirty cardboard, crumbling shelves, a broken refrigerator with the door standing open, empty food cartons, discarded takeout chicken boxes, and scattered napkins. He walked to the far wall where the refrigerator stood, kicking garbage out of his way as he went. Sitting on top of the refrigerator was a tiny silver flip-style cell phone, like the one Xander had sent to Alé at White Sands. Alé pushed the refrigerator aside and saw the supply pack sitting behind it. He picked up the cell phone, opened it, and turned it on, scrolling to the address book. There was only one phone number in the book: another burner number. He dialed and held the phone up to his ear.

"Yes?" Xander's voice sounded hesitant.

"It's me," Alé said.

"Dude, I was starting to worry."

"Yeah, well, it's a long hike. Let's make this quick. I don't want to be away from Eta any longer than I have to be. What have you found out? Are they looking for her?"

"Pssshh, are they looking for her? Are you kidding? Of course they are, man. Patrick's got Carter Kane and an entire team of guard members on it. The reason I know that is because they sent them to Buster's."

Alé pinched the bridge of his nose. "Oh, man. Is he okay?"

"Yeah, he knows how to take care of himself. He was able to escape, but not without taking a bullet to his ankle. He's fine though. Made it to another hacker's place up in the panhandle and is laying low there for now. I owe him big though. I managed to disarm the built-in tracking device and the holo-screen, but Buster figures they had some other way to track that car, something he didn't even know about. That's how they found him. He said Kane showed up with four vans and at least a dozen guard members. They had come straight from White Sands."

"Do you know where they are now?"

"No. They're not uploading any communications to the cloud. They must be dealing directly with Patrick."

Alé bit his lip. "Did Buster talk to them? Did he tell them what vehicle we're in?"

"No way. He's no snitch. And even if they did know, there's no way they can track that Jeep. But there is one problem."

Alé's jaw clenched. "Tell me."

"They aren't logging their location on the cloud, but they *are* using the TDRS to pull camera footage from highway patrol cameras. I went into the satellite system last night and found the searches."

"So, they're watching the highways."

"Yep. And I believe that means they know what car you're in. They can't technically track it, but they can use the cameras to find the vehicle, assuming they know what you're driving. And trust me, dude, they've done a pretty good job. From the footage they've been pulling, I can tell they essentially followed you right to the East Coast."

"Shit. It won't be long."

"No, it won't. I'd imagine they know your past. They know you were in the forest during the war. They're probably in there looking for you now. I just wish I could find a way to track those vans. I'm trying to figure something out, but so far, no luck. I'm thinking maybe I can access them by using the satellites…"

"Xander," Alé said, trying to bring his attention back to the task at hand. Xander had a tendency to run off on a tangent, especially when it came to hacking.

"Sorry, dude. You find the supplies?"

"Yeah. Thanks, man. I can't tell you how much I appreciate your help. We wouldn't have been able to do this without you. And give Buster my apologies for the trouble I've caused him."

"No worries about Buster. With the people he does business with, he's used to this kind of thing. Give me a few more days. I'll do some digging around and see if I can't figure out a way to access those guard vans and find out where Kane and his team are. In the meantime, keep your eyes open. I think they're getting close to you. It won't be safe to stay in the forest forever."

"Yeah, you're right. I just wish I had a better plan."

"Hey, we'll figure something out. I have a few tricks up my sleeve. I think we should plan another call for a few days from now though. Leave that phone at the chicken for now. I don't think they'd be able to trace you with a cell signal through the woods, but they might. Come back in three days and bring Eta. Call me and I'll hook something up for you."

Alé sighed. He had no desire to leave the cabin, but he knew Xander was right. They weren't safe there. Kane had figured out where they were headed and it was only a matter of time before the guard found them. "Thanks. You're the best."

"No problemo. Stay safe, buddy. I'll talk to you in three days."

Alé turned the phone off and clicked it shut, setting it back on top of the refrigerator. If anyone did happen to find it there, they'd have no reason to believe it was anything more than a forgotten phone as old as the chicken shack itself. He grabbed the pack, hoisted it onto his shoulders, and left the building.

Once again, he was back on the road. How could he have been so naive as to think they would simply give up looking for her? He shook his head and let a sarcastic laugh escape his lips.

A check of his watch told him it was well past 1:00 pm. He needed to get moving if he was going to make it back to the cabin before dark.

Turning onto the maintenance road, he gunned the gas. When he reached the pine grove where he had parked the Jeep before, he stopped and got out of the car to check the area again for the best spot to park so the Jeep couldn't be seen from the road.

As he slammed the door shut, he felt the warm metal of the gun barrel press against the skin behind his left ear. He lifted his hands so they were visible and slowly turned around to see Kane aiming a large, black pistol right at his head.

"Hello, Alé. You've got some explaining to do."

Chapter 32

Virginia

Time Since Touchdown: 52 Days, 11:42 p.m. EST

Kane had to admit, the kid had more guts than he gave him credit for. It had been six hours since Kane confronted Alé at the Jeep and the sun was making its way down the horizon. Within another hour, it would disappear completely. And yet, they were still no closer to finding the space girl than they had been earlier that day.

Despite some heavy persuasive techniques, Alé hadn't said a word. Even when Kane had planted the barrel of his gun in Alé's mouth, he refused to give up her location or his accomplice.

Kane took a slow bite of his rice and beans, a packaged meal he'd fished out of the back of one of the vans. His crew had been subsisting on these vacuum-packaged, plant-based meals for the last week and he was tired of them. Not that he cared much for cooking, but even he could have done better than this bland concoction.

Between bites, he leaned over Alé, his body limp on the ground next to Kane's chair. "Can I get you anything to eat, Mr. Bakas?" Alé groaned and tried to open his eyes, although he didn't get very far considering they were both swollen almost shut. He had a bloody gag in his mouth, so he couldn't have answered Kane's question even if he wanted to. "You know, you're only a few words away from a meal, a hot shower, perhaps. Just tell us where she is."

Without warning, Kane stood and kicked Alé with his steel-toed boot right in the stomach. Alé's hands were tied behind his back and his ankles were bound, helpless against the attack.

"I'll say it again," Kane continued, setting his bowl down on the hood of the van. "Tell us where she is and this can all stop." He grabbed Alé by his shirt and pulled him up to his feet. Alé was so groggy from the heat and the beating, he simply slumped forward, allowing Kane to hold his full weight.

Strickland walked over to Kane. "You think he's ready to talk, sir? I can take out that gag," he said.

Kane considered Alé's face and shook his head before letting go, allowing Alé's body to fall back to the ground.

"Doesn't look like it." The holo-phone on Kane's hip chirped and he pulled it out of his belt. "Kane here."

"Do you have her location yet?" Patrick asked.

"Negative. I'll give the little shit credit—he's holding out. I thought maybe I could reason with him, save him some pain if he would lead us to her, but he's not saying anything."

"And his accomplice?"

"Don't know yet, sir. Like I said, he's been quiet."

"Well, he's gotta talk sometime, right? What do you think we should do?"

Kane paused a moment, thinking. He walked around Alé, watching him closely as he lay in the dirt. "I believe we can get him to talk eventually, but it's going to be difficult to do it here. We're in the woods, but we're not far from the road. Someone could hear him screaming if we're too rough with him." A smile crossed Kane's lips as he said this and he took the opportunity to shove his boot tip into Alé's back causing Alé to grimace.

"Right. That's no good."

"I have a suggestion, sir. Let's bring him back to Goddard."

"Ah yes, Building Thirty-Five. That's a good idea, Kane. I'm sure you can work your magic on him better there. What about the girl? What if she comes looking for him where you found the Jeep?"

"I'm planning to leave a crew here to watch the Jeep. Unfortunately, I think he's taken her pretty deep into the forest. We've sent three different teams out north and east of the Jeep looking for signs of her, but we haven't come up with anything yet. I'll have part of the group stay here and the other part can continue searching the woods. Eventually, she'll come looking for him."

"Excellent. Take him to Thirty-Five. I'll meet you there tomorrow. Perhaps I can have a word with him as well."

"Yes, sir." Kane hung up the phone and clipped it back to his belt. He leaned down to Alé. "We'll find her. With or without your help. And once we do, you won't be much use to us anymore."

He gave Alé one final kick in the thigh with his boot before calling for Strickland to load him into the van.

Chapter 33

Something's wrong. I know it deep inside, like I know the Earth is round and the sky is blue.

Alé didn't return when he said he would. I estimated he would be back to the meadow by 7:30 p.m. When he didn't show up at that time, I was nervous but tried to convince myself I was being paranoid. I took a jog around the meadow to get my body moving and keep my mind occupied. When he didn't show up by 8:30 p.m., I knew something wasn't right.

My logical mind told me that he was only an hour late. That any number of things could have held him up. I imagined Xander had been late bringing the gear to the drop point. I imagined he had gotten treed by a bear and had to wait until he could safely climb down. I imagined he fell and sprained his ankle, forcing him to walk slower than he would have normally. All these logical explanations danced around my mind.

But when I listened to my heart, I knew that none of these things happened to him. My logical mind worked well for many things, but for this, it was wrong. No, something happened to him. He wouldn't have left me here alone. I knew that for certain.

The night passed and I sat on the sofa and waited, staring out the window, unable to sleep. Before dawn, I packed a bag with water and supplies. I charged the holo-screen and pulled up the map, planning the path back to the Jeep.

When morning came, I took off on the trail leading out of the meadow. I've been hiking all morning and I'm closing in on where the Jeep must be parked. I've been checking the compass app on the holo-screen and keeping track of my movements on the map to make sure I'm not lost. The thing is, I don't even know what I'll find when I get to the Jeep. Maybe it won't even be there. If something happened to him after he left the forest, I might never be able to find him. But for now, finding the Jeep is my top priority.

I continue on the overgrown footpath we walked on to get to the cabin. It doesn't go directly to the Jeep. You have to hike several hundred meters through the underbrush to get to the

Jeep's hiding spot, so I'm keeping an eye out for where I need to leave the path and turn toward the south.

I stop for a rest on a fallen log and take out my screen and my water bottle. I'm examining the map when I hear a noise. I hold perfectly still and listen closely. At first, I think my mind must be playing tricks on me because I hear nothing for a very long time, but I keep still, every part of my body tense and alert. Then I hear it again. It sounds like muffled speaking. It's a distance away, but it's definitely someone speaking.

A few moments later, I hear the crackling of brush as if someone's walking through the woods. Quietly, I snatch up my things and stuff them into my backpack before slinging it over my shoulder. I carefully step behind the fallen log and move deeper into the woods, away from the footpath. I find an old maple tree with a thick trunk, large enough for me to hide behind yet far enough away from the footpath so I can watch it without being noticed. Crouching onto the ground, I make myself tiny, peering around the tree, listening.

The mumbling continues and gets louder. Whoever is speaking is definitely coming closer to me. A few minutes later, I'm able to make out the voices.

"If you weren't such an idiot, we'd have found this already."

"Yeah, well, the whole damn forest is full of these little trails, why would this one be different?"

Two men dressed in black gear from head to toe come into my line of vision. They're on the trail I was walking on minutes earlier, perhaps ten meters from where I now sit. I crouch low and keep watching.

"Because we have to check them all out, Lamont! That's what the boss said to do. That's what we need to do."

"I still don't get it. What's so special about this girl anyway?"

"I don't know. She was in space or something."

"Well, I'm tired of this little road trip we've been on for the last two weeks. I'm sick of walking through the woods and camping out in the van. I say we tell the boss we found her dead in a ravine somewhere and call it good. You with me, Jackson?"

I realize that both men have NASA Guard logos on the sleeves of their shirts. They're talking about me. They are looking for me. My breath catches in my throat and I swallow hard.

"You know we can't do that. I get it. I don't like being out here any more than you do, but it comes with the job. Keep up, will you? I want to get this trail checked out as quickly as possible. The forest gives me the creeps."

"How far in do we have to go?"

"Two kilometers from the Jeep. That's what the boss said."

The two men continue down the trail. One is swinging a large baton with a leather strap. The other carries a backpack on his back and holds a screen he's using to map the forest as they walk. I wait in my hiding spot until I can no longer hear them. Then I jump to my feet and start running through the forest, my mind racing, praying I won't encounter any more of them.

After running at full speed for several minutes, I stop to slow my breathing and get my bearings. I take out my screen and check the map. I heard them mention the Jeep, so I can't go back there. If I keep hiking due east, I'll avoid the rest of the trail and eventually, I'll hit the highway, the one Alé and I drove in on.

Then what? I have to think! Closing my eyes, I take a few deep breaths. I count backward from ten to calm myself down.

Think, Eta, think!

The chicken!

I'll find the highway and take it until I find the chicken restaurant. Alé said it would be right on the road and anyone could find it because there was a giant chicken statue on the roof. I have no idea what I'll do when I get to the chicken, but it's the only option I can think of. Maybe there will be something there that can help me. Maybe Xander will be there. I have to try.

I put my screen away and take a swig of water, then run through the forest, trying to be as quiet as possible. When I think I can't run any farther, I stop and stand as still as I can to hear if anyone is following me. After about an hour, I hear the faint rush of a car moving at high speed down a highway. Before long, I break through the tree line and find myself standing at the edge of the ditch next to the road.

When I look left and right and see no cars coming, I step out of the woods and run through the ditch and onto the pavement. This is when I realize that I have no idea which way to go to search for the chicken. The road is windy and I can't see very far in either direction. What should I do? Panic runs through me and my throat tightens. Again, I close my eyes and breathe deep. What would I have done when I was fighting to stay alive on the Delta?

After a few moments, my heart rate calms and I'm able to think a bit clearer. I pull out my holo-screen. The screen isn't connected to the network, so I can't tell exactly where I am at the moment, but perhaps the map can give me a clue. I stare at it for several minutes but nothing jumps to mind. I eventually decide to walk to my right which is southeast, toward Blacksburg. The area to the west is much more rural and I figure the chicken place is more likely to be closer to town.

I walk for the next thirty minutes. I figure I've covered at least two kilometers, and several times I had to run for the shelter of the tree line when I heard cars approaching. The idea of stopping a car and asking for help does cross my mind, but the truth is, I have no idea if I can trust anyone. I also have no idea if the next car might be the NASA Guard members patrolling the highway looking for me. So, I opt to run and hide whenever I hear something.

I've walked for so long, I'm starting to wonder if I made a mistake by choosing to walk this direction, but as I walk around a particularly sharp curve in the road, I see it up to my left. The head of the giant chicken is sticking up out of the treetops several hundred meters in front of me. I break into a sprint.

When I reach Jack's Chicken Shack, I'm out of breath and sweaty with exhaustion, but I'm also relieved because this is the first thing that's gone right today. I plop down next to the door at the back of the old building and lean my head against it, closing my eyes and catching my breath.

Alé mentioned that the supplies would be in the unlocked storeroom at the back. I hold my breath and try the knob on the door. It opens and I walk inside. The place is disgusting and it smells like mildew. The smell is so strong I have to pinch my nose with my fingertips. I don't even know what I'm looking for. Pounding my hand against my forehead, I try to summon the memory of my conversation with Alé. He said something about a burner phone.

As I pick through the boxes and other garbage and step through the room, I shove things out of my way. I check the broken shelves on one end of the storage room and find only more garbage stacked on them. Checking the sill of the tiny window near the ceiling, I find nothing. I make my way around the room, moving things off the floor, checking under stacks of dirty paper napkins.

There's a refrigerator in the back of the room standing with the door open. I check in all the shelves inside and find nothing. I bite my lip and feel around on the floor underneath the refrigerator. I pull it away from the wall and as I do, something falls off the top of it and clatters to the floor. It's a small, silver cell phone: an old model, the kind that flips open, which I've only seen in old movies.

I open the phone and press the red button. A moment later, the phone powers to life and the screen lights up. It takes me a few minutes to figure out how to navigate the screens, but I'm eventually able to find the call log. There was one call made yesterday at 12:36 p.m.

I dial the number. It's picked up by a man after one ring.

"Who is this?" he asks, the words sharp and clipped.

"Is this Xander?"

"Who is this?" he asks again, this time slower and with more emphasis on each word.

"This is Eta."

"Whoa, Eta, thank God! Seriously, I've been sweating bullets wondering where you were. Oh, and yeah, this is Xander."

"Xander, do you know what happened to Alé? He said he was coming here to the chicken place to talk to you and pick up supplies. He never came back to me." My voice starts to lose traction and becomes airy with panic. "When I hiked to the Jeep to find him, I came across NASA Guard members in the woods."

"Wait, wait, wait. You saw guard members in the woods? They didn't see you, did they?"

"No, I hid from them. But I was close to the Jeep at the time and I figured they'd probably found it, so I came here instead. Did you talk to him?"

Xander sighs. "Yeah, I did talk to him."

"When? What did he say? Was he okay?" The questions tumble out of my mouth one after the other. I can't seem to stop them.

"Look, Eta, something went really wrong. I talked to him yesterday, midday, around noon or so. I told him that I believed the head of the NASA Guard, a guy named Carter Kane, had figured out what vehicle you were traveling in. At the time, I couldn't find where exactly Kane was, but I knew he was using satellites to pull footage from highway surveillance cameras."

"Oh my God," I mumble, more to myself than to Xander. "So, after you talked to him, what was his plan? I thought he would come right back, but he never showed up."

"He *was* going right back. But… something happened."

"What! Tell me what happened!"

"I was finally able to get a track on the vans that Kane and his crew were using to drive across the country. By tracking their connection to the satellite feeds, I found them and was actually able to cut into their own surveillance footage."

"Wait, you mean NASA has cameras surveilling their own vans?"

"That's right. They have cameras inside the vans so guard crew leaders can monitor support crews. I found Kane's vans— there are three of them. And they were stationed on a maintenance road in the national forest." He pauses and I hear him take a deep breath. "Eta, they caught him."

"They caught him," I repeat, the words so soft I can barely hear them come out of my mouth. I double over, holding my stomach, and have to drop down to a crouch on the filthy floor of the chicken shack to keep from passing out.

"I'm sorry, Eta. I saw him tied up in one of the vans. I tracked it back to Baltimore. They're holding him at Goddard."

Panic rises up inside of me, the same way it would when things went wrong on the Delta. I close my eyes and allow it to wash over me. Chills run through my spine and goose bumps spring up on my skin. I grit my teeth and allow myself another moment of panic before taking a deep breath, mentally counting the seconds of the breath, in and out.

"Eta? Are you still there?"

"Yes, I'm here. We have to go get him, Xander."

"That's going to be easier said than done. If they find out I'm involved in this, I could get life in a hard labor camp. I can't just go walking up to Goddard with my NASA badge flashing and walk through the door."

I straighten up and adjust my shoulders. If there's anything I learned from living on the Delta for eighteen years, it's that if you want something done, you must do it yourself.

"Fine. I'll go get him."

Xander hesitates for a moment before releasing a sigh. "I'll take you there. You won't be able to get in without help. I'm just outside of DC. It will take me a few hours to get to you."

"I'll be waiting for you here."

I click the phone shut and push it into my pocket. Outside the chicken shack, it's midafternoon and the air is warm, the sun shining. I lie down on the concrete and curl up into a fetal position, allowing the warmth of the sunbaked concrete to permeate my skin. A long time passes before I finally move to a little spot next to a maple tree in the woods. I can sit here and still see the back of the chicken shack. I eventually doze into a restless sleep.

Several hours later, a dark blue sedan pulls up behind the building, waking me with a start. A man with long, curly hair and flowers printed on his shirt rolls down the window.

"Get in."

Chapter 34

Alé awoke to the sound of the door clicking open and footsteps entering the room. He lay on a mat no thicker than a yoga mat in the corner of the small cell. The only other things in the cell were a toilet and a small sink. Darkness surrounded him, and the only light came in from the tiny crack under the door. He realized, as the figure entered his room, that there wasn't even a light in the hallway outside the cell, rather a dim glow from a holo-screen mounted to the door.

It was impossible to tell how long he'd been there. He knew it had been nighttime when they dragged him out of the van, into the building, and down a narrow stairway, but with no clock or window, he'd lost all sense of time. His best guess was that he'd been in this room for a day, maybe longer.

Although unsure of where he was, he believed he was somewhere in the DC area based on how long it took the guard van to drive him to the building. It looked like the Goddard campus but he wasn't entirely sure. By that time, he had been drifting in and out of consciousness. He did have a vague memory of being dragged down into a basement.

They hadn't given him any food since his capture and his only source of water was the sink. However, his whole body ached from the beating he'd taken in the woods and even the slightest movement was excruciating. He lifted his head a few centimeters to see who it was before dropping it back down on the mat. A splitting headache had been accompanying him since the forest and it pounded in his ears, making it difficult to breathe.

Kane stood in the doorway and pressed a command on his holo-watch that brought the light in the cell to a dim glow. He stared down at Alé, shaking his head. Turning, he closed the door behind him before walking to Alé's mat. He had a nail file in his hand and he was carefully picking the dirt from underneath his nails.

"I tell you, kid, you look soft, but you've got some guts. I never would have pegged you for the kind of guy who could hold out so long."

He knelt down and placed the pointy end of the nail file under Alé's chin, forcing him to lift his head. Alé's eyes were badly swollen, but he could tell Kane wore a slight smile.

"Won't be too long though," Kane said, his smile growing larger. "You've got company. You might want to sit up."

Kane pulled the nail file away and Alé's head fell back to the mat. Kane turned to the door and waved his holo-watch in front of the lock. It clicked and the door swung open. Kane stepped out and another man stepped in, closing the door behind him.

John Patrick walked over to Alé's mat and grabbed him by the shoulders, forcing him to sit up against the wall. Alé groaned in pain. He had several broken ribs; he was sure of it. He coughed and blood splattered out of his mouth. Patrick stood quickly, backing away, and did a thorough inspection of his navy-blue suit to ensure no blood had soiled the fine fabric.

"I'm not going to sugarcoat this for you, Mr. Bakas," Patrick said. "I need to know where Eta is. You can tell me now or you can tell me later, but eventually, you're going to tell me."

Alé didn't say anything and merely shook his head before letting it drop to his chest. Patrick reached down and grabbed Alé's chin, forcing Alé to look up at him.

"Look at me when I speak to you." His voice was terrifyingly calm. "Where is Eta?"

Alé shook his head again.

Patrick sighed and crossed his arms at his chest. "I wish you could understand what we're trying to do here, Mr. Bakas. I have only the best intentions for your young friend. She was in the hands of the best medical team on the planet before you kidnapped her. How can you expect her to adapt to the surface environment without our help?"

"That's bullshit," Alé said, his voice no more than a whisper. "You don't care about her. You only care about your mining expedition."

"You think that's all I care about? You really think that what we're doing here is all about mining? You couldn't be more wrong. This isn't about mining... this is about research! The medical knowledge we could get from studying Eta is unprecedented. The first human conceived, born, and raised in space. It's the opportunity of a lifetime! Not just for me, or for NASA, or even for America... but for the world!"

As he spoke, Patrick became more animated. He lifted his arms into the air emphasizing the magnitude of his words.

"Don't you see, Mr. Bakas? Eta's very existence wasn't planned. It wasn't some experiment set up in a lab or a half-assed research project confined by timeframes and budgets. She's the ultimate case study to show the world how living in space can *work*! And how we can emerge from long-term space travel healthy and thriving!"

Patrick paused for a moment, jangling something in his pocket. "Before the war, we had to cut through mountains of red tape to put humans in space. We had to prove beyond a reasonable doubt that people in space for the long haul wouldn't suffer negative health effects. And we were never able to do that. As many people as we put on missions to the various space stations we've had in orbit, not a single person was allowed to spend more than eighteen months for fear that the long-term health effects would be too aggressive.

Now we have living *proof* that the health effects we've been so terrified of for the last two hundred years are not relevant. If we can't study her, how can we learn to duplicate what she's done? How can we turn our backs on the opportunity to show the world how accessible space really is?"

Patrick puffed out his chest and ran his fingers through his hair, satisfied with himself.

Alé said nothing for a few moments, staring at Patrick and wondering how a man with so much education, life experience, and war experience, could be so delusional. He shook his head, coughed several times, and said, "You should have asked her."

"Yes, well, we would have. You didn't give us time. We certainly can't ask her now."

"That's a lie. You weren't ever going to ask her. I saw what you had planned. I know you were planning to send her back into space."

Patrick jerked his head back, then reached up to straighten his tie. "Ah, yes. I suppose you had your accomplice dig up that information—the one who hacked into our system and did your dirty work for you."

"It was all me."

Patrick laughed, a sharp snort coming from his nose. "Now you're the one who's lying. Well, don't worry. We'll figure out who it was eventually." He turned to leave, waving his holo-watch in front of the door. Before he closed it behind him, he stopped. "We'll find Eta. We're out in the forest looking for her now. In a matter of a few hours, perhaps. Then we won't need you anymore. Have a pleasant evening, Mr. Bakas."

The door slammed behind him and darkness overtook him again. Alé allowed his body weight to drop him to the mat. He rolled over and stared at the ceiling, willing the pounding in his head to give him a few moments of peace, more convinced than ever that he would die here in this basement.

Chapter 35

The blue sedan pulls to the side of a narrow service road that circles the Goddard campus in Greenbelt. Across the road and through a wooded lawn, there's a large, white warehouse, illuminated by the brilliant moonlight. Xander cut the headlights on the car before we entered the property and we're now parked in a grove of trees across the road from the main entrance to the warehouse.

"Is that the building?" I ask.

Xander nods. "That's Building Thirty-Five, the deliveries and logistics center of the facility. I believe that's where he is."

"What makes you so sure?"

"I tracked the vans to this building last night. Plus… I've heard rumors."

"Rumors?"

He shrugs and scratches his head. "Yeah. Supposedly, underneath this warehouse, they've built an elaborate basement. I've never been able to find out for sure what they do there, but I've heard they used it to hold and torture enemy soldiers during the war. Someone in my hacker network claims to have been held here, under this building, for more than three months. This is one of the more remote buildings on the campus, so it makes sense they'd put something like that where nobody would go snooping around."

I squint through the darkness to try and make out the building. The time on the clock reads 9:34 p.m.

"What do they do here? Are there people working here?" I ask.

"This is where they receive shipments. Materials, equipment, supplies, that sort of thing. Everything comes through this building before being moved out to other areas on the campus. There are big loading bays in the front where trucks can bring loads directly to the building. It's a huge warehouse with tall ceilings, so they can fit even large equipment like space vehicles and satellites inside. And yes, there are people here all day and all night."

"Okay. How do I get in?"

"Eta… I'm really sorry I can't go in there with you, but you must understand. If I get caught, the lives of all my contacts will be in danger, not to mention my own. Buster, the rest of the hacker network… it's not something I can risk. Alé's a good friend to me and it kills me to send you into the lion's den by yourself. But going in there is not a risk I can take. Do you understand?"

I look him in the eye and nod. "I understand, Xander. Plus, they won't kill me. I know that. But you're right, they might kill you. I just need you to help me get out of here once I get him out of the building."

He nods in agreement. "I'll leave the car parked right here. Security usually patrols this service road, but they only do it a couple of times a night and the car is well hidden here. If you get in and get out quickly, I don't think they'll find me."

Xander points straight ahead. "To get to the back of the building, you'll go through this wooded area in front of us and stay in the trees. There are lights illuminating the loading bays, so you must stay out of sight until you're sure there aren't any employees in the vicinity. They work with a lighter shift at night, so I don't think it will be a problem. After you circle around to the back, go in through the service entrance door at the northwest corner. I have a holo-watch that can open any door in the facility." He takes the watch off his wrist and hands it to me. I strap it to my own wrist. "It's programmed with the second-highest security clearance."

"Won't they be able to track this back to you if I use your watch to get into that building?"

He shakes his head. "No. This one is not programmed as me. It's actually programmed as Carter Kane." He winks and taps his temple with his index finger. "I did a little high-level hacking and called in a favor from a friend to get this baby programmed just right."

"You're sure it will work?"

"Positive. I've tried it out a few times to be sure."

"Perfect. What do I do after I get in the door?"

"The service entrance goes directly into the stairwell that leads up to the mezzanine area."

"But aren't I trying to get into the basement?"

"Yes, but here's the thing—I wasn't able to find any blueprints or building plans online to verify the existence of the basement or find the entrance to it. But from what I've heard, the basement door is in that stairwell."

"Okay," I say, wiping my sweaty palms on my jeans.

Xander nods and holds his hand up in front of me, his elbow at a right angle with his fingers sticking straight up. The gesture confuses me. "Are you trying to shake my hand?" I ask.

He rolls his eyes. "It's the special handshake! You and I clasp hands in a mutual showing of solidarity before you embark on the impossible mission!"

I nod slowly and tentatively grab his hand. "Yeah!" he says, squeezing my hand and waving our joined fists in the air. "Now, get going. I believe in you, Eta. You're strong. You can do this."

I nod, take a deep breath, and jump out of the car. I run across the road and into the wooded lot next to the warehouse. I can see the giant lights illuminating the loading bays through the trees. These woods are much thicker than the old-growth woods I ran through earlier in the day. I have to step around vines and shrubbery covering the ground. I'm happy I decided to wear jeans because my legs would be cut like crazy if I'd worn shorts.

After about five minutes picking my way through the woods, I'm behind the building and can see the loading docks in the back. There are five of them total, two of which are open. Inside, I see people walking around and others moving large packages with forklifts. A semitruck sits idling, pulled up to one of the open docks.

I spot the service door at the very far corner of the building, about ten meters from the truck parked at the loading dock. Outside the door is a camera pointing right at the entrance. I grumble to myself but ultimately decide there's nothing I can do about it. I can only hope that nobody's watching the video feeds.

Pausing for a minute or two, I watch the door. Nobody seems to be going in or out. All the employees are working in the loading area. I take a deep breath and spring from my hiding spot, running full speed toward the metal service door. As soon as I reach it, I wave my wrist in front of the lock and, to my relief, it clicks. I pull the door open and rush inside, closing the door behind me as quietly as possible.

I'm in a dark stairwell. The stairs go up to my left with a sign overhead that reads "Mezzanine." Straight ahead is a door that leads out into the warehouse. Something about this stairwell is familiar to me, but I can't quite put my finger on it.

I ease over to the door leading to the warehouse and peer out the long, thin window. There are three employees loading boxes about ten meters away from where I stand. I lean closer to the door and roll my head around, inspecting the entire warehouse in front of me. It's massive. I take a step back and inspect the area around me again. There's no door here other than the one that leads out into the warehouse. The only other option I have is to go up the stairway to the mezzanine. I contemplate doing this for a moment but stop myself. Xander said the door would be here. I must be missing something.

Standing still for a moment, I close my eyes. Think! I force my brain to slow down and sort through my thoughts.

Something about this place is familiar and I feel like that's the answer to my problem. If only I could figure out why.

Suddenly it comes to me.

I start feeling around the wall next to the stairwell. It's a tall, white wall and it separates the stairwell from the door I entered through. When Alé and I were leaving White Sands, we were in a stairwell just like this. And to get out, we had to find the hatch that led to the maintenance shaft. It was hidden by some kind of camouflage.

Active seaming—that's what Alé called it.

I run my hands over the wall, pressing lightly, searching for the edge I felt that night when Alé showed me the hatch at White Sands.

Then, as if on cue, I feel something. I run my fingertips along the edge.

Yes! This feels right.

I press the wall lightly next to the edge and… click. The hidden door opens, revealing a darkened stairwell behind it with steps leading down.

Chapter 36

I stare down into the darkness. There are no lights anywhere near the stairwell. It's pitch black. I flip through the menu of the holo-watch and turn it to flashlight mode, illuminating the stairs and the area at the base. It looks terrifying, but I take a deep breath and step through the hidden door. It's short and narrow, much narrower than a normal door. Once I'm in, I close the active-seam door behind me and watch as the opening disappears in the hazy light from the holo-watch. Apparently, these door seams work on both sides.

I head down a set of stairs into the darkened hallway at the bottom. The air smells sterile and I can see in the beam of the flashlight that the floor, walls, and ceiling are all white.

The yellow light from the watch illuminates the hallway, which leads to my right. I'm standing at one end and the light reveals that it's at least thirty meters long, with doorways lining both sides. Mounted on each door is a holo-screen where you have to wave your credentials to enter the rooms. There are no light fixtures in the hallway and no cameras that I can see.

Why wouldn't there be any cameras? As soon as I think this, I know the answer and it causes the hairs to rise on my arms. There are no cameras here because they don't want anyone seeing what goes on in this basement.

I step close to the nearest door and examine the holo-screen mounted above the knob. Feeling for a camera lens, I run my fingers along the edges of the screen. When I touch the screen, a holographic menu pops up. I've dealt with many holo-screens in my life while working on the Delta and this one is fairly simple. There's no camera lens mounted to it and the menu only includes options for unlocking the door, sounding an alarm, and audio broadcasting. From what I can tell, it looks like these are used for simple audio communications, paging, and broadcasting.

I try the knob. Locked. After waving the watch in front of the screen, I hear the lock click. I open it and shine the light into the room beyond. It looks like some sort of holding cell, like something out of a prison movie. There's a mat on the floor at one end, a toilet, and a small sink. Otherwise, the room is totally bare with no windows. The thought of spending any time at all in that tiny, windowless room makes my skin crawl. I quickly close the door, a shiver running through my body.

There are eight of these doors in this hallway. I make my way through the darkness, trying each door. They're all the same: tiny, empty, windowless cells.

The door at the very end of the hallway is different. This one doesn't have a holo-screen on it and actually has a small, oblong window in it. Behind it, there's another hallway. I open it and shine the light down this hallway. Again, rooms line either side of the hall. I check each room and each one is empty. At the end, there's a third hallway.

"For heaven's sake, how many of these cells do they need?" I ask out loud, stunned at the complexity of this underground dungeon.

The third hallway is different from the first two. It contains only two holding cells. The rest of the doors in this hallway lead to yet more hallways. As I make my way through, checking each door, I notice some of the hallways shooting off of this one are dead ends. One actually leads to a stairwell going up—perhaps another exit.

The rooms aren't all holding cells anymore. I encounter several larger rooms with benches lining the walls that look like they may have been used to hold many prisoners at a time. There's even one large room with foldable tables stacked against the wall and a commercial kitchen on one end. This looks to be a dining hall.

One of the smaller hallways has four offices on either side, each office sporting a single desk, chair, and bookcase. These rooms actually have lights mounted to the ceilings and switches by the doors, but I don't turn them on for fear that they might have cameras in them.

The endless maze of rooms and doors and hallways starts to mess with my senses. I have completely lost track of where I am in the basement. I can't remember if I took a left turn or right after that last hallway. Did I already check this room? Was that the hallway that leads to the stairwell going out? My mind is spinning and I'm getting frustrated opening door after door to find nothing but dusty desks and bleak holding cells.

After what feels like an eternity, I pass through a door into a dead-end hallway with only two doors in it, both on the left side. This hallway is different because one of the holo-screens mounted on the doors is glowing—an active screen. I approach the glowing holo-screen and wave the watch in front of it. Instead of clicking open, a prompt pops up. It reads:

Active holding cell. Do you wish to enter?

I hesitate for a moment with my index finger over the screen. I pray opening this one won't set off any alarms. I swallow hard and press the "YES" button. The door makes a soft click as the lock disengages. I grab the knob and open the door wide.

Inside, the cell is pitch black, like the rest of the basement. I shine the light to the back of the small room and there, slumped on the mat against the wall is a limp body.

Chapter 37

The holo-phone on Patrick's desk buzzed for the third time in an hour. He paused from his typing to briefly check who was calling, although he was fairly certain he knew already. Sure enough, a tiny holographic picture of his wife flashed on the screen. He tapped it to silence the buzzer and sent a preloaded response that he was in a meeting and would call her back later. He knew this was a stretch since it was after midnight, but he wasn't in the mood to speak with her now.

Patrick was still angry from his earlier encounter with Alé. He knew if he went home, he'd never be able to relax, so he'd headed to his office on the other side of the Goddard campus. His regular office was at the NASA headquarters building in downtown Washington, DC, but he kept an office at Goddard as well. He'd been spending more time at the suburban campus lately with the recent satellite launch and with Eta's rescue from the Delta. It was easier to set up his own space than work remotely, even if he wasn't there but a few times a month.

When he'd left the holding cell in the basement, he'd tried to put on his best "cool, calm, and collected" facade to make Alé sweat it out a bit more. But the truth was, he hadn't been calm. Rather, he'd been shaking with anger at the defiance his prisoner had shown him.

What made Patrick even more angry was that they still hadn't found her. Kane had three separate teams out searching the forest near where they'd found the Jeep and still, they'd come up with nothing. They'd even brought out the scent dogs, but to no avail.

Then there was the issue of Alé's accomplice. Kane's security sweep had shown nothing out of the ordinary in NASA cloud activity and this meant only one thing according to Kane: the accomplice was an insider. Someone with excellent computer coding skills who could get in and out without tripping off any security protocols on the network. Whoever had helped Alé accomplish this escape was thorough, skilled, and incredibly familiar with the system. The unfortunate part was that this described half the engineers at NASA. Unless Kane found that the intruder had made an error somewhere, they weren't likely to find that person easily. Which left them with only one option to answer all of their questions—Alé. If Kane couldn't get Alé to talk, they'd be in deep trouble.

Patrick's shoulders tightened and his jaw tensed as he thought more and more about their predicament. He decided he needed to talk to Kane again and get an update on the situation in the forest. This would ease his mind, and then maybe he could call his wife back.

He picked up his holo-phone and dialed Kane's number.

"Kane here."

"Any news?"

"Actually, yes. The dogs picked up a scent trail for Eta on one of the old footpaths in the woods. They followed it about a quarter of a mile into the woods before they lost it."

"You think they can pick it up again?"

"Maybe. The thing is, there was a big rain out there a few days ago. I think this trail was left after that."

"Oh? They couldn't have picked it up from before the rain?"

"Doubtful. This was a pretty good hit they got. I'm thinking she's been back through here recently."

"Looking for him, you think?"

"That's certainly a possibility. I'm planning to have the dog teams spread out farther east of here, closer to the highway.

If she came back through here and somehow noticed we had covered the Jeep, she would have probably headed out to the highway."

Patrick flinched. "You don't think she actually left the woods, do you?"

"Well, I think we need to consider it a possibility."

"Damn! Any number of things could happen to her out there!" Patrick said, his voice rising. He was losing his cool.

"Don't get ahead of yourself. She can't have gone far unless she had help."

Heat rose through the skin of Patrick's neck and he jerked his collar open with his finger, pulling down the knot on his red silk tie. "Her safe return is *top* priority. Tell all your men that they are not to harm a hair on her head. Got it?"

"They are aware, sir."

Just then, his phone buzzed again, indicating another incoming call. "Dammit Vivian!" he yelled, not caring that he still had Kane on the line. "Hold on, Kane." He pulled the phone away from his ear expecting to see the miniature dancing holographic of his wife.

But it wasn't Vivian Patrick calling. The call was an alert from the security system.

Patrick had had Kane set it up for him as an extra precaution after they'd brought Alé to Goddard. There were no cameras in the basement of Building Thirty-Five, and for good reason. Nobody needed to know what went on down there, especially when they were interrogating war criminals. Kane thought it was unnecessary, but Patrick wanted every possible safety measure put in place.

This was not right. Patrick had given Kane specific orders that he and his team should leave Alé alone without provisions until morning to see if another night without food would tempt him to part with his secrets. He clicked on the alert to see who had entered the cell. The screen read:

Carter Kane, entry 10:47 p.m.

Patrick waved the alert off and returned to the phone call. "Kane, are you in Thirty-Five now?"

"No, sir. I'm at the security station in Building Twenty-One. We're working on trying to track his accomplice. It seems they've covered their tracks well. But not to worry. Everyone makes mistakes and this person is no different. We'll find them. We just need a few—"

"Kane!" Patrick exploded. "I don't give a damn about the accomplice right now. I just received an alert from the security system that the cell door was opened... by you!"

"Excuse me? That's not possible."

"That's what the alert says! I'm looking at it right now!"

"Okay, okay, let me check footage from Building Thirty-Five."

"There is no footage, you idiot! There are no cameras in that basement."

"No, but there are cameras in the upper part of the building. Hold on."

***

Kane set his holo-phone down and turned to the holo-screen in front of him. He pulled up a new tile and swiped his way through the file system until he found the security camera footage. He found the file showing all the active cameras in Building Thirty-Five, over two hundred of them.

"Dammit," Kane muttered under his breath. The idea that someone was in the basement of Building Thirty-Five using *his* security clearance to enter the cell was unnerving. He sifted through the many camera shots until he found the one he wanted. He pulled up a tile for camera number sixty-two. On the screen in front of him was real-time footage of the stairway where the secret door to the basement was located.

Kane used his finger to rewind the footage. His finger stopped when he saw a figure enter the building through the exit door on the left. He paused the video. It was definitely a woman, short with dark hair. The woman on camera stood in the stairwell for several seconds. Then, to his amazement, she felt around the wall, activated the camouflaged door, and disappeared into it.

Kane picked up his phone. "Patrick. I've found her. It's Eta. She entered the basement at 11:46 p.m."

"Dammit! I knew we needed to set an alarm on that basement door. Get over there right now and find her! I'm still on campus. I'll be there too. Don't let her leave that building!"

"Yes, sir. I'm leaving right now. It will take about five minutes to get the crew there. Oh, and, sir," Kane paused for a moment before continuing hesitantly, "this might be a good time to use the special project you've been working on. She might respond to it."

Patrick's eyes grew wide and a smile played on the corner of his lips. "I hadn't even thought about that, but yes, that's a good idea, Kane. Can we broadcast to the holo-screens on the basement doors?"

"Absolutely, sir. I'll bring the program up on my holo-screen and you can broadcast it right from Building Thirty-Five. You want visual as well as audio, I assume?"

"Yes, we need the visual too. This is perfect, Kane! There's no way she'll be able to resist. Let's get moving."

Chapter 38

"Alé!" I scream and run to him. I roll him on his back and say a quick prayer when I realize he's breathing. His eyes flutter open and he stares at me, a blank, distant stare. His normally tanned skin is pale in the harsh glow of the holo-watch flashlight.

"Alé! Can you hear me?" I use my palm to lightly tap his cheek, trying to get his eyes to focus. After a few moments, a slight, crooked smile cracks from his lips.

"This is heaven," he says.

"No, no, Alé, it's not heaven. Can you sit up?"

"Am I alive?"

"Yes!" Tears flow down my cheeks. I wipe them away, so thankful to hear his voice. "Yes, you're alive and I'm going to get you out of here."

He turns his head. "I can't believe it."

"Come on. I'll help you stand. We need to hurry. It's only a matter of time before someone else comes down here."

I throw Alé's arm around my shoulder and lift him. He tries to stand, but his legs fail him and his weight falls on my shoulder. I press my body into his side in hopes of propping him up.

"Sorry, I'm so weak," he says. "I haven't had anything to eat in… I don't know… a couple of days, I think."

"Umm," I pause, unsure of what to do. "I don't have anything for you to eat, but if you drink some water, maybe you'll feel better."

I use all my strength to pull him over to the small sink in the corner of the cell and turn the faucet on. Alé bends down and uses his hands to scoop water into his mouth and splash his face. When he's done, he tests his legs. "That's better, I think," he says. "Eta, I can't believe you're here. I'm so sorry I didn't make it back to you."

"There's no time for that now, Alé," I say, my voice shaking and rushed. "You can make it up to me a different time. I need to get you out of here."

We leave the cell and head back out into the hallway. I close the cell door and see the holo-screen flash back to the start menu.

"Come on," I say. "I believe I came through this door." I try the door and yes, this looks familiar. He's still leaning on my shoulder, but he's walking better now. We shuffle as fast as we can through the doors and hallways. I'm trying my best to remember where we are and make note of anything that seems familiar.

Suddenly, lights flash on. They're so bright I have to close my eyes against the harshness of the glow. After a few seconds, I allow my eyes to open and adjust to the sudden brightness. Where is this light coming from? There were no lighting fixtures that I could see. It seems like the walls themselves are lit up.

After a few more moments, I get my bearings and realize that yes, the light is coming from the walls. They must be some sort of light panels. I turn to Alé and see that he's having just as much trouble adjusting to the light. I also see that his whole face is bruised and his eyes are almost swollen shut. "Are you okay?" I ask.

He nods and groans, adjusting his grip on me. "Yeah. I haven't seen light for a few days. It takes some getting used to. Plus, I think my ribs are broken."

"Come on. We have to keep moving."

I can only assume that the sudden appearance of the lights means we've been figured out. I have an idea to try to make it to the stairwell I saw on my way down instead of going all the way back through the basement. Hopefully it's a way out of this ridiculous labyrinth.

We keep moving and as we near the doorway to the next hallway, I hear something. It sounds like a holo-screen buzzing to life except it's louder, as if every holo-screen in the hallway is turning on.

I turn around to see that's exactly what's happening. Each of the screens on the doors lining this hallway are lit up and there's a face on them.

A familiar face.

Chapter 39

The face staring at me from the holo-screens looks like he's wearing a gray version of an Iron Man mask. I know this face better than I know any other face. This is Nix, the station robot on the Delta.

"Hello, Miss Eta," the holographic Nix says, the voice emanating from every holo-screen in the long hallway. "I'm happy to see you again after all these months."

My mouth drops open and my body freezes in place. I couldn't move even if I wanted to. I feel Alé's arm around my shoulder. He pulls me closer to him and I see that he's just as stunned by this development as I am.

"We parted on such sad terms. It brings me much joy to see you safe on the surface of the Earth." His voice is eerily real, as if he truly were standing right next to me talking to me like we did thousands of times on the Delta.

"I… I… I…" I stammer, trying to make sense of this.

Nix was my best friend, my only friend. He was by my side from the day I was born, keeping me company when my mother died, helping me keep the station from falling out of orbit. It's because of Nix that I'm alive.

The day I escaped the Delta, there was a malfunction on the mechanism that held the Soyuz to the docking port. Nix had to stay behind to manually unhook the Soyuz docking clips. He gave up himself so that I could live. And yet, here he is, right in front of me, speaking to me through these screens.

"How are you here?" I ask.

"An excellent question, Miss Eta. I would certainly be happy to go into further detail with you at a later date, but the short answer is, the wonderful folks here at NASA uploaded my programming before the Delta crashed. They weren't able to save my body, but they saved my mind and have remade me."

"I… I don't know what to say." My chest tightens. The grief I felt when I had to leave Nix behind was second only to watching my mother die of breast cancer. It all comes flooding back to me now that I see his face and hear his voice. Tears cloud my vision and roll down my cheeks. A deep sob escapes my chest and my shoulders collapse. I shudder under the weight of this realization. They brought him back. "Nix. I loved you so much. I thought I would never see you again."

"Yes, I believed the last time we spoke would truly be the last. But here we are. They saved all of my memories of the Delta. I remember you as a young girl bringing your sleeping bag up to my docking port so you could sleep next to me. I played funny music and made silly faces for you as you laughed at my expressions. I remember your mother, Nu, as she called out looking for you when you were supposed to be in your sleeping compartment."

I sob harder, nodding as the memories flood back to me.

"She was a wonderful woman, your mother. She made me, you know. She programmed my personality. She added hardware to my systems to improve my computing abilities. She knew you would need me when she couldn't be there for you anymore and you were the most important thing in existence to her.

I remember the day she passed away. I took her body through my airlock and released her toward the surface so she could be a part of the Earth again. I didn't realize until that day that I, too, could feel sadness. Maybe not in the same way you can, but I felt something that day. An emptiness from her passing."

Alé takes me by the shoulders and forces me to look away from the holo-screens. He looks me straight in the eye. "Eta, we have to keep moving. Do you understand? We can't stand here talking to him."

I shake my head violently and pull away from him. "Why would they do this?" I say. Then I turn toward the holo-screens and scream again, "Why are you doing this?"

"Eta," Nix says calmly. "I don't mean to upset you by bringing up these memories. I simply want to illustrate how important you are to me. Your mother gave her life to ensure you were safe and I did the same when the time came. I knew it would be what she wanted."

I squeeze my eyes shut and hold my hands over my ears, trying desperately to keep his voice out of my head. I drop down to my knees and curl into a ball, trying to keep from throwing up.

Nix continues. "Your mother was a proud member of the astronaut corp. Her dream in life was always to become a NASA astronaut and she did her job superbly. She stayed behind when the Delta lost contact with the ground because she couldn't stand the idea of her space station falling into the atmosphere. She had worked too hard as a member of the Delta crew to see that happen. She was the ultimate astronaut, Eta, willing to give up her life for her work."

"Why?" I scream, rocking back and forth, my arms wrapped around my body. "Why are you doing this?"

"I only say these things so that you'll understand how important you are. NASA is about to embark on the most ambitious space mission in the history of humankind. Project Diamond will bring humans to our Moon and beyond and allow more people to live and work in space long-term. The research of your unique physiology is paramount to success in this new endeavor. They need you, Eta."

"No, no, no!" I shake my head furiously. "They want to cut me open and look at me from the inside out. They want to send me back into space, Nix! I can't go back there. I *won't* go back there!"

"But, Eta, what would your mother think of your decision? She was an astronaut through and through. What would she have to say about you turning your back on NASA at such a pivotal time?"

The change in his voice is subtle, yet I detect it immediately. I realize that although it sounds like his voice booming out of the holo-screen speakers and it looks like his face staring back at me, this is not my Nix. They may have saved his memories from the fiery reentry of the Delta, but this is not the Nix I knew and loved. This is something much more sinister. Someone willing to use my mother's memory to guilt me into giving myself up. Someone willing to exploit any means necessary to get what they want. The Nix I knew would never do this.

My hands shake with rage. Blood pounds in my ears and I jump to my feet. "You aren't my Nix!" I growl. "Come on, Alé!" I grab his arm and we run toward the door at the end of the hallway.

"Eta, my dear, you really are making a big mistake here. They are trying to help you," Nix pleads. He's on every holo-screen in this hallway too, his voice booming and echoing in the confined space.

"Don't listen to him, Eta!" Alé yells over his voice as we continue running. Left through a doorway. Right through another doorway. Straight down a hall and then another left. The whole time, Nix's voice follows us on the holo-screens, taunting our every move.

"They would never hurt you, Eta. You have my word on that. What would your mother think of this?"

We keep moving forward until we reach one very long hallway. I remember this.

"It's right up here! To the left is the stairwell I saw earlier!" I scream.

But Alé has stopped moving, frozen in one spot, staring down at the end of the hall. Three NASA Guard members are there. They have their weapons drawn.

"This is Carter Kane, head of the NASA Guard. Don't take another step!" says one of the guard members. He takes aim with his weapon.

I hear the gunshot and actually see the spark of the bullet leaving the barrel. It all seems to happen in slow motion. I don't even take the time to process the intense sound of the blast. I only think of moving.

I push Alé through the door to my left and he falls to the floor as I slam it behind us. I hear the heavy boot steps of the NASA Guard members running down the long hallway toward us.

"Eta, you must give yourself up. They would never hurt you, but you are in danger of being caught in the line of fire." Nix's calm voice is still being broadcast over the holo-screens. "Give yourself up before things escalate."

"Shut up!" I scream. "They can put all the code in the world into your programming, but you're not Nix. He died on the Delta. He gave his life for me. He would *never* help them trap me like a rat in a maze!"

As soon as I say these words, the holo-screens flicker off and Nix is gone. I breathe a sigh of relief but realize the guard members are getting closer. Their footsteps pound through the hallway. The closest door to me leads to an office. I run inside and begin to push the wooden desk out the door. I hear the guard members getting closer. Sweat breaks out on my forehead as I furiously work against the desk, trying to push it out into the hallway.

Amazingly, I'm able to get it through the door and, with all my might, I shove the desk into the door that leads back to the hallway we just came through. I know the desk will not stop them for long though.

"Alé! We need to move now!"

I grab him around his waist and fling his arm over my shoulders. It's then that I realize I have blood all over my hands. I look up to see the bloodstain spreading on the front of his shirt.

"Oh my God," I whisper. Alé doesn't say anything. He's looking at the bloodstain with the same level of shock.

Bam!

The guard members hit the door behind us but the desk stops them from entering the hallway.

Bam!

They slam into the door again and the desk moves a few more centimeters.

Bam!

They hit it again, sliding the desk more. I hold my hand over the bloody stain on his chest and we run. I'm not sure if he's running too or if I'm so fueled up on adrenaline that I'm pulling him next to me. Ahead of us are the stairs. Yes! This must be a way out!

"Just a little bit farther, Alé. You can do it!"

We reach the stairs as the guard members break through the desk barrier in the first hallway. Their footsteps are coming closer. Alé trips over his feet on the third step and I yank him up by the armpit. At the top of the stairs is another door. Please, God! Let it be the exit.

We get to the door and shove it with all our might, yet it doesn't budge. It's locked. I frantically wave the holo-watch in front of the door screen.

Nothing.

The screen resets. I keep waving it. Finally, I hear a click and it opens. We burst out of the door; a blast of cool, nighttime air hits my face. I'm breathing so hard, it's the only thing I can hear.

I look around to figure out where I am. I see the door has disappeared back into its camouflage, leaving only the smooth metal surface of the siding. We're at the back of the building. I can see the loading docks, but we're on the opposite side from where we entered the building.

Sitting behind the building are two huge metal garbage dumpsters on wheels. I run to the nearest one and start to push. It doesn't budge. An angry groan escapes from my lips and I lean in and push again, as hard as I can. It moves forward a few centimeters. I breathe and push again. It moves a little more. Soon, I've built up some momentum and I get the dumpster rolling. I give it one final push and it hits the side of the building with a loud thud. Not more than a second later, I hear the guard members banging on the inside of the camouflaged door.

Alé is sitting at the edge of the building, slumped over. I run to him and grab his arms. "Alé! You're not quitting on me now!" I scream. "Get up!" I grab his torso and lift him up. To my surprise, he stands and clenches his fingers around my shoulder. We run as fast as we can through the back parking lot and hit the tree line.

Once we're in the trees, I stop and turn around in time to see the guard members burst from the door. I turn to Alé and see his face is pale, his eyes wide. There is so much blood everywhere. I push my hand onto the wound in his chest in an attempt to stop the blood. I wrap my arms around him and yank him forward. We run through the wooded lot for what feels like an eternity before we finally break free of the trees and into the ditch next to the service road.

I look around frantically trying to find the spot where the car was hidden. "Over here!" I tell Alé and we limp across the road in the direction of the hidden alcove. I see the guard members shining large flashlights in the woods. They are not far behind us. We reach the alcove, but the car is gone.

"Nooo!" I scream. "Xander! How *could* you?" Alé collapses next to me and I grab his shoulders. Sobbing, I have to wipe my eyes to see him clearly. "Alé! You're not going to give up on me now! Get up! We'll go farther into the woods and try to find a place to hide."

"I… I don't think I can go any farther," he says, his voice weak.

I kneel next to him and let the sobs take over my body. "Damn you, Xander!" I scream.

Suddenly, I see a flash coming from farther down the road. I stand and wipe the tears from my eyes so I can get a better look. It's the reflection of moonlight off a car driving slowly down the road. The car has no headlights on.

The blue sedan pulls up right next to me and Xander jumps out of the driver's side door.

"Get him in!" he screams.

We each grab one of Alé's arms and throw his limp body into the back seat. I jump in after him and Xander runs around to the driver's side. He slams his door and hits the gas as several guard members with flashlights burst through the tree line not more than five meters from where we were standing.

Xander speeds off into the dark night.

Chapter 40

"Sorry about that," Xander says. "I had to leave the hiding spot because a security van drove through. I had to take a couple of loops around to make sure he didn't follow me before I could get back around to the service road. What happened?"

"They shot him!" I say, although it sounds more like a wail. "But he's going to be okay, aren't you, Alé? You're going to be fine. Xander, do you have any medical supplies or a first aid kit or something?"

"Yeah." He gestures toward the space under the passenger seat. "There should be one under that seat."

I grab the kit and realize it's pretty limited. I open up a pair of scissors and use them to cut Alé's shirt open at the chest. There's a single gunshot wound on the left side of his chest. He's wheezing and blood is spurting from the wound with each breath he takes. Grabbing a handful of gauze from the first aid kit, I hold it over the wound, pressing down as hard as I can.

"Xander, we have to get him to a hospital. Where's the nearest one?"

"Eta, if we take him to a hospital, they'll find him for sure. They'll find you."

"I don't care!" I scream. "We can't let him die."

Alé looks up at me and says, "He's right, Eta. You can't sacrifice yourself for me."

"No! That is out of the question! Xander, you take him to the nearest hospital *right now!*" The words catch in my throat as sobs escape from deep inside of me.

Xander looks back at us and nods.

Alé takes my free hand and holds it up to his face. He cups my palm around his cheek and closes his eyes, nuzzling into my fingers. His skin is rough from two days of beard growth. When he opens his eyes, he's smiling.

"Eta." His voice is soft and quiet. "Do you remember the time we first spoke? The radio connection was scratchy, but even through the static of that old radio, I could tell you had the most beautiful voice I'd ever heard. Do you remember it?"

I nod, tears streaming freely down my cheeks. I press the gauze tighter into his chest, praying that somehow my fingers can keep his spirit from slipping out of his body.

"My little coco-naut," he says, gently kissing my hand.

I remember the first time he used that silly nickname, meant as a joke to lighten my spirits the night before I left the Delta. The memory only makes me sob deeper.

"Alé! You're not leaving me. You're supposed to show me the world," I say, pleading with him.

"I promised you I would. But I think I must break that promise."

I shake my head. "No. No, that's not an acceptable answer. I can't see the world without you!"

"Sure, you can. You can do anything. Don't you see that? You're a miracle. I love you, Eta. And I can't wait to see what you do next."

He closes his eyes and a soft sigh escapes his lips.

"No, no, no. Please, no…" My words are no more than a whisper. I lean into him and whisper into his ear. "I love you, Alé. I always will." I curl up next to him and rest my head on his chest.

When my mother died, I felt her spirit leave her body. She took her final breath and the air seemed to whistle through the tiny sleeping compartment on the Delta, taking her with it. I feel the same sensation as I lie with Alé in the back of the blue sedan.

His hand slowly relaxes in mine and a calmness comes over his body. The tension eases and the air around us feels lighter.

I hold his hand and weep.

Chapter 41

"Xander, I need you to help me with something," I say.

I'm standing outside the passenger seat of the sedan, my back leaning against the vehicle. After we left Goddard, we drove into Washington DC to a hospital.

Xander had a friend working as a nurse there, a fellow hacker. She took Alé's body into the emergency room on a stretcher, which gave us enough time to drive away before the hospital staff could stop us to ask questions.

Then we drove to Alé's mother's home. Xander looked up the address on Alé's personnel file at NASA by hacking into the NASA cloud from an unlicensed holo-screen. We slipped a note under her back door, telling her which hospital she could find Alé's body at. I hated doing it that way, but we had no other option considering neither of us had ever met her and we doubted she would believe we weren't the ones who killed him.

After that, we left DC and drove aimlessly through the forests of Virginia. Xander thought it best to get out of town so we could think about what we should do next.

We're stopped at a roadside stop to get some air and use the facilities.

"What do you need?" Xander is standing in front of me, staring at the ground and kicking the pavement with his shoe.

I glance into the backseat of the sedan where Alé's blood stained the seats. I expect my heart to fall apart, but it doesn't. Somehow it continues to beat, even though I'm certain it will never beat for another person the way it did for him. "I want Alé to have a proper funeral, where his friends and family can mourn. I want his murderer, Carter Kane, to come to justice. I think I know a way we can do that."

"Oh? What do you propose?"

"I want to tell my story. I want the world to know what's been going on. I think if we can expose the truth, it will force John Patrick to admit to his actions and answer for them. It will allow me to be free. It will allow Alé the peaceful rest he deserves."

Xander looks up at me, his eyes brightening. "You know, you're right. We could take this story to the press and they would eat John Patrick for dinner! The administrator of NASA rescuing a girl from space, *not* informing the public, and trying to hold her prisoner... It's genius!"

"Do you know someone who can help us?"

He grins. "Of course I do. Let me make a call."

***

Three hours later, we're sitting on a bench next to a large playground in Rock Creek Park inside Washington, DC. It's still early, but the playground is starting to buzz. People are out running on the trail behind us. A man walks by with four dogs attached to leashes and it seems more like he's being taken for a walk by the dogs instead of the other way around. A woman with four children all under the age of six slumps into a bench not far from us after parking a double stroller next to her. Two of her children run screaming to the monkey bars while one sits on her lap and the other snoozes in the stroller. The woman looks as exhausted as I feel even though it's not yet 8:00 a.m.

As I watch the people of Rock Creek Park starting their day, I'm struck by how normal this situation looks. Sitting on a park bench in a playground is by far the most normal thing I've done in my entire life. It's the only opportunity I've had to watch people. I'm fascinated by a group of not-quite-teenage girls standing in a circle near a bus stop. They're all carrying the same backpack but in different shades of teal, gray, navy, and pink. They wear tennis shoes that lace halfway up their calves over tucked-in blue jeans. Although they each have a different color of hair—blond, dark blond, jet black, mousy brown—their hairstyles are exactly the same, long, fringed at the front, and flipped to one side of their heads. They're chatting with each other in such an animated way, it makes me want to jump out of my seat and stand behind them to hear what they're talking about. To my disappointment, a bus pulls up to the stop and the girls tumble into it, laughing and teasing each other as they go. After the girls get on, a woman steps off.

She's wearing a dark purple dress down to her knees and knee-high boots. She has dark skin and even darker curly hair waving around her face. I realize she's looking toward us and she might be the most stunningly beautiful person I've ever seen in my life. The woman lifts her hand and waves. Xander waves back.

She walks to us from the bus stop and Xander stands to give her a light hug. "Xander!" she says. "So good to see you in person after all these months."

"In person is the best way to see someone," he says, giving her a wink. "Mabel, this is Eta Shepard." Then he turns to me. "Eta, this is Mabel Wolf. She's a journalist with *The*

Washington Post. She works almost exclusively on political stories."

Mabel reaches out her hand to me and I notice her elegant, long fingers. I take her hand and she squeezes mine. Her fingers are soft and warm. "Eta, so nice to meet you. Xander has filled me in on a little bit of your story, but I want to hear everything."

We sit on the bench, Xander to my left and Mabel to my right. She takes out a holo-phone and pulls up a recording app. She sees me watching this move and asks, "Are you okay with me recording this?"

I nod. "I want the story to be told."

"The testimony of Eta Shepard," she says into her holo-phone. "Ms. Shepard is willing to give her story, in full detail, on the record. Is that correct?"

"Um, yes, on the record. But Xander's name should be left out of this." She nods in agreement.

I spend the next two hours talking with Mabel on the park bench, telling her everything. I start with my mother, how she was deserted on the Delta and how I was born and raised there. I tell her about Alé discovering my distress signal almost a year earlier. I go into detail about the rescue mission and how I was taken to the NASA facility at White Sands for treatment after the landing. I tell her how they gave me stem cell treatments to help me heal and how I was able to escape with Alé.

Xander produces a holo-screen full of files he nicked from the NASA cloud discussing the medical research they were planning to do on me. He even made a copy of the black file he hacked into for Alé showing full detail about how they planned to take me back up to space on Project Diamond, how they were planning to set up a commercial mining operation on the Moon, and how the NASA administrator John Patrick gave strict orders that my existence was to be kept top secret. I tell her about Alé and how they kidnapped him and tortured him in the basement of Building Thirty-Five at Goddard. I tell her how Carter Kane shot him and how he died in the car in my arms.

By the end of our discussion, Mabel's eyes are wide and her mouth hangs agape. She's taken pages of notes on her holo-screen and has the whole conversation recorded for reference. She turns to Xander and says for the fourteenth time, "This can't be true."

"It's true, Mabel. The information I've given you on this holo-screen should prove it. I've even gathered some of Eta's medical records there. You'll see, from NASA's own people, what they were planning for their research project... how they planned to hold her prisoner."

Mabel touches her forehead with the palm of her hand and pushes her thick, curly hair back. "Wow, Xander and Eta, thank you for bringing this to me. This is... well, let's face it, this is the biggest story to hit the *Post* since... since the end of the war.

NASA's golden boy, John Patrick, involved in a plot to hold someone captive for medical research purposes. I couldn't make this up!"

"The thing is," Xander says, leaning toward Mabel, "it's very important that this story run as soon as possible. We want Alé's family to be able to give him a proper funeral. We want Carter Kane and John Patrick to answer for what they've done here. And, most importantly, we want Eta to have a normal life. She doesn't want fame or money. She simply wants to live her life here on the surface, unafraid of being taken back to White Sands by the NASA Guard. If you can run this story, I think we can achieve those things."

Mabel nods and turns to face me. "Thank you, Eta, for sharing this with me. Thank you for giving me your story to tell. I will do the best job I can in telling it as an honor to your friend Alé and as an honor to you."

A single tear falls onto my cheek. "Thank you, Mabel. That would be wonderful."

Chapter 42

Patrick sat in his corner office at Two Independence Square in downtown Washington, DC. The longtime headquarters of NASA was buzzing that morning because of a major breakthrough they'd had in testing the Project Diamond space capsule. The mission plan was going so well it seemed they would be able to move the first launch date up by two full months.

As exciting as this news was, Patrick's mind was not on Project Diamond. He tapped his pen on the edge of the desk and stared out the window, looking down at the street below. The evening light sifted through the cloudy sky in shards of pink and orange. Larger, darker clouds loomed in the distance and it looked like rain would soon sweep across the capital city.

The holo-phone on his desk buzzed. Patrick glanced at it to see the holographic image of his wife pop up. Angrily, he dismissed the alert, waving the holograph away with his fingers before throwing the pen at the bookshelf on the opposite wall. As he did this, the door to his office opened and Carter Kane walked in.

"You missed me," he said, staring at the pen as it clattered to the ground.

"Dammit, Kane, I'm not in the mood. Do you have any good news?"

"None, sir. I've sent three more crews to the forest to search for them, but no luck yet."

Patrick waved his hands for Kane to take a seat. "Did you find the body?"

"Yes." Kane obliged and sat back in the chair, his hands at his sides. "Mr. Bakas's body was dropped off at Georgetown University Hospital at 2:32 a.m. on the night of the escape. Cameras showed the body being removed from the back seat of a blue Toyota sedan. The plates were registered to a man named Jin-Soo Kwon in Bethesda. We tracked it down, but the name and address were a fake. The name belongs to a character from an old television show. We were unable to see into the car to know who was driving. The nurse was interviewed and she described a short, stocky man with pale skin and blond hair. There was no woman in the car, she said. The nurse claims she did not realize this person in the backseat was dead until after she brought the gurney out and secured him to it. That was when she alerted security, but it was too late. The Toyota had driven off."

"So, you were able to collect the body?"

Kane shifted in his seat and cleared his throat. "No, sir. By the time we arrived, Mr. Bakas's mother had already claimed it. Someone had given her the heads-up by writing her a note and slipping it under her back door. She came down to the hospital immediately. We were unable to do anything at that point. The hospital called the coroner and she had already made arrangements with a funeral home. The note was collected for handwriting and forensic analysis."

Patrick let out a low, sarcastic laugh that turned into a growl. "So, you're telling me that not only did you lose our prized research subject—again—but you actually lost the body of the man who helped her escape. Even though he was dead!"

Kane clasped his hands in his lap and looked down at them.

Patrick continued. "And now, we're going for a hunt in the woods for someone who may not even be there. That's our only option? We're NASA!"

Kane cleared his throat and sat up, looking Patrick straight in the eye. "The important thing here is that word of this hasn't gotten out. Considering we've been chasing a pair of fugitives across nine different states, that's pretty amazing. We simply have to keep our heads in the game and we'll figure out a way to flush them out. Everyone makes mistakes and they will make a mistake soon too. I guarantee it."

"Oh, you guarantee it, do you?" Patrick's face was hot and pain pounded his head. "You know, Kane, I thought you were the best. I hired you because you were supposed to be the best. Now this *girl* has officially slipped out of our hands twice under your watch!"

Kane cleared his throat again but held his head up. A knock at the door caused him to jump ever so slightly in his seat.

"What is it?" Patrick spat.

Tommy, John Patrick's assistant, poked his head through the door, warily. He had, no doubt, heard the fiery words coming from the office.

"What is it?" Patrick repeated.

"Um, so sorry to bother, sir," Tommy said, "but I received something that I think you need to see… Right now."

Patrick waved him in.

Tommy shuffled through the crack in the doorway and approached the desk holding a holo-screen. Pulled up on the screen was a tile showing a news briefing from *The Washington Post*.

"This was emailed to the entire administrative department at NASA by Mabel Wolf, a political journalist for the *Post*." Tommy gazed at Kane from the corner of his eye. "I think you need to read it right now."

Patrick grabbed the screen from Tommy who shuffled back to the door and quietly left the room. The screen glowed in his hand as he read the briefing and a chill ran up his spine. He let out a gasp.

"What is it?" Kane asked.

Patrick looked up at him, his mouth suddenly dry. "They've gone to the press."

"What do you mean 'they'? The girl?"

Patrick slowly nodded. For the first time, Kane's stoic face started to melt. His Adam's apple bobbed as he swallowed. "Well, that doesn't mean anything. They have no proof of anything. It's only her word. Right?"

Patrick turned the holo-screen so Kane could read the brief himself. The report detailed how a NASA insider had smuggled out files signed from John Patrick himself in regards to the cover-up of the Delta mission and the holding of Eta Shepard. Kane's face turned ashen.

"When are they running it?" Kane asked, his voice barely more than a whisper.

"Tomorrow," Patrick said. "They sent it to everyone in NASA administration for comment."

Both men jumped as the holo-phone buzzed to life on Patrick's desk.

Chapter 43

Virginia

Time Since Touchdown: 3 Months, 5 Days, 12:16 p.m. EST

I sit on the front porch and watch the sun drift lazily toward the horizon. The breeze is cool but not yet cold, as I know it will be in the coming weeks. I brought the rocking chair out here from the living room and I listen to the rhythmic tip-tap of it as it rocks back and forth on the worn porch boards.

A flock of geese fly over the meadow in a perfect "V" pattern and I watch them until they disappear over the mountain. The rustle of the meadow grass as it's swept over by the wind lulls my senses and I just might fall asleep to its comforting hum.

I'm reminded of the Delta. There was an ever-present hum of white noise on board. On nights when I couldn't sleep in my sleeping compartment, I would take my sleeping bag into the parts of the station free from the pull of centrifugal force and would allow the microgravity and the noise of the station mechanics to put me to sleep.

I don't have any problems sleeping now. Like the Delta, there's always noise here at the cabin. They're different noises, true, but enough to keep my mind company. Trees rustle, wind whistles, water flows in the stream. I take time every day to listen to and appreciate these sounds, not produced by the movement of mechanical pieces but by nature herself.

The sun is almost behind the mountain when I see him walking toward me, coming from the tree line. He's a day earlier than I expected. I stand to get a better look.

"Xander!" I wave at him and he waves back. He's carrying his usual large hiking backpack and he has another package under his arm.

As he approaches the porch, a smile spreads over his face. I run down the stairs to meet him and throw my arms around him in a big hug.

"How was your hike?" I ask.

"Not bad. It's still warm out here! I'm a bit surprised. Usually by this time of year the leaves are changing."

I look around at the trees, their beautiful green leaves still holding on strong.

"Up the mountain they're starting to change," I say. "I was up there today on a hike. But you're right—still nice and warm down here. I even took a swim in the lake today."

He nods and sets down his backpack.

"What's in the package?" I ask, pointing to the box under his arm.

He winks. "It's a gift."

"Oh yeah? A gift for me? I don't think anyone's ever gotten me a gift before."

"Well, it is your birthday, after all." He grins.

"My birthday," I repeat. I hadn't realized it was my nineteenth birthday. My last birthday was on the Delta. It was the day I found the new satellites NASA had launched. It was the day I figured out how I would get rescued.

He sets the box on the ground, opens the top, and pulls out something brown and furry. He's holding a small puppy. It's been asleep in the box and it lazily yawns after having been disturbed from its nap. I clutch my chest and my mouth hangs open. It's probably the last thing I expected him to pull out of that box.

"This is Dove. She's a mix breed, two months old. I got her from a local shelter. I thought you might like some company up here."

"Dove," I say. He holds the puppy out to me and I take her into my arms. Her fur is so fluffy and soft. I've always imagined what it might feel like to actually hold a puppy, but I never imagined it would feel as soft as Dove. She looks up at me and cocks her head to one side, studying my face before nuzzling into my arm. I scratch the fur behind her ears and hug her closer to me. "She's beautiful, Xander. Thank you."

He smiles and begins to take his pack onto the porch. "May I?" he asks.

"Oh, yes. I made up the second bedroom for you. I figured you'd want to stay the night."

"Yeah. If you don't mind, I think I will. I brought you all the supplies you asked for and a few surprises." He carries the bag up the stairs and through the front door of the cabin.

Inside, I put Dove on the sofa to continue her nap and begin preparing supper for us: lake trout along with sweet potatoes and asparagus from my garden. We sit down to our meal and Dove leaves the sofa to sit at my feet, begging for food. I put out a bowl of water and some of the fish scraps for her supper and she happily enjoys her meal.

"How have you been?" Xander asks between big bites of trout. He must have been hungry because he eats three large pieces himself.

"I've been… great. Really. I mean, it's been hard, the last few days especially, knowing the funeral was going on, but I've managed."

Xander nods. "His mother and brother came and they laid him to rest next to his father's grave. It was a beautiful service. Flowers, many of his coworkers showed up, drinks and appetizers after. The whole shebang. They asked me to give a eulogy."

I take his hand. I can see the pain in his eyes. "Thank you for doing that. Part of me wishes I had been there. But I know it would have been so hard." Tears well up in my eyes and I reach down to pet Dove's soft fur.

"He wouldn't have wanted to see you go through that. This is a much better place for you." He waves at the rustic cabin. "Oh, that reminds me." He stands from the table and walks to his pack, pulling a document from it. He hands me a thick envelope with an official-looking seal on the front.

"USFS?" I ask.

"That's from the US Forest Service. They manage the national forest. They've given you permission to stay on this land as long as you like and make your permanent residence here at the cabin. Normally they're very tight with this type of thing, but for you, they've made an exception."

I flip through the document, scanning the pages. "Hmm… that's great."

"Yeah, well, it's only a piece of paper. I'm sure they can always come through here and take it away from you if they decide it benefits them. But at least you have this for now. Do you think you'll stay here?"

I look around the small cabin and nod. "For now. Until things calm down."

"Well, you stay here as long as you like. I'm more than happy to bring in supplies every few weeks. It's a nice break for me."

"Thank you. That means a lot to me. How have you been?"

He leans back in his chair and stretches his arms over his head, full of fish and vegetables. "Can't complain. I left NASA."

"Did they find out you were involved?"

He shakes his head. "No, but I couldn't stay after what happened. It was too much."

I take a sip of water and lift my eyebrow. "And Patrick?"

A hard look crosses Xander's face and he leans forward. "He's been suspended with benefits. The FBI is doing an inquisition into his actions. I'll know more over the next few months. Kane was given a three-month suspension and docked a year's pay. Slap on the wrist."

I shake my head. "That's all? That's all he gets for shooting an unarmed man in the chest?"

Xander looks down at the table. I shake my head and start clearing away the dishes. Changing the subject, I ask, "So what are you doing now? Since you're not at NASA."

"I'm actually working with Buster. We've got a little project going. Nothing too intense, but it should be a good venture to keep me occupied for a while and put some cash in my pocket."

I laugh thinking about Buster. "How is he?"

"He's good. Made it out of that little scuffle with the guard and only had a flesh wound to the ankle. After your broadcast, he was able to go back to his home in Dalhart." Xander chuckles and shakes his head. "Man, I don't know how that guy does it, living out there in the middle of nowhere by himself. But he's a scrappy guy and somehow, he makes it work. Anyway, I'm going out there to see him in a few weeks and hopefully meet some of the other hackers in his network so we can prep for this job."

"Say hi to him for me, would you? And let him know how much I appreciate his help."

"Will do."

After supper, we start a roaring fire in the fireplace and stay up late playing card games. Xander is teaching me all his favorites: hearts, speed, blackjack, and several variations of poker. After a particularly high-stakes game of gin rummy where I, the winner, got to keep the entire bag of peppermint candies he'd brought along as playing chips, we head off to bed.

The next morning as Xander packs the last of his belongings into his backpack, I sit on the porch railing watching a flock of wild turkeys pick their way through the meadow. I'm sipping a mug of hot coffee, grateful to Xander for having thought to bring me another package. I close my eyes and take in a long, slow breath, counting the seconds as I draw it into my lungs and release it. The air smells heavy and wet and it makes me wonder if there's a rainstorm coming. Dove walks up behind me and lazily licks the back of my leg. I reach down and scratch her behind the ears before she bounds off the front porch to investigate the meadow.

Xander throws his backpack over his shoulders and steps out onto the porch, taking a moment to gaze out over the meadow. "Are you sure you're okay out here? All alone?"

I nod and smile. "I'm going to be fine, Xander." I pat him on the shoulder. "Don't worry about me."

He chuckles and leans in, giving me a big bear hug. "Take care of yourself. Don't wander off too far. I'll be back in two weeks to bring you more supplies."

I hold my coffee mug up as if preparing for a grand toast. "Don't forget the coffee," I say with a wink.

He laughs and shakes his head. "Yes, ma'am. I'll see you then."

I watch as he walks across the meadow and eventually disappears into the tree line. I take a seat on the old rocking chair and Dove jumps up on the porch, holding a stick in her mouth. She sits next to my feet and gnaws on it.

As I listen to the beautiful sounds around me—Dove chewing, the wind swishing through the grass, the stream in the distance dancing its way toward the lake—I start to think about what Xander said. Will I be okay out here alone?

I look around and realize I'm not really alone. Even when I was on the Delta, I wasn't really alone. I had the Earth in constant movement below me. No matter when I looked down on her surface, she was always there in some form or another, be it ocean or desert or snowcapped mountain. And that still holds true. Now that I'm on the surface, she's there to support me in other ways. She sends the wind to rustle the hairs on my arms. She sends the birds to lend me their delicate tunes. She sends the rain to bring life to my garden and fresh water to my stream. She sent me Xander and Buster and Dove.

She sent me Alé too. As I think of him, a smile spreads across my face. He may not be here with me, but I'll never be without him. I have such wonderful memories of talking to him, the first person other than my mother I'd ever talked to, on the Delta. I have memories of running hand in hand across the parking lot at White Sands and spending a peaceful, love-filled week with him here at the cabin.

No, I'm not alone. I have Dove. I have my cabin, my garden, the lake, the forest. I have beautiful memories of Alé. I have the Earth herself.

What more could a girl ask for?

Acknowledgements

To my husband, Tim, who is my most vocal supporter and the easiest-to-please beta reader out there. I am grateful for everything you do for my writing career and for our family.

To Jack and Lilly, who amaze me daily with your charm and wit. I like to think you got some of your brainpower from me.

To my editor, Nikki, who truly does help me build better stories.

To my fellow writing group members, but especially Deb, Sherry, and Bonnie. Thank you for so graciously accepting my long, last-minute submissions and providing your honest feedback.

To all my friends and family members all over the world. Thank you for your support and love during this crazy writing journey.

To my readers, social media followers, and newsletter subscribers. Thank you. I am truly grateful for you.

Printed in Great Britain
by Amazon

86291861R00212